YOU'LL MISS ME When I'm Gone

YOU'LL MISS ME
When I'm Gone

RACHEL LYNN SOLOMON

SIMON PULSE

NEW YORK   LONDON   TORONTO   SYDNEY   NEW DELHI

SIMON PULSE

An imprint of Simon & Schuster Children's Publishing Division
1230 Avenue of the Americas, New York, New York 10020
First Simon Pulse hardcover edition January 2018
Text copyright © 2018 by Rachel Lynn Solomon
Jacket photograph of young women copyright © 2018 by Ildiko Neer / Trevillion Images
Jacket photograph of leaves copyright © 2018 by BSANI / Thinkstock
Helix interior illustrations copyright © 2018 by julichka / Thinkstock
All rights reserved, including the right of reproduction in whole or in part in any form.
SIMON PULSE and colophon are registered trademarks of Simon & Schuster, Inc.
For information about special discounts for bulk purchases, please contact
Simon & Schuster Special Sales at 1-866-506-1949 or business@simonandschuster.com.
The Simon & Schuster Speakers Bureau can bring authors to your live event.
For more information or to book an event contact the Simon & Schuster Speakers Bureau
at 1-866-248-3049 or visit our website at www.simonspeakers.com.
Jacket designed by Sarah Creech
Interior designed by Mike Rosamilia
The text of this book was set in Palatino.
Manufactured in the United States of America
2 4 6 8 10 9 7 5 3 1
Library of Congress Cataloging-in-Publication Data
Names: Solomon, Rachel Lynn.
Title: You'll miss me when I'm gone / by Rachel Lynn Solomon.
Other titles: You will miss me when I am gone
Description: First Simon Pulse hardcover edition. | New York : Simon Pulse, 2018. |
Summary: Eighteen-year-old twins Adina, a viola prodigy, and Tovah, a future surgeon,
find their relationship tested when they learn that one of them will develop
Huntington's, the degenerative disease ravaging their mother.
Identifiers: LCCN 2017008359 |
ISBN 9781481497732 (hardcover) | ISBN 9781481497756 (eBook)
Subjects: | CYAC: Sisters—Fiction. | Twins—Fiction. |
Huntington's disease—Fiction. | Sick—Fiction. | Jews—United States—Fiction. |
Family life—Washington (State)—Seattle—Fiction. | Seattle (Wash.)—Fiction.
Classification: LCC PZ7.1.S6695 You 2018 | DDC [Fic]—dc23
LC record available at https://lccn.loc.gov/2017008359

FOR MY GRANDPARENTS,

all five of them:

Phyllis, Howard, Bess, Dorita,

and Hertzel

Fall

One

Adina

I USED TO THINK HIS TOUCHES MEANT NOTHING. WE brushed arms in the hallway of his apartment, and I let myself believe the space was simply too narrow. Our hands tangled and I figured it was because we reached to turn the sheet music at the same time.

Then his touches started to linger. I could feel the warmth of his palm on my shoulder through the fabric of my dress after he told me I'd played beautifully, and I convinced myself of something else: he has touched me far too many times for it to be happening by accident.

Today I will make it happen on purpose.

My bus turns onto his street. He lives on a hill claimed by two Seattle neighborhoods, Capitol Hill and the Central District. This hill and I, we go way back. I walked up it the year of the snowstorm when the buses stopped. I slipped down it once, skinning my knee to save my viola case from smashing to the ground. Arjun saw it happen from his fourth-story window, and he rushed down with a Band-Aid with a cartoon character on it. He explained the Band-Aids were for "the little ones," his younger students. It made me laugh, made me forget about the smear of my blood tattooed on the concrete.

I mutter "thank you" to the driver as I step off the bus, my boots landing in a puddle that splashes water up my sweater tights. It's the first good rain of the fall, the kind that pummels windows and roofs, making a house sound like it's preparing for war. It is sweet, fresh, *alive*. I've been waiting for it all month.

Arjun buzzes me inside, and I press the faded elevator button between numbers three and five. By the time the doors swing open, my hands are damp with sweat. To relax, I play a Schubert sonata in my head. I've hummed eight measures before I feel calm enough to see him.

"Adina! Hello," Arjun says, pulling the door wide. "I was starting to think you got lost on the way up."

"Elevator was stuck," I lie. My lungs feel tight, like I sprinted up the hill.

"Old building. Happens to me all the time." He grins, brilliant white teeth between full lips. "Ready to make some beautiful music?"

"Always."

A collared shirt peeks out the neck of his burgundy sweater, showing the lines of his broad shoulders. The sweater looks so soft, makes me imagine what it would feel like to touch him on

4

purpose. *I could do it now.* But I don't have the courage yet. The sight and sound of him have turned my muscles liquid.

I follow him to his studio, where portraits of composers, all grim and serious—possibly because most of them were dying of typhoid or syphilis—stare down at me. With trembling hands, I unbuckle my viola case and arrange my music on the stand in front of me. Arjun sits in the chair opposite mine. The ankles of his pants inch up, exposing his argyle socks.

Our first lesson was three years ago, but it wasn't until I heard him play that he became someone I think about every night before I fall asleep. Dreamed about. I try very hard to forget that he is twenty-five, my teacher, and entirely off-limits. Sometimes, though, when he looks at me after I finish playing, I swear he feels the same pull.

His lips tip into a grin. "Don't make fun of me, but I had studded tires put on my car last weekend."

"No!" I gasp.

He shrugs, sheepish. "Have to be prepared for the worst, right?"

I shake my head, laughing, and relax in my chair. Each winter he prepares for an apocalyptic snowstorm, since he'd never seen snow until his first winter in Seattle. It doesn't snow in Gujarat, the state in India where he grew up, or in New Delhi, where he played in the symphony.

"It's September," I say. "You're absurd. Besides, we probably won't even get snow this year. We only got, what, half an inch last year?"

"And it shut the entire city down! We'll see who's absurd when you're stuck in your house for days and you haven't stocked up on nonperishables."

"You'd share your protein bars with me."

"Maybe," he says, but he's smiling. He snaps his fingers. "Do you remember the New Year's Eve symphony showcase I told you about, the one for musicians under twenty-five?"

I nod and scoot to the edge of my chair, my heart hammering allegro against my rib cage. The showcase will feature the best soloists in the Pacific Northwest. I play in the youth symphony, but the viola is typically a background instrument. Rarely do I get the spotlight to myself.

"It turns out," he continues, "that the director is a friend of mine. I sent him some clips of you playing, and he was quite impressed. He can fit you in for an audition Friday after school, if you're interested. Three thirty."

I do some quick mental calculations. If the buses aren't delayed, I should be able to make it home by sundown. By Shabbat. And even if I know the audition is more important, my family doesn't have the same priorities. In their minds, tradition beats everything.

"Are you serious? Yes, I'm interested. Thank you!" This is the first genuine happiness I've felt in weeks. I turn eighteen this weekend, a birthday I have been dreading, and the genetic test is a couple days after. That test is the reason I need to make a move with Arjun now, before everything could change. Before I find out if the disease that is stealing the life from my mother will do the same thing to me.

"Test," a word I've always viewed with mild annoyance, doesn't have a fraction of the weight it should.

"You deserve it." His dark eyes hold mine, replacing thoughts of the test with images of what we did last night in one of my dreams. "Have you decided where you're applying yet?"

"Peabody, Oberlin, New England, the Manhattan School of Music." My father, who unlike my mother doesn't believe someone can make a living off music, has begged me to apply to at least one state school. *Just in case*, he says. In case what? In case I fail spectacularly at being a musician? Conservatory has been my path since fourth-grade orchestra, when I fell in love with the mellow, melancholy sound of the viola. It was less obvious than the violin, less arrogant than the cello. Bass I've only ever seen played by guys with huge egos, as though the instrument is inversely proportional to penis size and they're trying to make up for their shortcomings. Each year my orchestra classes shrank as kids discovered they liked other things more than strings. And each year I was the one my teachers asked to play solos—never mind that violas don't usually solo. I vowed to become one of the first to do it professionally.

"Solid choices," Arjun says.

"And Juilliard, just for the hell of it. I'm still working on the recordings." Arjun and my school orchestra teachers will write my letters of recommendation. To my other teachers, I am simply a body in a seat. I'm always waiting to stop pretending to take notes on Chaucer or entropy or the quadratic formula so I can go to orchestra, or on Wednesdays, to go to Arjun.

"You'll get an audition. I know you will."

I pull at a loose thread on my tights, exposing a triangle of skin. My nerves unravel too many pieces of clothing. The truth: conservatory applications will have to wait until my test results come back. Right now, the uncertainty of it all is paralyzing.

Arjun pages through his music as I get to my feet, positioning the instrument under my chin. He likes his students to stand while playing so we are always performing. I warm up with scales, dragging my bow along the strings in smooth, fluid motions. Then I move on to Bach, Mendelssohn, Handel. Soon my feet are rocking back and forth, my fingers flying up and down the instrument's neck, the room full of sound that tugs at something deep in my chest. I breathe in minor chords, out major chords.

Sonatas and concertos tell stories. They make you feel every possible emotion, sometimes all within a single piece. They're nothing like three-minute pop songs with predictable patterns and manufactured sounds. They are joy and tragedy and fear and hate and love. They are everything I never say out loud.

"Your C string is a little sharp," Arjun says after one piece. "Linger on that last note for a few more seconds," he says after another. Every few bars, I steal a glance at his face. The looks he gives me are all fire, warming me down to my toes.

After I play my final piece, Debussy's "La Fille aux Cheveux de Lin," translated in English as "The Girl with the Flaxen Hair," Arjun stays silent. It is a delicate, emotional prelude. The flaxen-haired girl is a symbol of innocence.

I love irony.

I put down my bow and lay my viola in my lap. His eyes are half closed, dreamy, like he wants to stay inside the song for a while longer before rejoining the real world.

Nearly a minute passes before he says, "That was incredible. Flawless."

"I practiced a lot." Three, four, five hours a day, except on Shabbat, of course.

"It shows."

The rare times I've heard him play, he's been flawless too. Arjun's hand is on the desk, and before I can let myself overthink it, I cover it with mine. His skin is so warm. My hands are always ice; my twin sister, Tovah, and my parents make fun of me for it. I have dead-person hands, they like to joke. Even in the summer, even when I'm playing viola, they never heat up. But if my hands are too cold now, Arjun doesn't say anything.

So I take a deep breath and lean in. I want to bury my fists in his sweater and wrap my legs around his waist and push our hips together. I want to forget everything happening at home, the way Tovah seems to do so easily. But I restrain myself. I simply bring my lips close to his, waiting for him to move the last inch. I imagine he would taste like all decadent things you aren't supposed to have too much of: tart cherries, espresso beans, wine the color of rubies I once saw in his kitchen. My adrenaline spikes, anticipating the rush that comes with doing something you're not supposed to do and getting away with it.

Something I'm well versed in when it comes to guys who are older than me.

Suddenly he pulls away. A miniature orchestra inside my chest strikes an ominous minor chord. I'm seriously considering moving in again when—

"Adina." His accent, the one I love so much, clings to my name like it belongs there. Like that's the way my name was always meant to be said. "This . . . You know it can't happen. I'm too old for you, and I'm your teacher, and . . ." Any other reasons get lost in the wave of shame that begins to turn my face hot.

His words crash and explode in my skull, making word confetti. Making me feel tiny and stupid and worst of all, *young*.

"I—I'm sorry. I . . ." *I thought you'd kiss me back?* How could I have gotten this so wrong? I was so sure. I was *so sure* he wanted this too.

His lips make a tight, thin smile. A smile that says, "Hey, it's okay," but nothing is okay. I am going to combust. I have never been this embarrassed in my life. He won't meet my eyes, and his hand drops to his lap, leaving mine cold, cold, cold.

"I should go. I'll go." I pack my viola as fast as I can. Suddenly I'm fourteen years old and in Eitan Mizrahi's bedroom. Except that time, I got what I wanted: I was able to change his mind.

"That's probably a good idea," Arjun says to the floor. Clearly there's no changing *his* mind.

As I race down his hallway and into the elevator, my heart,

10

which swelled when I laid my hand on his, shrinks to the size of a pea. Maybe it even disappears completely. It occurs to me he might be so uncomfortable that he'll drop me as a student. Give up on me. I'd have to find a new teacher, and no one understands my music the way he does.

♪ ♫♩

It's not until I get back on the bus that I wonder why, if he was so eager to shut me down, it took him so long to move his hand from mine.

Tovah

I USED TO THINK BEING A TWIN MEANT I'D NEVER BE the center of attention. That I'd always share the spotlight with my sister or fight for control of it. For a long time, I didn't mind sharing. I hid behind Adina while others praised her for her music, her poise, her looks.

Then my shyness mutated, and I started wanting to be seen too. We tried to share the spotlight until she got jealous. Until something shattered our entire family, and in the aftermath she ruined the precarious balance between us. Turned us into two girls who share some DNA and nothing else.

Tomorrow, when we turn eighteen, Adi and I will take a genetic test that tells us whether we've inherited our mother's Huntington's disease, the asteroid that knocked our family out of orbit four years ago. The black hole slowly swallowing her up.

Tomorrow I take the next step in knowing whether it'll one day swallow me, too.

But tonight I skate.

Lindsay whizzes by, black hair streaming behind her. Four years on the track team have made me somewhat athletic, but I don't have much grace. I never know what to do with my arms.

"Have you noticed," I ask Lindsay when I catch up to her, "that we're the oldest ones here?" There are two other birthday parties at the rink tonight. Mine is the only one that doesn't require parental supervision.

"Considering I'm the same size as most of them, I was feeling like I finally found my people." At four ten, Lindsay's more than a half foot shorter than I am. She wears tiny T-shirts and matchstick jeans and carries a bucket of a purse the size of her torso. "Admit it. You're having fun."

It was Lindsay's idea to have my birthday here, and I'm grateful for the distraction. Great Skate is a relic from the 1980s. Neon orange carpet in the dining area, strobe lights, outdated music collection. It smells like foot spray and fryer grease. Adi and I spent birthdays here as kids, eating oily pizza and hoping the guys we liked would ask us to skate with them. At that age, holding a guy's clammy hand while Aerosmith's "I Don't Want to Miss a Thing" played from the rink's scratchy speakers was the most romantic thing I could imagine.

"I'm . . . trying," I say after grappling for the right word.

Though my sister and I ignore each other most days, Great

13

Skate isn't the same without her. If no one asked us to dance during couples skate—or more accurately, if Adi didn't like the boys who inevitably asked her—we'd glide around the rink with our arms linked, pretending we didn't care. And after a few laps, we didn't. We were the independent Siegel sisters! We didn't need boys.

We slow down as we approach Lindsay's boyfriend, Troy, and his friend Zack, both wobbling on their skates near the rink entrance. Lindsay, Troy, and I are proud AP kids who've spent most of high school preparing for college. Advanced classes, student council, after-school sports, and as many other extracurriculars we can squeeze in. When Lindsay started dating Troy at the beginning of sophomore year, Zack, whose only AP class is Studio Art, joined our group.

Given what this birthday means, I hoped tonight would be just Lindsay and me, but I'm used to sharing my best friend with Troy. While there's nothing wrong with him, sometimes I want to be selfish. I'm just not brave enough to tell her.

Lindsay drags her toe to stop and tugs on Troy's Seahawks sweatshirt strings. "I can't tell if you guys are pathetic or adorable."

"Pathetic," Troy grumbles. "That group of fourth graders has lapped us four times. I think I'll stick to writing about others' athletic achievements." Troy's the school newspaper's sports reporter, and he can rattle off statistics about all of Seattle's teams. None of them ever seem to be winning.

"I prefer adorable." Zack wobbles and nearly loses his bal-

14

ance. His wavy russet hair falls in his face, and he has to grab the wall for support. "Nailed it."

"Have you been finger painting?" I ask, gesturing to his hands. His knuckles are smudged blue and yellow.

Zack examines them. Grins like he's just realized he's a mess. "It's mixed media, and I happen to be using my fingers."

"Sounds like finger painting to me."

"That's because you're not an ar-*tiste* like Zack is, Tov," Lindsay puts in.

"Hardy-har. Got any big plans now that you're eighteen?" Zack says. "You can pierce or tattoo anything. Vote. Go into an *adult* store." His mouth quirks up when he mentions this last one, and when his thick-lashed hazel eyes catch mine, I feel my cheeks grow warm.

"I'll be keeping it pretty tame," I say. He doesn't know what my actual, life-changing turning-eighteen plans are.

A group of five girls skate by with arms locked around one another. "Don't break the chain!" one of them shouts, and the others giggle.

"Oh, to be nine," Troy says in a mock-wistful tone. "Those halcyon days when we didn't know what integrals or derivatives were . . ."

"Don't remind me," Lindsay says. "I have at least three hours of AP Calc waiting for me at home. And about a trillion college essays."

This is what AP kids do when we're not in school: talk about school.

"I bet Tovah's already finished her college apps," Zack says.

Even in AP land, I'm a shameless overachiever. I have no problem embracing it. I love when everyone begs to peek at my meticulous study guides or when I'm the first person in class to turn in a test.

"The one that matters, yes. I sent it in last week." Johns Hopkins University in Baltimore has been my goal since seventh grade, when I went to a summer program there for girls interested in science and medicine. My favorite professor was a surgeon who let us watch an open-heart surgery, and while some of the kids shut their eyes, I was riveted. I'd always loved science class the most, but this—I was watching her physically fix someone. It felt powerful. Important.

Since then I've shadowed as many local doctors as I can, and I volunteer at a Seattle hospital. Because I applied early decision, I'll hear back in December. Biology program at Johns Hopkins, and then, if all goes well, med school there too. The next five to ten years of my life perfectly planned out.

"I bow down to you." Zack attempts to do so and almost topples over again.

The sight of this nearly six-foot-tall guy stumbling on skates tugs at my heart. Makes it race faster that its usual sixty bpm. My mind, in all its infinite logic, reminds me this crush can't become anything more than that. My future is too much of a question mark to drag someone else into my life.

Textbooks and exams don't have emotions. They're much safer.

The music stops midsong, and the DJ booms over the speakers: "Helloooooo, and thanks for coming out to Great Skate tonight! Everyone having a grrrrrreat time?"

All the kids yell back that yes, they are.

"I can't hear you," the DJ taunts in that way all announcers love to do, and we all bellow back, though Zack rolls his eyes at me. "We have a few birthdays here tonight. Can Sienna, Nathan, and . . . Tovah come up here?"

He hesitates before saying my name, the way most people do when faced with an unfamiliar word. It's not hard to pronounce, but I don't like how he utters it: like he's questioning it.

I glare at Lindsay. "You didn't."

She tries to make her pale-green eyes innocent. Fails. "Get over there, birthday girl," she says, laughing as she gives me a push.

"I despise you," I tell her before skating to the middle of the rink along with the two kids, who blink up at me like I'm, well, an adult at a skating rink full of children. I grind my teeth—my worst habit—and cross my arms, wishing I could shrink to the size of a third grader. My sister, who prefers the company of string instruments to people, would hate it even more.

"How old is everyone turning?" the DJ asks.

Lindsay's filming a video on her phone. A playful smile bends Zack's lips, which I've imagined kissing only when I feel like torturing myself.

"I'm ten!" yells Nathan, and Sienna one-ups him with, "Eleven!"

17

"I'm, uh, eighteen," I mutter, which gets a few laughs and gasps from the kids.

Eighteen. It's supposed to be a lucky number. Hebrew letters have numerical value, and the word "chai," meaning "life," is spelled with two letters that add up to eighteen. It's a word we toast with—"l'chaim!"—and carry around on necklaces. Since my mother's diagnosis, eighteen has meant something different. It doesn't mean luck or life. It means the opposite. The worst thing that could possibly happen, multiplied by eighteen, raised to the eighteenth power.

I don't know the Hebrew word for that.

The DJ leads everyone in "Happy Birthday," and I suffer through thirty more seconds of humiliation. As I skate back to my friends, the DJ says, "Now it's time for you to find that special someone for our couples skate."

The lights turn red. Seal's "Kiss from a Rose" starts playing, though none of us are old enough to remember when it was actually popular. If it ever was. My taste is more nineties grunge, thanks to my father's lifelong Nirvana obsession. No one else in our family can stand Kurt Cobain's growl or distorted guitar.

Tonight the couples skate fills me with more dread than it did when I was twelve. Lindsay and Troy are already slowly circling the rink. The kids pair off, their nervous laughter mixing with Seal's velvety vocals. I envy their naive confidence.

Zack's gaze meets mine. His eyebrows lift. My heart plummets.

"I'm going to take a break," I say quickly. He can't ask me to skate with him—because I can't say yes. Before he can reply, I clomp off the rink.

Before entering my house, I kiss my fingertips and touch them to the mezuzah on the doorpost.

My parents are watching an Israeli movie in the living room, subtitles on for my dad's benefit. Adina and I speak Hebrew with our mother, who was born in Tel Aviv and lived there until right after her mandatory military service. We call her Ima and our father Aba. He's American and not quite fluent in Hebrew, though he's been taking classes for years.

"Yom huledet sameach." Ima wishes me a happy birthday as Aba pauses the movie. Her head jerks upward. Twice. Three times.

It doesn't look too unusual unless it happens thirty or forty times a day.

Huntington's makes her body do things she can't control, makes her temper unpredictable, makes her forget names and conversations. I never know if something I say will make her furious, or if she'll remember tomorrow where I went tonight. Or if one day she'll forget my birthday altogether.

"Todah," I thank her.

"Eich ha'yah?" Aba asks in stilted Hebrew.

"About as fun as skating with a few dozen small children can be."

He smiles, and then an alarm on his phone beeps. "Time for kinuach," he says.

A while ago Ima insisted we call her pill regimen "dessert" so she wouldn't sound as sick. There's no cure for Huntington's, but the meds reduce her symptoms. Mood stabilizers and antidepressants, plus antinausea pills to combat the side effects.

I was fourteen when Ima was diagnosed. She'd been acting strangely for a while, dropping cups and plates, forgetting conversations we'd had. Yelling at us when she'd only ever been gentle. Huntington's is a genetic disease that slowly kills the brain's neurons. There's no way to tell when symptoms will appear or how fast the disease will progress, though usually people start showing signs in their forties or fifties. Sometimes before then. People gradually lose the ability to walk and talk and swallow food. In the final stages of the disease, they're confined to beds in assisted living facilities. Time between onset and death is ten to thirty years, and there's no cure.

Though her symptoms aren't grave now, the reality that this disease is fatal has only started to sink in over the past few years.

I leave my parents to their movie and head upstairs to my room. When I flick on the lights, I jump: my sister's standing in the middle of the room like she's haunting the place.

"You scared me," I accuse, and she rolls her shoulders in a shrug that suggests she's not actually sorry. I swipe an orange plastic case off my desk and shove in the night guard my dentist makes me wear for bruxism: grinding my teeth too much, especially while sleeping. It's caused by stress, but my hectic

20

schedule will have been worth it when I'm accepted to Johns Hopkins.

"I wanted to talk to you."

She hasn't been in my room in a while. With the light on, she scrutinizes the walls, the photo collages of me and Lindsay and a few other friends. My shelves overflow with medical books and Jewish texts. A printout of next week's Torah portion, Ha'azinu, on my desk so I can study it before services. Then there are the academic achievement awards and middle school Science Olympiad medals. Framed above my desk is my most prized possession: a ticket from a Nirvana show my dad went to when he was my age.

I'm not sure what's on Adina's walls. I haven't been in her room in a while either.

"Fine. Talk."

Adi regards my bed as though she doesn't know if she should sit or not. Pushing some of her hair off her shoulder, she settles for standing, crossing one ankle behind the other. We're fraternal twins, "te'omot" in Hebrew. It's similar to the Hebrew word for coordination, which when it comes to us is wildly inaccurate. We share some features: same long thin nose, same curves. Adina's always been more comfortable in dresses that accentuate the lines of her body, while I prefer loose clothes that disguise mine. We have the same thick almost-black hair, though mine is coarse and hers is like silk. I chopped it into a pixie when I started high school, but Adina keeps hers long, curls twisting halfway down her back. Even if I wanted to look like her, I never will.

21

Her dark eyes are hard on mine. She has Ima's eyes, while mine are light blue like Aba's. After a couple agonizing minutes of silence, she says, "I don't want to take the test tomorrow."

"Are you fucking kidding me?" The night guard goops up my words. Makes them less sharp than I want them to be.

Not knowing has to be worse than a positive result. We can prepare for the worst. We can't prepare for an unknown. Not taking the test means even more years spent wondering, wondering, wondering if we're going to end up like Ima. If we take it, there's a chance for relief. To know that we've been spared.

As little as we talk these days, I'm too scared to do it alone. This fate binds us as sisters, as twins, though the rest of our lives have spun in opposite directions. It's something we have to do together—or not at all.

"I keep thinking about how much happier I'd be if I didn't know." Her arms hug her chest. Adina's prone to big, dramatic emotions. If she thinks she's played poorly in a show, she whines and slams doors, sometimes even cries. I'm thirty-six minutes older than she is, but the gap between us could span an entire geologic era. "I'm not ready."

I pull a pair of pajama pants from a dresser drawer. Slam it shut. *"Adina."* I snarl her name as I whirl around to face her. "We've had four years."

"I want to keep focusing on viola. If I don't take it, I won't have to worry as much about the future, and—"

"You know why you have to take it with me," I interrupt her. "You owe me."

22

The heaviness of her debt sags between us as we stare each other down. She knows what she did. Knows the balance between us is permanently skewed. And that means I get what I want now.

Adina's jaw quivers. "I was hoping for a little empathy. But clearly I went to the wrong place."

"So you're done in here?" I ask as I start unbuttoning my jeans. Her puppy eyes won't win her any pity.

"I'm done," she says crisply. I shut the door behind her. There's nothing left to talk about. There's only tomorrow.

✖✖✖✖✖

Adina glances away as a nurse jabs needles into our veins, but I watch the glass vials fill with red. I've never been squeamish. It'll make me an excellent surgeon.

I cling to the statistics. There's a fifty percent chance each of us will test positive. A positive result means someone will develop Huntington's. Fifty percent isn't the worst probability, I try to convince myself. A fifty percent chance of rain in Seattle doesn't always mean a downpour; sometimes it means gloom and gray skies. I pray for gloom and gray skies.

In three weeks, we'll know if neither or both or one of us is going to die the same way our mother will.

Three

Adina

A FAMILY OF THREE LINGERS IN THE STRINGS SECTION of Muse and Music, where I work part-time. The parents murmur as they scan price tags. Their young daughter touches all the most expensive instruments.

"You look like you could use some help," I say.

The parents look relieved. "Hailey's always been musical," the mother says, placing a hand on her daughter's shoulder. "She's nine now, and we'd like to sign her up for music classes."

"We told her she could pick any instrument," the father says, "but I'm afraid neither of us knows how to play anything, so we're a bit lost."

"I want to play the violin." Hailey points to a Windsor. "I like this one."

"What do you know about this?" the mother asks me.

"Windsor is good quality. Solid choice for a beginner. But," I say, bending down to Hailey's level so we're eye to eye, "*everyone* plays the violin. You're going to be one of twenty violins in your school orchestra, I guarantee it." Her hand drops from the Windsor. "Do you really want to be like everyone else, or do you want to be unique?"

She shakes her head. I have said the magic words. "I don't want to be like everyone else."

I grin like I am about to tell her a secret. "How about the viola?"

I show them a Stentor, a Mendini, a Cecilio. The makers' Italian names waterfall off my tongue. Then I go over rental rates. "If she's planning on playing it long-term—and you said she's very musical—purchasing the viola outright will cost less than an entire year of renting."

Hailey likely has a long life ahead of her to play viola. To become a soloist, even, if she truly devotes herself to the instrument. If I test positive, if I develop the disease one day, when will I have to stop playing? That's what I haven't been able to get out of my head since the blood draw a few days ago.

"You've made our decision very easy," the father says.

I make commission on every sale, and I make a lot of sales.

The deal I struck with my parents when I turned sixteen was that if I wanted to continue taking private lessons and playing in the youth symphony, I had to pay half. Ima encouraged my music, but Aba wanted me to experience the "real world," which did not revolve around long-dead nineteenth-century composers. But I've always been more comfortable

25

with long-dead composers and string instruments than with anyone with a beating heart.

My manager, Oscar, swoops over once the family leaves. "Can you work your magic on that guy over in guitars? He's been here for more than an hour."

The guy is the stereotype of a moody acoustic guitarist. He hunches on a stool with an Ibanez in his lap, strumming a Bob Dylan song, shaggy black hair falling in his face.

"You know," I say as I approach, "if you own it, you can play it any time you want."

He plucks another few chords. "I've been in here awhile, huh?"

"I love Dylan." I do not, but music tastes are sacred. There is no more immediate connection you can make with someone than learning they like the same composer, the same band, the same vocalist as you. "And that's a great instrument."

When he finally glances up at me, his eyes rove over my body. Up. Down. Up. From my hips to my chest to my reddest red lipstick, a shade called Siren. Men have been looking at me in ways they probably shouldn't for a long time. Seniors leered at me in the halls even when I was a lowly freshman. I developed early, wore underwire when all the other girls were still in training bras, and I have never looked my age. The attention typically makes me feel important. Wanted. Like I can be a star onstage instead of an invisible piece of an orchestra. Usually, I adore being looked at, but today it irks me. Arjun's rejection and the impending test results have stripped some of my confidence.

"Can't afford it now, unfortunately." He sets it back on the wall. "Do you play . . . Adina?" His gaze lingers on the name tag above my breast. Today I wish I could paste it to my forehead.

"I play viola."

"Don't tell me you're into *classical music*." He says *classical music* the way someone might say *using pliers to pull off your fingernails one by one.*

That sets me off, makes me wish I'd told him how overrated I find Dylan. He has probably never listened to a classical piece in its entirety. He probably equates it to elevator music. Music without a soul or a heartbeat.

"I *am* into classical music, in fact," I say. "It's been around for more than a thousand years, its composers have more name recognition than whatever 'indie' music you're listening to right now, and symphonies sell out millions of performances a year. So go ahead, tell me classical music is tedious or boring or inferior."

He shrugs, jamming his hands into his pockets. "I gotta go," he mumbles, pocketing a few fifty-cent guitar picks as he leaves. If he dares come back, I will report him.

Music snobs who hate classical music mystify me. Classical music is everything to me, and since viola is what I've devoted my life to, I don't tolerate critics. Without viola, I'm not sure who I'd be.

♩ ♫♩

The nearer doomsday draws, the harder it is to keep my nerves inside. My tights develop so many holes, I have to buy new ones.

While Tovah has a whole group of close friends, I only have my mother to confide in. On a day off from work, I visit Ima's fifth-grade classroom. I need some kind of reassurance from her that I am strong enough to handle this.

My first fourteen years carried no tragedies, but Tovah and I still consoled each other during rough times, like when Papa, Aba's father, passed away. We only saw him a couple times a year, but I couldn't wrap my mind around him being suddenly *gone*. Tovah, sad but logical, told me to focus on my good memories of him, hugged me when I cried. Later, I was there for her first heartbreak: when she lost in the final round of the regional Science Olympiad in seventh grade. Silver was a prettier color than gold anyway, I said to her. The other day in her room, I noticed the medal still hung on her wall.

Tovah had no kind words for me then. I should have expected as much. She claimed, as always, that I am the one to blame, but she is the reason we no longer share secrets or inside jokes.

At her desk, Ima slashes assignments with a red pen, her hand trembling. Errant scribbles mark up the margins. She probably has only a couple years left to work, and she loves her classroom more than anything. I help my mother out at least once a week, but I doubt my sister has ever set foot in here.

"How were your students today?" I ask Ima in Hebrew.

"Today was movie Monday." Words used to fly from her lips at warp speed. Now, even in her native language, they're slow, plotted, like her mouth is full of honey. "We started *Singin' in the Rain*." Each Saturday after sundown, Ima and I watch a classic film together; we watch *Singin' in the Rain* at least twice a year. Classical music and classic films: I am an anachronism. "Did you know I wanted to be a tap dancer when I saw it as a kid in Israel? I taped shekels to my shoes and practiced in the street."

"I didn't know that."

My vision of Israel, and my mother's home in Tel Aviv, is blurred. She rarely talks about growing up there, snatches of memories that sound distant as fairy tales. Her mother, who we now suspect had Huntington's too, died when Ima was young. After she served her time in the military, Ima moved to the States for college and never returned. Another thing I cannot picture: my ima holding a gun.

Her past terrifies and fascinates me, but she's having one of her good days, and I don't want to destroy it with a question that could leave a bruise. Huntington's is okay to talk about, and yet my mother's life in Israel is off-limits.

"Why didn't you do it?" I ask. "Become a tap dancer?"

"I have no grace. Not like you, Adina'le." In Hebrew, adding "le" to the end of a name turns it into a diminutive. Her mouth tips into a wicked grin. "I caught two kids passing love notes back and forth this week."

"Really? Who?"

"Caleb and Annabel."

"Didn't you send Caleb to the principal last week for putting gum in Annabel's hair?"

"Don't you remember fifth grade? That was how you told someone you liked them."

Fifth grade: passing notes to Tovah, scribbled in Hebrew in case they were intercepted, tree tag at recess, giggling during sex ed, being sent out into the hall to calm down, not being allowed back inside until we were "mature enough" to handle talking about vaginas and penises. Fifth grade was, quite possibly, one of our best years.

"I had so many boyfriends in fifth grade. I could barely keep track."

Ima laughs. She has the best laugh of anyone I know. It's deep and throaty and makes me feel as though I'm truly funny. I'm only ever funny around her—and Arjun.

"I need to ask you something." I take a deep breath. There's not enough time between me and our next doctor's appointment. I want to pile weeks and months and years on top of each other until I'm confident I can be okay with either outcome. "Would anything have changed for you if you were diagnosed earlier? Or if you'd gotten tested and you knew you were going to develop it?"

Ima purses her lips as she ponders this, loosening the knitted scarf around her neck. Years ago she declared she was going to knit all of us sweaters and scarves and blankets, but soon found she didn't have the time. Now she has too much of it; her health has made her drop commitments at our synagogue and with her friends. During our movie nights, her needles clack as old Hollywood stars sing and dance onscreen. Half-finished projects hang across the back of the couch and kitchen chairs.

"It might have. Maybe I would have gotten my teaching

certification sooner, or I wouldn't have wasted my time on jobs I didn't care about." Ima changed majors three times in college, then bounced from job to job before going back to school to become a teacher. It's strange how aimless she was, considering both Tovah and I have known our paths for so long. We didn't inherit the wandering gene from her. "But if you're asking if it would have changed my decision to have children, I can't answer that. I can't imagine a life without you and Tovah in it."

I don't want the machala arura, the damn disease, to sneak up on me, but I am also not sure I want to plan my own funeral. If I don't find out, though, perhaps I'd wonder every day if I might soon start losing control over parts of my body.

"Knock-knock." Another teacher pokes her head inside the classroom. Mrs. Augustine, who I had for fourth grade, has red spiral curls streaked with gray. "Do you need help with anything, Simcha?"

"Thanks, Jill, but my daughter's helping me today."

Mrs. Augustine squints at me through huge purple glasses. "Is that Adina?"

I hold up my hand. "Present."

She laughs as though I have made a hilarious joke. I haven't. "How's high school treating you?"

"All right. Only eight more months of it."

"Your mom says you're keeping busy with the violin, and of course we're all so proud to hear about your sister. I heard she was a National Merit Scholar!"

31

"She was," I say through gritted teeth. I don't bother correcting her about the violin.

Everyone always talks about how noble Tovah's pursuits are, how brilliant her mind is. We need more women in STEM, after all, and apparently Tovah is going to singlehandedly solve the imbalance. She is going to save lives—but I am going to enrich them.

"Well. I'll leave you two. Simcha, we're still on for the faculty breakfast next week?"

"I never pass up pancakes," Ima says with a big smile, which doesn't leave her face until Mrs. Augustine's heels *click-clack* out of earshot. Then she turns back to me. "I brag about both of you," she says, as though she can tell from my stiff posture that Mrs. Augustine's words have hit a nerve. "You know how much I treasure your music."

Logically, I know my parents don't play favorites. But I have always believed my mother understands me better than she will ever understand my sister.

"I'm no National Merit Scholar, but thank you."

"You are at least a hundred other good things. Don't let what she said bother you, okay?"

I shrug. Ima returns to grading her assignments, and I start cleaning the classroom. As I push the vacuum across the carpet, I force my thoughts somewhere happier. I can still feel the warmth of Arjun's hand beneath mine. Wouldn't he have moved away faster if he didn't like me? The thought builds me back up, restores my confidence.

As far as I know, Arjun doesn't have a girlfriend, though last year he hinted at it. Occasionally, he used the pronoun "we," which sent shivers of envy through me. *We* are going to the farmers' market Saturday. *We* are going to the symphony next week. I was only a me.

Once when I used the bathroom, I found a tube of wild rose–scented moisturizer in the medicine cabinet. Did she simply leave it there one day, or did she regularly spend the night? Was she moving in? I squeezed a dime-size amount onto my palm. I wondered if Arjun liked when she wore it. If it made her skin soft when he touched her with his long, beautiful fingers. Then I panicked. Arjun might notice it when I got back to the studio, so I turned on the water and scraped my hands until they no longer smelled sweet like Arjun's girlfriend.

When I checked a few weeks later, the lotion was gone, and when Arjun talked about his weekend plans, his "we" turned back into an "I."

"Adina?" Ima's yell penetrates my eardrums over the vacuum's roar. I switch it off. "I've been calling you!"

"Sorry," I say. "The vacuum—"

She interrupts, waving me over. "Come here for a second." Before Huntington's, she was even-tempered, but now her moods shift quickly. It's jarring when she raises her voice.

Above her desk is a window with a view of the playground. "Do you hear that?" she says.

Whatever it is, I probably couldn't hear it over the wail of the vacuum. "Hear what?"

"The barking." She sounds exasperated. "I've been listening

33

to it all day. I think there are some dogs on the playground."

There probably are. Too many people in Seattle let their dogs go off-leash. Last week at the bus stop, a collarless mutt yapped at me for a full fifteen minutes before the 44 bus arrived.

I've always had excellent hearing, able to pick up nuances in songs, detect when a single string is slightly out of tune. But right now I only hear the wheels of the janitor's cart squeaking down the hallway.

"They have to be somewhere out there. Under the slide maybe? It could be dangerous with so many kids around, especially if the dogs are strays."

"Ima, I don't hear them."

"Oh! There they go again." She pushes open the window, letting in a cool breeze. "Get out of here!"

Then I realize it: The barking isn't real. The dogs aren't real.

I've never been alone with her when she's—*hallucinating.* The word itself is terrifying. It has too many syllables; there is no simple word to explain how complicated and scary it is. Aba's always been around, and Aba, who takes notes during Ima's doctor's appointments, always knows what to do. Whenever this happens at home, I flee the room as fast as I can.

She's sticking her head out the window, flapping her arms wildly. I rack my brain, trying to remember how Ima's specialist told us to handle her hallucinations. We're supposed to tell her that we believe she's really hearing this, but I can't go along with it. I have to snap her out of this somehow.

"They're not real. They're not real, okay? You're imagining

34

it." I want her to believe *me*, not whatever's going on inside her head.

"Go back where you came from!" She climbs on top of her chair to fit more of herself out the window. "That barking! I can't stand it, Adina. It's dreadful."

"Please," I implore her, steadying the wobbly chair with my hands. "Be careful."

Her head whips around. "Don't just stand there. Help me! Azor li!" Continuing to mutter under her breath, she stumbles off the chair and tears out of the classroom.

"Ima!" I chase after her, punching open the metal doors to the playground. A few kids on swings stare at the strange teacher crouching on the woodchips, peering underneath the slide.

"I can't find them," Ima says, "but I can still hear them!"

This could be you someday, a voice at the back of my mind warns.

I swallow around a knot in my throat. *It'll be okay soon. We'll get through this and we'll go home and have dinner and I'll practice for my audition. Aba will take her to the doctor and they'll change her medication and everything will be fine.*

"We'll find them." Cold air bites at my cheeks and nose. "I'll help you, okay?"

Then, certain I'm doing this all wrong, I yell and wave my arms along with her. Together, we shoo the imaginary dogs.

Four

Tovah

THE HUMAN BODY IS MADE UP OF MILLIONS OF microscopic puzzle pieces, and in med school I'll have to memorize them all. Understanding what makes us work has always brought me comfort. I seek out the *why*, and I learn the answer.

It's why AP Bio is my favorite class. Today I snip the hinges of a frog's mouth and open it up, spelling out words to Lindsay so she can label our diagram. Esophagus, pharynx, vomerine and maxillary teeth. She half covers her face as she scribbles on the worksheet.

"I can't watch," she says.

With latex-gloved hands, I open the frog's body cavity. "Look, you can see its stomach and pancreas! And that curled-up thing is its small intestine."

I try to sound enthusiastic, but with the test results more than a week away, each day brings me closer to solving my own unknown, and this lab isn't distracting me the way I'd hoped it would. Nothing can. At synagogue over the weekend, I sat on a hard bench in the sanctuary with the rest of my family while Rabbi Levine spoke. I love weekly services; I love the way Hebrew sounds when the entire congregation recites it together. But when I left the synagogue, I couldn't remember what the Torah portion had been about. I never space out like that.

At the lab station next to ours, Henry Zukowski and Evan Nakayama are pretending to make the frogs talk.

"I feel funny," Henry says in a high-pitched voice as he puppeteers a frog's mouth.

"Do I have something on my face?" Evan says in the same tone, and both of them cackle. I roll my eyes.

"Please be mature and respectful, or I'm taking the sharp objects away!" Ms. Anaya calls. She stops by our station. "Tovah, careful with your incisions! You nicked that little guy's left atrium! Why don't you give Lindsay a turn?"

Heat flares on my cheeks, and I clench my teeth. Ms. Anaya's my favorite teacher; she loves biology so much that all her sentences seem to be punctuated with exclamation points. She's never criticized me before. I can't even be good at what I'm supposed to be good at, and I have a feeling I won't be back to my old self until we get our results.

Well. Depending on what those results are.

"Sorry," I mumble. I try to pass the scalpel to Lindsay, but she shakes her head and clings to her pencil.

"You okay?"

37

"I need some air." I peel off my gloves, toss them on the table, and snatch my backpack. In my rush, my backpack knocks something hanging off the edge of a lab table. Someone gasps, maybe me, as a metal tray flies off the table and a frog plummets to the floor.

The classroom goes silent for a split second before erupting into noise. "Oh my God!" and "Did Tovah Siegel seriously just do that?" and "I'm gonna throw up."

Ms. Anaya tells us to have respect for everything we work with in the lab, especially anything that used to be alive. I've taken away whatever dignity that frog had left.

"Tovah," Ms. Anaya says gently, "I'll take care of this. Why don't you go get cleaned up?"

Cleaned up? I have no idea what she's talking about until I notice the frog's not just on the floor—some of it is on my sweater, too.

"Lindsay, could you help her?"

Lindsay springs to her feet and steers me outside. I'm still speechless, but I love her for not laughing. I love her for not complaining about how vile she must find this. I love her for helping me scrub the sweater as best we can with generic pink soap and school bathroom water that has two temperatures, cold and ice-cold.

"Thanks for helping," I say.

"Always."

Lindsay has some spare clean clothes in her gym locker, though her long-sleeved shirt stretches too tight across my too-big breasts.

"You look fine," Lindsay says as I tug at the shirt in the locker room mirror. "I know you hate them, but I wish I had your boobs."

"Take them. Please." My curves aren't something I've ever been comfortable with—and sometimes I think it's because my body looks so much better on Adina.

Lindsay's phone buzzes with a text as the bell rings. "Troy's heading to the parking lot. Lunch at Mario's?" All seniors with at least a B average can get off-campus passes.

"Oh." I'm not feeling supersocial at the moment, so I lie: "I have some work to finish up before fifth period."

She's giggling at something on her phone, no longer paying attention. "Sure. Okay."

Lindsay's mine until her boyfriend comes along, and then I'm microscopic.

I bundle myself in a peacoat so the shirt looks a little less obscene. I'm not hungry, and I don't feel like facing the cafeteria. The table of student council reps, where Lindsay and I usually sit when we don't go off campus, is always the loudest. This year I'm a senior rep, which means I have to go to a couple scintillating faculty meetings a month and report back to the rest of the council. It isn't glamorous, but I needed a leadership role on my résumé.

I roam the school. Near the math wing, I scoop up a discarded copy of our student newspaper, the *Roar*. I pause before pitching it into the recycling bin. Next to Troy's article about our football team's "devastating loss" last week is a photo of Adina.

It's part of a series the paper does highlighting student achievements. She never told me she was being interviewed, but that doesn't surprise me. The piece calls her a "prodigy," which isn't news. In the photo, she's wearing her usual Adina smirk, this look plenty of guys reading the paper have likely said lewd things about. Though I'm sure few of them give a shit about classical music.

She gets all this praise because she has this innate talent, this natural musical ability. I know, because I don't have it. I've had to work for every bit of my success in high school: studied for hours for the PSAT and SAT and ACT, campaigned for a seat on student council, fought for a volunteer position at the hospital.

Not for the first time lately, I wonder if waiting for the test results would be easier if we could talk. But there's no way I'd initiate that conversation after everything that's happened between us.

I ball up the newspaper and toss it in the bin.

Eventually I wind up in the art hallway. Most of the student work on the walls is pretty good, though I don't know anything about composition or color theory.

"Admiring my work?"

The voice makes me jump, and I spin around to face Zack Baker-Horowitz. He's wearing my favorite jacket of his, a tweed blazer with elbow patches, over a faded green T-shirt that makes his hazel eyes more jade than brown. He's holding a cardboard plate and a slice of cafeteria pizza.

"Which one's yours?" I ask.

"These three." All of them are mixed media with various random objects that go off the edges. They're imperfect but interesting. He props an elbow on the wall next to his work, his body less than a foot from me.

I examine each piece, aware he's watching me, waiting for my verdict. It makes me wonder if he craves a compliment from me, though he's the one applying to art school. An agonizingly logical part of my mind wonders, *How will he make any money doing that?*

"I don't get it," I say finally.

A little wrinkle appears between his brows as he frowns. "There's nothing to *get*."

"Isn't art supposed to have some deep meaning?"

"I don't think it always needs to." With his free hand, he points at one of the pieces. "I like to draw connections between ordinary things. I'm experimenting with different ways of telling stories using paint and found objects I've been collecting. Receipts, grocery lists, stuff like that. It's an exploration of the mundane."

"So your art is mundane?"

He cracks a smile, exposing a small gap between his two front teeth that I find adorable, and moves his elbow off the wall to nudge my arm. Though my jacket is so thick I can barely feel it, my stomach does backflips. I wonder what it would feel like to touch him longer than a split second. "Exactly."

41

Really, my crush on him is more of an admiration. In the spring when we both run track, he pushes back his hair with neon sweatbands and strikes dorky, flashy poses at the finish line that make me laugh. I can't date him, so I'm resigned to appreciating him: his confidence and his jokes and his long eyelashes. And his vintage jacket, of course, because he has his own style and I can appreciate that, too.

"You're not at lunch with Lindsay and Troy?" I ask.

"Nah." He stares at the ground for a moment. "You know that whole B-average thing? I'm sort of working on that. Last week I had a bad test . . . or three."

"Oh." I chew the inside of my cheek, feeling guilty for assuming a B average was easy to maintain. In my AP classes, kids weep over Bs. I'd weep over a B too, but I've only ever gotten a B-plus in Introduction to Drawing, actually, which I took freshman year to fulfill an art elective. Somehow, the introduction was too advanced for me. Mrs. Willoughby insisted we were graded on effort and not talent, but still, it was clear my apple and orange baskets looked like cerebral hemispheres, not fruit.

He must sense the awkwardness because he changes the subject. "Happy New Year, by the way." Rosh Hashanah, the Jewish New Year, is tomorrow. My family will spend hours at our synagogue, both morning and evening, to observe it.

"You too. Doing anything for it?"

One of Zack's moms is Jewish, but his family is pretty secular, while I was raised Conservative Jewish. We have this running joke that he'll never be as Jewish as I am. Obviously it isn't an actual competition, and if it were, well, I've already won.

Conservative Judaism isn't at all related to American politi-
cal beliefs; "conservative" simply means we conserve Jewish tradition. We obey halacha, Jewish law, but we're flexible enough to
adapt as society progresses. "Tradition and change"—that's the
motto of the movement. My family and I keep kosher, observe
Shabbat, pray multiple times daily, and attend synagogue
weekly, though much of our spirituality takes place outside of
that. We're a people with a history, thousands of years of culture
and traditions.

There's this phrase "klal Yisrael," which means "all of
Israel," that all Jews are connected. I'll admit I'm drawn to Zack
partially because he's Jewish too, one of fewer than ten kids in
my thousand-person school who are.

"I get presents. Does that count?"

"Barely." Gift giving isn't a typical part of Jewish holidays.
Some families exchange gifts on Chanukah because of its prox-
imity to Christmas, but we haven't done that since Adina and I
were kids.

"Then I'll have to impress you with my Hebrew," he says, and
I lift my eyebrows, a challenge. He clears his throat. "L'shanah
tovah . . . Tovah."

"Kol hakavod," I commend him. "And nice pronunciation."
I'm sweating in my coat, but I refuse to reveal Lindsay's triple-XS
shirt.

"L'shanah tovah" means "for a good year." My name means
"good" in Hebrew, hence the double Tovahs. Adina's name

means "delicate and refined," because of course it does. My name's definition is boring in comparison.

L'shanah tovah, Tovah. I like the way he said it. Maybe *good* isn't so bad after all.

"You know, we've been doing this thing for a while," Zack says. "This our-best-friends-are-dating-so-we-might-as-well-hang-out-with-each-other-too thing."

"Yeah . . ." Though we don't hang out just the two of us, not ever. "We have. It's like we each got a bonus friend."

"Bonus friend. I like that." Zack's fingers fidget with his plate. I've never seen him nervous, not even before a track meet. "I wanted to ask you something. Bonus friend to bonus friend. Do you . . . maybe want to see a movie sometime? With me?" When I don't respond right away, he continues: "Or it doesn't have to be a movie. Most movies these days aren't that good anyway. It could be dinner. Somewhere kosher! Or we could go to a science museum—you're into that kind of thing, right? Or an art museum if you wanna make fun of some famous masterpieces . . ." At last he trails off, ripping the plate crookedly in half.

My jacket is suffocating me, my temperature probably well over thirty-seven degrees Celsius. I can handle the joking around. I can pretend the elbow bumping happened by accident. But this is impossible to ignore. As much as I want to say yes, I can't. What's the best possible outcome here—we have a spectacular first date, and then he has to comfort me if/when my life falls apart at the end of the month? He plays the role of supportive boyfriend because he'd be an asshole not to? That isn't how I

44

want to begin my first relationship. If I'm ever going to be with Zack, I should be entirely unburdened.

"I, um." Telling him about the test flashes across my mind for an instant. Then this would turn into a pity party, and I don't want that. "I—can't," I say, because *Ask me again in ten days* would require more explanation than I'm capable of giving.

"Oh. That's fine. Never mind, then. It was just an idea. Don't worry about it." He flicks his hair out of his eyes again and spins to head down the hall. "See ya."

"See you," I mumble.

Zack's meaningless art stares down at me. He was wrong: it does mean something. It means that inside his mind is all this creativity and life and energy. All this color. It's not mundane at all. It's a reminder that today I got too close to him, and I won't make that mistake again.

Five

Adina

TODAY ARJUN IS MUCH TOO FAR AWAY, MY MISTAKE HEAVY between us. There's too much space between our chairs. The legs are bolted to the floor and we are chained to the backs like prisoners.

"I think we should talk about what happened last week," he says, more to my music stand than to me. His voice makes it clear we are not going to talk about how he's fantasized about me every night since that afternoon.

I grip my bow too tightly. I've been dreading this lesson.

"I'd rather forget it," I say. "Please. I shouldn't have . . . whatever. I misinterpreted things. It was . . . a mistake." My tongue trips over the lie. A mistake is accidental. This is not who I am; he has taken my confidence.

Arjun looks relieved. "I was worried you wouldn't come back. I hope you know how much I enjoy working with you. Professionally."

Professionally. The word has a hard edge to it, like it is trying to prove itself to me. I give him a professional nod in return.

"I just want to play," I say *professionally*, so I do. I play Bach and Bartók and Giorgetti and Simonetti and of course Debussy's "The Girl with the Flaxen Hair." At my audition last week, this prelude earned me a spot in the New Year's Eve showcase, but I haven't allowed myself to feel victorious about it yet. I will play two pieces for the showcase, but the Debussy is my show-stopper. If I audition for conservatory, I'll play it there, too.

I don't know what I was expecting, but it wasn't this. I thought—*hoped*—he'd tell me he was wrong, that he does have feelings for me. Evidently, I know nothing.

It's not just that I want to kiss him. It's that I feel more connected to him than I do to anyone else. I've spent my entire life feeling different because I speak another language, because I don't celebrate the same holidays as most people, because I don't call my parents Mom and Dad. Arjun, who immigrated to the United States as an adult, knows what it is like to be tied to a complicated country. There is a lot of good in India, he's said, but also a lot of bad. Israel is similar. I've never met a person who doesn't have a strong opinion about its politics. They always have to share it with me, like there's something I can do about it, like being half Israeli makes me a representative for an entire nation, an entire people. I don't feel fully American, but a language and half my genes can't be enough to tie me to a place I've never been.

Arjun has no praise for today, only critique, though I know I cannot be playing quite that poorly. Perhaps he is trying to more solidly establish himself as the teacher, and me, the student. For the first time, I am relieved when our hour is up.

On my way to the bus stop, I buy a cheeseburger from the food truck parked across the street. I am in desperate need of food therapy. It greases up my fingers and tastes perfectly, excessively salty. The guy at the counter knows me, since I've been coming here after some lessons for nearly a year. He asked for my number once, but greasy food truck guy isn't exactly my type. I have an incurable fondness for musicians.

No one knows I don't keep kosher when I'm not at home. After Ima's diagnosis, it stopped seeming important. Why did God care what I ate? Why did separating meat and dairy, and a hundred other provisions, matter when my mother was suffering so much? At home I observe Shabbat because it means so much to my family. But the day of rest makes me restless, and the services at synagogue are too long. I'm not sure what I believe in anymore, or what I ever believed in, but it's not anything as insignificant as this. When I move out, I will eat whatever I want and practice any time I want. Even on Shabbat.

♪ ♫♪

A blessing spills from my lips, meaningless. I murmur along as Ima leads us in the hamotzi over the braided loaf of challah, but the words are hollow, even if I love the way they sound.

Ba-ruch a-tah A-do-nai e-lo-hei-nu me-lech ha-o-lam, ha-mo-tzi le-chem min ha-a-retz.

Prayers in Hebrew are sung in minor keys. They lilt up and

down; they tremble. When I was small, I could trace the ribbon of Ima's voice even when we sang in large groups at synagogue. It was more confident, more on-key than any of the others. I always wished I could sing, but my vocal cords have never cooperated. That is another reason I fell in love with classical music: no lyrics.

Yom Kippur, the Day of Atonement, began on Shabbat this year. The holiest day of the year—to everyone in my house but me. Ima didn't fast because the ill don't have to, but I've been fasting all day, unable to sneak food past my parents. The last thing I put in my stomach was a bottle of Gatorade yesterday, which helps prepare the body for a fast.

Earlier today we sat through services at our synagogue. Shabbat is sunset Friday to the appearance of stars Saturday night every week, twenty-five hours that endlessly drag. No phones, no computers, no money, no fun. Some Conservative Jews drive on Shabbat, but my family likes the tradition of walking to and from synagogue when we can. The exercise is good for Ima.

"Amen," Ima says, and we all echo her. Her fingers twitch as she reaches for her fork, and her head jerks back and forth.

We're breaking the fast along with my parents' Israeli best friends, the Mizrahis. Gil Mizrahi works with my father at Microsoft, where they are both software engineers, and his wife, Tamar, is a real estate agent and the synagogue gossip. Before dinner, I overheard her telling my parents about Devorah Cohen's daughter, who supposedly left college because the workload was stressing her out. The real reason was that her TA had gotten her pregnant. Since Ima got sick, people from synagogue have visited her regularly, including Devorah Cohen and her daughter, so I am unsure how to react to this rumor.

I add beef brisket, potatoes, and salad to my plate while my father pours wine for Tovah and me. When we were little, we drank grape juice on holidays, but we graduated to wine after our b'not mitzvah—that's the plural of bat mitzvah. I used to get so bored waiting to eat on Jewish holidays, because when you are nine years old, you have no patience for prayers. One thing I never grew out of, I suppose.

Tamar Mizrahi asks us about college, and Tovah monopolizes the conversation with chatter about Johns Hopkins.

"There are so many research centers and opportunities for undergrads to actually get involved," Tovah says between bites. She's talking so fast she can't fully chew her food. I want to tell her *chew, then speak.* "And most of the med students have done undergrad there, so I figure I have a good chance of getting into their med school, too, which is what I want. Plus, I *love* Baltimore."

Please. She's been there once.

"I'm sure you're a shoo-in," Tamar says.

"We'll see!" Tovah chirps, though I detect a layer of nerves in her voice. I'm certain Tovah will earn a monster scholarship that will thrill Aba more than any of the schools I'm applying to—though I still haven't applied. But I mumble to Tamar about the conservatories on my list anyway. However, Manhattan School of Music doesn't have the same name recognition as

Johns Hopkins. People know Juilliard, maybe Berklee.

"Both your girls are so ambitious, Simcha," Tamar says to Ima, though she's looking at Tovah, smiling at Tovah. Gil is too. Tovah's accomplishments are tangible. Worthy.

"We got lucky."

Tamar tucks a wisp of hair back into the blond cloud on top of her head. "You're maturing into such a beautiful young lady, Adina. Such a precious figure. Do you have a boyfriend?"

"Nope." I pop the *p*.

"I always thought you and Eitan would make a good couple." She pierces a slice of brisket with her fork. Her eyes are the same deep brown as Eitan's. "You were both always so serious about your music. Him with the piano, you with viola. You know, he's teaching lessons to some of his students in Jerusalem in his spare time."

"Eitan's much too old for Adi!" Gil says. "How much wine have you had?"

Laughter. Too much of it. My face flames. There are no *beautiful young lady* comments directed at Tovah, who's staring down at her plate. Tovah is cute, with her pixie haircut and faint freckles. But her body language projects so much insecurity, like her skin isn't the right size for her.

I wonder if words like Tamar's make it worse.

A *clang* steals my attention. Ima's knocked two serving dishes into each other. "Clumsy me," she says, and my stomach twists.

"I'm only saying, it's a shame," Tamar continues. "A pretty girl like you should have a boyfriend."

51

"Adina is very busy with her music," Ima says. Rescuing me, because my mother is always on my side. I smile at her in thanks. "She doesn't need a boyfriend if she doesn't want one."

"How does Eitan like Israel?" Aba asks.

"Loves it. But he misses his mother's cooking. Would you believe it?"

More laughter. I drain my glass of wine.

"Whoa there." Aba winks at me. "Should I get you the whole bottle?"

"Please," I say, and he chuckles before drawing us all into a discussion on the history of Rosh Hashanah and Yom Kippur.

Before he met Ima, Aba didn't keep kosher or observe Shabbat, but the traditions were important to her, and therefore they became important to him. He studied Hebrew, though he's never mastered the language, and read tomes on the history of the Jewish people. These days he's more devout than she is. I suppose there's a reason he thinks we should keep putting on these shows of prayers and blessings. He thinks his faith, which hasn't faltered the way mine has, will somehow save us.

Wide-eyed, Tovah digests Aba's every word. If Ima is always on my side, Aba is always on Tovah's. I have heard this story dozens of times, so I chew my food silently. What Tamar said about Eitan hit too close to the truth. The Mizrahis' son was my very first crush. We talked about music and he laughed at my jokes and made hours-long dinners less boring. When I was fourteen and he was eighteen and we'd drunk too much wine after Passover, he invited me into his room. Said he wanted to show me a keyboard piece he was working on, that we could play a duet. It was a few weeks after Ima had been diagnosed. I felt like I had no control over anything in my life, except maybe this. Him.

I kissed him first, mostly to see if he'd kiss back. He did. And more. Zippers unzipped and buckles unbuckled and skin met skin. Everything felt good.

"Are you sure?" He was breathing hard. "You're only four-teen. . . ."

I hated the way the word sounded. *Fourteen.* "Do I look fourteen to you?" We both knew the answer was no.

I had already researched consent laws. In Washington, a fourteen-year-old can consent if her partner is four years older or less. Eitan had just turned eighteen, and I was a few months from fifteen. He told me again and again how beautiful I was. We were probably in his room for a grand total of eight min-utes; still, the ways he touched me made me love my body even more. Made me love the power I had over him. The first time didn't hurt much, but the second time was so much better, and the third, fourth, fifth, which happened over the next several months, were excellent.

I liked it so much. I liked him. I liked sex. Our families never figured it out, and Eitan went to college and I moped through my sophomore year, stalking his Facebook updates and wait-ing for messages, hoping we'd get back together when he came home to visit. And we did, but he always seemed to forget about me whenever he left.

I didn't tell Tovah, though we were still close back then. She was still giggling with her friends about how *cute* some boys in their class were, and what I had done felt so adult. I knew she wouldn't understand.

"Adina," Tovah says, and I blink. "Aba asked you a question."

"Oh. What?"

"He asked why the shofar is blown on Rosh Hashanah and Yom Kippur."

The shofar is a ram's horn, and all I know is that I can't stand the toneless way it sounds.

I shrug, Tovah sighs, and Aba asks if she can answer the question. Of course she replies correctly. Gold fucking star. Tovah plays along with this whole religious charade, doesn't realize none of it matters. Soon we'll get our results and none of this prayer will have changed a thing.

♪ ♫♪

Tovah and I are washing dishes in the kitchen after the Mizrahis have left and after Ima has taken her nighttime meds, which I refuse to call kinuach, the euphemism the rest of my family uses. I will call them what they are.

"You don't have to be such a brat about our religion," Tovah says, dragging a sponge back and forth across a plate.

Brat. For some reason that word stings more than "bitch." It sounds young, a kindergarten taunt. Tovah's insults haven't matured yet.

"And you don't have to be a sheep about it." I take the clean plate from her and start drying.

Tovah's grinding her teeth. I can hear the scrape of enamel against enamel, sending a shiver up my spine. She's quiet long enough for me to know I've stung her back.

"It's what I believe," she says softly. "How am I a sheep if this is what I truly believe in?"

I set the plate in the cupboard too loudly. "That's what I don't understand. How you can still believe after what God did to Ima?"

"God didn't do anything to Ima. That's what you don't understand."

I wonder how she can be so sure when she barely spends time with our mother. "I'm sorry I can't remember all the minutiae of this religion."

"*Our* religion," Tovah corrects, handing me another bowl. "Don't you care about where Ima came from?"

"Yes." I'm not sure how to explain to her that to me, being half Israeli and being Jewish are two very different things. Ima's pre-America life is a secret I want to uncover. It is personal, belongs only to her. This religion, with all its rules and regulations, belongs to too many people.

When Tovah passes me the next plate, her hands are too slippery and I can't grasp it, and it crashes to the floor. We stare at it on the ground, a mess of soap and shards. I'm not sure which of us dropped it.

Neither of us says it, but I am sure we are both thinking it: this is how it started for Ima.

"Perfect," I say. "That was a gift from Aba's parents at their wedding."

"Then you shouldn't have broken it."

"It slipped. It wasn't either of our faults." I run my tongue along my teeth, trying to calm down. "Let's just throw it away. They probably won't even notice. We have so many plates."

Tovah gets out a broom and dustpan. I decide I am done in the kitchen with her, so I go into the dining room to finish cleaning up. The thin ivory candles in the middle of the table are a third their original height. Jews are not to extinguish them; we are supposed to let them burn on their own instead. That's what I have been taught.

Tonight I lean over and blow them out.

Six

Tovah

I TRY TO TAKE A DEEP BREATH, BUT I CAN'T FULLY FILL my lungs. The air in the clinic is thin, sharp with disinfectant. One day I'll work in a place like this—unless my test comes back positive. Then maybe I won't get a chance to. I suppose I'll spend most of my life here either way, as a surgeon or as a patient. Will it always feel like it's suffocating me?

Aba rubs my back while we wait. "Hakol yihyeh b'seder," he says, trying to reassure me. "Whatever happens, we're going to figure it out together. Okay, Tov?"

When we got to the clinic, they put us in separate rooms. Said it was customary to give out results one by one so each person had ample time to process on their own first. Aba stayed with me, and Ima went down the hall with Adina.

I balance my elbows on my knees, my heart pounding so loudly I'm certain Aba can hear it. He always brags to his friends that I'm going to be a surgeon. "One Siegel will finally become a doctor," he'll say, because he failed to finish a PhD program in computer science. Genetics might seem like an obvious career choice for me, but I want to fix people who can be fixed. Who can get better. This right here is all too claustrophobic.

Aba tries to distract me with Nirvana trivia, something he used to do when I was little. I had such a sharp memory that he got a kick out of quizzing me on album track listings despite Ima's complaints that some of the songs weren't appropriate for a kid. Nirvana's music is raw and unapologetic, like someone turned Cobain's brain inside out and the lyrics were the thoughts he couldn't tell anyone else. Back when I had more free time, Aba and I spent hours listening to vinyl albums and watching documentaries and old concert footage. I couldn't believe he'd seen them in person, both because I couldn't imagine my L.L. Bean–clad father in a mosh pit and Nirvana seemed more mythological to me than tangible. Adina may have gotten a pricey viola for her bat mitzvah, but my gift was so much better: the ticket to that show Aba went to, the one still hanging above my desk. A connection to my dad and the music that Adina would never understand. Something entirely mine.

"Original band name?" Aba says now.

"Too easy. Skid Row."

"What are the only two songs Cobain doesn't have the sole writing credit on?"

"'Smells Like Teen Spirit' and . . . 'Heart-Shaped Box'?"

58

"First one's right. The second's 'Scentless Apprentice.'"

"Right. Right. I knew that." My leg is jiggling. I hate sitting still like this.

Once music was something Adina and I shared too: finding a song we both liked, staying up all night choreographing a dance that we promised to perform at the school talent show, though we were always too shy to actually follow through. Every so often one of us would strike a pose from the dance, and the other would burst into laughter. Once music brought us together, and now it's another thing dividing us.

Our fight on Yom Kippur is still fresh. Adina's not the first person to question how I reconcile faith with science. History is filled with scientists who were also people of faith: Ada Yonath, an Israeli woman who won a Nobel Prize for chemistry; Max Born, who helped develop quantum mechanics; and little-known theoretical physicist Albert Einstein.

God did not cause Ima's illness. God has limits, humans have free will, and the natural world isn't ruled by a higher power. After Ima was diagnosed, I realized blaming God would only cause me anguish. I had the power to decide how to confront that tragedy. I could turn it into something good—and I did, with my zeal for Johns Hopkins, my 4.0, my two-page single-spaced résumé. If I test positive, then I must be meant to accomplish something great in my shortened life.

Someone knocks on the door, and I spring to my feet.

Dr. Simon, the neurologist, and Maureen, the genetic counselor, enter the room together. Maureen had Adi and me

59

come up with a plan for testing negative and a plan for testing positive. She had to know we weren't at risk of harming ourselves. If I tested positive, I'd go to counseling every week and join a support group. I'd do everything doctors told me to do, appointments and supplements and experimental meds. If I tested negative, Maureen said it was perfectly natural to experience guilt. I was prepared to deal with that, too.

"Tovah. Matt," Maureen says to my father and me. "You don't have to stand up, unless you're more comfortable that way."

"Oh." I sit back down. Cross and uncross my legs. Cross them again.

Dr. Simon and Maureen take seats across from us. "How have you been doing?" Dr. Simon asks, tucking a dark curl behind her ear.

"Longest three weeks of my life," I say with a weak smile.

"I've heard that one before. I'm sorry. I wish this process were a bit speedier."

My smile turns into something more like a grimace, a hard line across my face. I wonder what it was like when Aba sat in a room like this with Ima. If it was a tragedy right away, or a relief to finally be able to name her symptoms.

"Do you want us to cut right to the chase?" Dr. Simon asks.

"Yes. Please." My heart hammers in my throat. I have my two plans. Whatever happens, I can deal with it.

I hope.

The moments before the doctor's next sentence span eons.

Glaciers melt and entire species go extinct. I'm certain she'll tell me what I've only let myself obsess about through research and in my nightmares.

"You will not develop Huntington's disease. You tested negative."

Seven

Adina

"ADINA, I'M SO SORRY.... YOU TESTED POSITIVE."

The room tilts. Sunsets and mountaintops burst from their frames and slide off the walls. Computers crash to the floor and lightbulbs explode and everything lands in a heap of broken pieces.

I blink, and the room repairs itself.

"Adina?"

My mother begins to sob, pianissimo at first. Her arms wrap around me, but I cannot get mine to do anything. *Positive.* The word has turned me to cement.

A masochistic laugh bubbles out of me. It's a quick noise, a *ha!* that almost sounds like I'm choking. Because it is funny, almost, that "positive" usually means something good.

"Adina," Dr. Simon says again, "do you understand what that means?"

Slowly I nod. Somehow I find my voice. "I—I have HD."

"You don't have it yet," Dr. Simon is quick to correct. "You won't have symptoms for a long, long time. You're only eighteen. You can still have a long, full, *normal* life ahead of you."

Only eighteen. I am as young as I often fear I am. I shake that thought away.

"Not exactly normal." The laugh returns. This time it sounds like a bark.

"We'll do all we can for you to make it as normal as possible," Maureen says.

Ima hugs me tighter. "Adi, I am so sorry."

It takes several more minutes for me to attach any real meaning to the words spilling out of the doctor's mouth. The room is thick with those words, consonants and vowels stacked to the ceiling. Entire sentences collapse on top of me.

You can still live a normal life.

Many people do.

You're so young.

Machala arura—the damn disease belongs to me now, too.

"We'll give you some time to process this as a family," Dr. Simon says.

As a family—oh God, how is Tovah handling this? My frustrations toward my sister vanish for a moment. If she tested positive too, she will surely develop some coping mechanism so it won't wreck her own meticulously planned future, and she'll share it with me and we'll get through it together the way she promised all those years ago. She broke that promise, but she can still make it up to me.

But when Tovah enters the room with Aba, her eyes are not red, and she hasn't been crying. Her shoulders are straight, relaxed, and she looks entirely unchanged by her result.

"You tested negative," I say, and a brief nod from her confirms it.

Opposite results.

It takes a split second for the reality to dawn on her. "Oh my God, Adi." My nickname sounds strange on her tongue. She hasn't used it in a while. "I can't believe it. Oh—oh my God." Her voice is soft, crackly. My usually articulate sister has no intelligent words.

Tovah sinks into the chair next to mine, bites her lip as she tries to think of something else to say. She is the one who is going to live a long and healthy and normal life. I am the one doomed like Ima, and perhaps it fits, since Ima and I are so close, for she and I to be eternally bonded in this way.

Tovah shifts toward me, apparently deciding to attempt a hug. It has been years since we touched like this, years since I have hugged the sister I spent nine months with in utero. She says my name again, this time into my hair, as I stiffen at the shock of her arms around me.

When she pulls back, pity has knit her brows together, and her eyes won't leave mine. I wonder if that's how people will look at me from now on, with sad eyes that say *I feel so bad for you* and at the same time *I'm glad what happened to you didn't happen to me.*

The conversation ping-pongs between our parents.

Ima: We're here for you.

Aba: We'll get through this.

Ima: Can we get you anything?

Aba: We can call the doctors back in. Or we can talk more about this at home. Or we can wait to talk about it. Do you want to talk to Rabbi Levine?

Ima: Rabbi Levine would be more than happy to sit down with you.

Aba: We can do whatever you want.

Tovah (whispered): Adi. Are you okay?

Tovah: Adina. Say something.

Aba: Maybe we shouldn't have let them do this so young.

Ima: They aren't young. They're adults. They deserve to know.

Aba: We thought about this possibility, of course, but we never thought . . .

Tovah: Please.

Too many people are talking. They are sucking the last of the air out of the room, leaving none for me. For once in my life, all I want is silence.

♪ ♫

I never wanted to know.

After Ima's diagnosis, Tovah and I talked about HD occasionally, but whenever she tried to convince me to take the test with her, I told her no. Over and over and over. Once we started high school, we pursued our passions with renewed vigor. I started private lessons and Tovah joined student council and track and

65

buried herself under mountains of homework. Distance grew between us, of course, but that was natural. We were busy.

Spring of sophomore year, Tovah applied to a half-dozen summer programs, including a study abroad with a STEM focus that would last an entire year. Her Johns Hopkins application had to stand out, which apparently meant abandoning our family. I wondered why she couldn't start a charity or invent something, the way people who get into prestigious schools always seem to do. This was what she wanted, though: to spend several weeks or months or an entire year away from our family. Away from me. When I asked her to stay, I only sounded selfish.

One evening when she was out for a run, her bedroom door open, her computer beckoned me closer. Her applications weren't difficult to find. The essays talked about how science helped her make sense of the world. What I couldn't get out of my head was that no one could make sense of what had happened to us.

She was the only one who knew what it was like to have a mother suffering from something you might suffer from too, and I had to keep her here any way possible—even if it made her angry. Anger, I could deal with. A missing sister, I could not. And she couldn't leave if she never actually sent in her applications.

Deleting the applications was the easy part. My engineer father ensured we knew our way around a computer better than our naturally tech-savvy peers. I erased every version she'd saved, made sure she couldn't recover them.

The hard part was what came after: the yelling and the slammed doors and the disapproving looks from my parents, especially Ima. Aba threatened to take away my viola, but I cried so hard he eventually reneged. I was grounded for an entire month.

Tovah retaliated. The night before my audition for the youth symphony, she shredded my sheet music. But it didn't matter—of course I'd memorized my pieces and easily made it in. Then it became war and we became children: locking the bathroom when we knew the other needed it, taking a long time to get ready and making us both late for school, eating all the leftovers when Ima made shakshuka.

A couple months after I deleted everything, she barged into my room and, in a venomous whisper, she said, "You're taking the test with me when we turn eighteen."

Quickly I shut my laptop, where I'd been watching old videos of Arjun's performances with the New Delhi symphony. "No. I'm not."

"You want me to keep speaking to you? Do this with me, and I will. I can't promise that we'll be close again, but one day I'm sure I'll forgive you. But if you don't take the test, Adina, you are dead to me."

"You can't be serious."

But she was. Then came the three words that would characterize our relationship from that point forward: "You owe me."

Sister guilt runs deep. I gave in, and for the next two years we stayed out of each other's way. We were polite but brusque.

No more late-night talks or inside jokes or entire conversations communicated only with our eyes. By trying to keep her here, I'd pushed her further away.

I have been holding out for that *one day* when she might forgive me, and it has been the loneliest time of my life.

Eight

Tovah

"I WANT TO GO HOME." ADINA TAPS HER NAILS ON HER viola case, the security blanket I just now realize she brought with her. "Tovah, can you take me?"

"I can do that," I say. My parents look as shocked as I feel, but at least they've stopped blasting her with questions.

"Take your time," Aba says. "Come home when you're ready."

Naturally, the elevator stops at every single floor on our way down to the lobby. I open my mouth a dozen times but have no idea what to say. *I'm sorry* is too trivial. Even the Hebrew version, ani miztaeret, which has always felt full of more emotion to me, doesn't fit. The ride is silent, except for the jazz piped in through the speakers. The soundtrack to getting bad news.

When we get in the car, Adina tucks her case between her knees and says, "I'm going to viola. Drop me off at Arjun's."

"Are you serious?" I assumed she'd have canceled her lesson.

It's started to rain, fat drops spitting against the windshield. I turn on the wipers.

Adi is a statue. Somehow that makes her words sharp as scalpels. "I want my fucking normal life, okay? Can't you let me have that right now?"

This shuts me up for the rest of the drive. *Pound-pound-pound* goes the rain. Drowning us.

"Do you want me to pick you up after?" I ask. "Or I could wait for you?"

"I'll take the bus home." She opens the car door, and I realize she forgot to buckle her seat belt.

Nine
Adina

APPARENTLY I HAVE FORGOTTEN HOW TO PLAY THE viola. I fuck up my beloved Debussy prelude for the eighteenth time in a row. I have ogre fingers that cannot find the right notes. The piece is meant to be played *très calme et doucement expressif*: calmly and gently expressive. There is no gentleness in me today.

"Try again." Arjun flips the sheet music back to the beginning. He taps a pen on the music stand with staccato clangs. "From this measure."

The prelude starts quiet, gets loud.

Crescendo.

The conversation at the clinic rings in my ears, warring with my prelude.

Decrescendo.

Soon there will be sessions and experimental medication and research studies. I might never be independent again.

Crescendo.

"Focus." Arjun's voice slices up my thoughts, juliennes them like vegetables. There is an edge to it. I've never played this terribly.

My bow slips out of my fingers, falls to the carpet. Silent tears burn behind my eyes, and I ball up one fist tight, tight, trying not to break down.

"Adina, are you all right? Is something wrong?"

Not something. Everything. The tremor in my fingers spreads up my arms, earthquaking my shoulders. *What if it's starting already?* No. No. That's ridiculous.

Sinking into the chair, I shield my face with my hands, hiding from Arjun, from the portraits of Beethoven and Dvořák and even Claude Debussy himself, who is disappointed I've botched his prelude.

Footsteps. Arjun is coming closer. Something touches my right shoulder—his hand. *Oh.* He rubs it tentatively at first, back and forth, then in circles. Everything in me becomes acutely aware of the few square inches of acrylic his fingers are stroking. My skin is electric beneath it. He has never touched me quite this way before, this intimate, this deliberate.

"Adina," he says softly, pianissimo. "Adi, please talk to me. I can't help you if I don't know what's the matter."

I drop my hand from my face to find he's kneeling in front of me. Concern has widened his eyes, and all his earlier harshness has disappeared. He is the Arjun I love again, the Arjun who gave me a cartoon character Band-Aid when I skinned my knee. I wish I could melt off this chair and into his lap.

The tension in my shoulders eases the tiniest bit, and he moves his hand away.

I've never wanted to tell anyone about this family heirloom of a disease. But I've always been able to talk to Arjun: when school is unbearable, when I'm frustrated with Tovah, when I've had a bad day.

I inhale, filling my lungs completely. "My mom . . . she's sick."

"Sick how?" He sits back in his chair and turns it toward me. Our legs are almost touching. He is wearing striped socks.

"Do you know what Huntington's disease is?"

"I've heard of it, but I'm not sure how much I know."

"Most people don't." Leaving out my own genetics, I explain what the disease is, how there is no cure. And then: "My mom has it. She was diagnosed four years ago."

"I'm so—"

"I have it too," I blurt, then backtrack. "I mean, I *will* have it. It's genetic, and I took a DNA test. A few weeks ago. I—I tested positive. I found out today." I stare at the floor. "And my sister tested negative."

Arjun blinks a few times. He lifts an arm as though to reach for me, but then drops it, as though hugging is crossing a boundary he's already made clear he won't cross.

"I . . . I had no idea." He shakes his head. "Sorry doesn't seem to encompass it, but I'm sorry. So sorry. That's . . ."

"Shitty. It's shitty, and there's no other word for it." There isn't enough air in this room either. I will never get enough air into my lungs.

"They find new cures for diseases every day," he says. "You're still so young."

There is the word I hate again: "young."

"It's not fair," he continues. "God, you're so talented. It's not fair at all, not to anyone."

"I know it's not fair. But—it's happening."

Silence for a few moments. I become more aware of how close his chair is to mine, and that nearness distracts me from everything else. Delicate black lashes frame his eyes, and I ache to run my fingers through his neatly combed hair, to mess it up.

I am not some vulnerable fawn, and I won't let my result turn me into one. I want to be a girl he cannot resist. So I scoot my chair a centimeter closer to his and say, "What happened that day I tried to kiss you?"

"Adina—"

"I'm serious. Why did you stop me?"

He sets his jaw, which is shadowed with stubble. "I told you. I'm your instructor. And you're only seventeen."

What he doesn't say: that he stopped me because he doesn't like me.

"I'm not seventeen. I turned eighteen three weeks ago." The age of consent in Washington is sixteen, anyway. I have looked it up.

"What?" A crease between his brows vanishes almost as quickly as it appears. Then he shakes his head like my age doesn't change anything. "It's not a question of whether I like you or not, or how old you are. This is—I don't do things like that. I *can't* do things like that."

"Kiss people?" Even when I am not talking, I part my lips, painted with an extra layer of Siren red, in the hopes he won't be able to look away from my mouth.

The forehead crease reappears. I'd like to iron it out with my lips. "Even if you weren't my student, it's still . . ." He gropes for the right word. *Wrong. Inappropriate.* "Unprofessional," he finishes.

I love seeing him flustered like this. I already feel more like myself. "You still haven't told me you don't want to."

"Adina."

He has to stop saying my name like that. Like a growl. Neither of us dares move for a long time. The power I discovered with Eitan, I want it with Arjun. I want to tell him all the ways I'd touch him, with my hands, with my mouth, how I'd make him feel so, so good. How he'd make me feel good too. How I'd wrap my legs around him in his chair and scrape my nails down his back . . .

"I think about you so much," I say. "I think about touching you all the time."

He grips the arms of his chair, skin stretching tight across his knuckles. My breath catches in my throat, my heart going more allegro than the final movement of a Brahms sonata. It's going to happen. It's finally going to happen. Then something changes in his face, and he gets to his feet, rolls up his shirtsleeves. Paces.

I get to my feet and follow him, weaving a few fingers through my wild hair, hoping he will imagine what it would feel like for him to do the same thing. He is only a couple inches taller than I am, and we are nearly eye to eye. There's half a foot between our chests. If we exhaled at exactly the same time, we'd be touching.

"I see how you look at me. How you're always finding ways to touch me. It's not accidental. I know it. Haven't you—haven't you thought about us? Together?"

I let my gaze drift toward his belt buckle so he understands what I mean by "together." Rest-two-three-four, rest-two-three-four.

He shoves his sleeves up even more, past his elbows, showing more of his bronze skin. "You've had a lot of stress today," he says slowly. "You should be spending this time with your family. Not here." He adds more distance between us, stands beneath Beethoven. "I'm so sorry."

I wish he'd stop apologizing.

"You want me to go."

"I think that would be for the best."

I bite down hard on the inside of my cheek, so hard I taste metal. "Arjun. Don't you find me attractive?"

He pauses, and for a second I'm certain he won't even answer me, considering he's skirted all my other questions. Instead he does something I've never seen him do: he rakes a hand through his hair and makes this sound halfway between a grunt and a sigh, this action that seems at once frustrated and flustered. It's not something Arjun the teacher would do. His hair is sticking up, but he doesn't seem to care.

He puts his back to me, so I can't see him when he speaks. "You need to go, Adina. Please. I'm not going to ask you again."

Somehow I buckle my viola back into its case and shove my arms through my jacket sleeves. Somehow I find my way to the door. Somehow I stumble down the hall and into the elevator, where I punch-punch-punch-punch-punch the first-floor button five times in a row.

Age seems to matter so much when you're young, but to me it's a meaningless number. I should be able to relate more to the kids at school than to my twenty-five-year-old teacher, but I don't. I can't tolerate any of their insipid conversations about who cheated on who and who asked who to homecoming and who drank so much they threw up at whoever's party last week.

This, with Arjun, isn't going to happen. I have a finite number of minutes before I start dropping plates the way Ima did at the beginning, before I lose coordination in my fingers, before I can no longer stand in front of an audience and do the only thing I've cared about for years. Despite all that, I cannot have what I want.

I hate him for sending me away.

Ten

Tovah

I HATE MYSELF FOR LETTING HER GO. I'M NOT certain of many of my emotions today, but I'm positive about that one.

Positive. I have to strike that word from my vocabulary. I'll never be able to use it casually.

Rain pelts the windshield, wipers slashing across it. My vision blurs. A car behind me honks. I'm in a loading zone, so I circle the block and find a new parking spot. Turn the wipers off so I can hide underneath a layer of rain-spattered glass.

Why couldn't we both be lucky?

For a few minutes after Dr. Simon delivered the news, I was overwhelmed with relief. My mind swelled with possibilities. I could date. I could have children. I could grow so old my hair turns gray, then white, then falls out. Before, I never let myself think about my future unless it involved Johns Hopkins. A one-track mind made the past four years easier. But suddenly there were so many choices.

"Even a negative result can be complicated," Dr. Simon said, but I didn't understand what she meant until I saw Adina.

Adina, who I cut out of my life after she deleted my applications. After she said, without words, that her dreams mattered more than mine. I'd been jealous of her much of our lives, but I kept it buried. She set hers loose. She was the prodigy, the center of attention, the girl with the spotlight bright on her beautiful face. Clearly she couldn't stand to see me getting something I wanted. While I've missed her, I haven't been able to forgive her.

Somehow I figured that whatever happened, we'd deal with it together, despite our recent history. Maybe because we're twins. Maybe because you think the worst-case scenario is impossible. You're invincible. Nothing can touch you, not death, not disease, not losing your best friend. Or someone who used to be your best friend.

I text Lindsay the results and wait a few minutes for a reply. Nothing comes. Then I scroll all the way down to the last name in my contacts. Zack. Suddenly I want to talk to someone who knows nothing about my family and this disease.

I type **Hey**, hit send, and immediately panic. Who just says *hey*?

My phone vibrates.

Hey.

I'm racking my brain for a response when another message appears.

What's up?

After a minute of deliberation, I type back, **Homework. You?**
A minute to come up with two boring words. I'm brilliant.

**Hunting for the perfect canvas board. Dragged Troy.
We're gonna grab pho later, if you want to join. Don't worry,
NOT A DATE ;)**

His messages seem so effortless, like he doesn't proofread
them a dozen times before hitting send. I'm seriously considering
saying okay when I get another text from Aba asking where I am.

Back to reality.

Another time. AP Bio calls.

Before I pull back into traffic, I study my face in the rearview
mirror. I examine each freckle. Each pore. Each blemish. What
decided Adina tested positive and not me? Was it somewhere
between the gene that coded for dark hair and the one that gave
me blue eyes?

On the drive home, my foot punches the gas pedal in sharp
bursts, the car throwing me forward and backward at every
light.

Today we got answers, but they've only sparked more
questions.

The first time our lives changed was April of eighth grade. Our
parents sat us down in the living room and explained that Ima
had finally been diagnosed with something called Huntington's
disease. The whole conversation made me feel selfish, because
by the end of it, when Adi and I learned we were at risk too, I

80

hated that I couldn't be sad only for my mom—I had to be sad for myself, too.

There was a girl in my earth science class whose mother had breast cancer. With enough chemo and possibly a mastectomy, her mom might get better. She could go into remission. There was no way to stop what was destroying Ima.

"You can ask any questions you want," Ima said, but the only question I had was *why?* And there wasn't an answer to that one.

After my parents had gone to sleep, there was a soft knock on my door. Adi tiptoed into my room and climbed into my bed. Back then, we still spent a lot of time together, but it was mostly outside of school. Our parents had both of us tested for the gifted program, and I got in and Adi didn't.

Viola was the only future she saw for herself. Part of me wondered, sometimes . . . if she became famous one day, however famous violists can become, what would that mean for me? I tried violin in fourth grade when she picked up the viola, but I didn't have the patience for those long songs, and I had no rhythm. I was on a downbeat when everyone else was on an upbeat.

Adi pulled the sheets tight around both of us, and for a while neither of us spoke. "I'm so scared for Ima," she said finally. Her tears soaked the too-big Science Olympiad T-shirt I wore to bed.

"Hakol yihyeh b'seder," I said over and over, stroking her soft hair. *Everything is going to be okay.* We didn't usually speak Hebrew with each other, only a few words scattered here and there. It sounded more reassuring in Hebrew, though.

"How do you know?" she asked.

"I'm older. Naturally, that makes me smarter," I said, making her laugh at the old, unfunny joke. "Whatever happens, we'll deal with it together. Okay?"

Adi's toes touched my legs beneath the sheets. Her feet were icicles. "Do you think we should get tested?" Ima and Aba had said it would be up to us when we turned eighteen.

I was quiet for a long time. I'd only recently made a five-year plan. More like a ten-year plan, considering I'd be in med school for a while. What did Ima's diagnosis mean for that future I'd already grown so attached to?

By the time I spoke again to tell Adi yes, she'd fallen asleep. A few weeks later, she told me she didn't want to know her fate. But I didn't just want to know; I needed to know. Most people never get to know their futures like this. Over the years it would start to hit me that getting tested and having the answers wouldn't mean everything was okay. Ima was still sick. For a short time, though, I believed the test would spell out my entire future.

When I get home, I'm antsy. I can't focus on homework and my parents are talking about Adina in hushed tones. So I put on the special sports bra that fits my double-Ds like a shield and go for a run. My typical route: Burke-Gilman Trail along Gas Works Park, northeast through the University of Washington, Seattle's huge public college, then back to Wallingford, the neighborhood we've lived in since Adina and I were born. Nirvana's *Bleach* pulses against my eardrums.

It's nine degrees Celsius outside. I refuse to measure anything in Fahrenheit. All scientists use Celsius, which is much cleaner and simpler. Water freezes at zero, boils at 100. I try not to think about how cold it is. Instead I focus on the reason goose bumps are prickling my arms: the tiny muscles attached to the hair follicles are contracting, making the hairs stick straight up, causing my skin to pucker.

I run track in the spring, and the rest of the year I jog almost daily to stay in shape. I started running track in middle school because I knew I wouldn't be able to get into Johns Hopkins with advanced classes and a 4.0—I had to be extraordinary. An AP kid and a scientist and an athlete and a student council rep and a hospital volunteer.

Some people love running to clear their heads, but I usually relish the extra time to think. This afternoon, though, my head fills with thoughts I can't control. How Adina's feeling. What this means for her future. What I'm supposed to say to her besides *I'm sorry* a hundred times because it'll never be enough. How getting a disease named after you is clearly a great accomplishment, but it's not quite the same as claiming a star or a city.

Siegel disease: the tendency to overanalyze everything.

⬥⬥⬥⬥⬥

Chinese takeout containers are spread across our kitchen table. My fortune declared WEALTH AWAITS YOU VERY SOON. Aba got the same one.

It's after seven p.m. when Adina gets home. Aba jumps to

his feet, and Adina shrinks away like a frightened cat. "Hey, Adina. Do you want some hot and sour soup? We saved you some."

"Not hungry." Her knuckles are white on the handle of her viola case, and her red lipstick is stark against her ashen face.

I push a piece of broccoli around my plate.

"I know how you feel," Ima tries.

"No," Adi says, and I notice she doesn't look directly at Ima, "you don't."

Ima's head is jerking up and down, up and down, up and down. *That will never happen to me.* Instead of relief, I feel a tightness, like my entire body has been mummy-wrapped.

Adina aims her gaze at me. "This is your fucking fault. I didn't want to know. I told you I needed more time."

Language, I expect one of my parents to say, but the warning never comes.

"I . . ." I grip my chopsticks, unsure what to say. She took the test because I asked her to. Forced her to. But the results were decided a long time ago, imprinted in our DNA.

"Adi," Ima says, "this is no one's fault."

Adina ignores her. She places her palms flat on the table and angles herself closer to me. I'd be able to see her pores if they weren't microscopic. "You wanted to know so badly, and you made me do it with you—why? As punishment? Or because you couldn't handle doing it alone?"

Both. That's the truth.

I snap my chopsticks in half. Maybe she sealed her own fate

84

when she pressed delete. *No*—I force the illogical thought from my mind.

"You would've wanted to know eventually," I say, but my assertion is half-hearted.

She snorts. Smacks the table. "Because you know me so well?"

"Girls," Aba says quietly. "Let's all give each other some space, okay?"

Without saying anything, Adina spins around and climbs the stairs to her room, her door slamming shut.

Give each other some space. That's the problem, though, isn't it? There's too much space between my sister and me, an entire galaxy I fear our results have made impossible to cross.

Eleven

Adina

SOMETHING IS DIFFERENT ABOUT ME. I CAN'T SEE IT, can't feel it, but I know it's there. It has been hiding in me for eighteen years. I've gone eighteen fucking years not knowing I am a ticking time bomb.

The day after we get our results, I skip school. My parents told Tovah she could stay home too, but she had a quiz in AP Statistics and a test in AP Bio and a presentation in AP Lit, and naturally, she couldn't miss any of them.

"If you want, I can keep you company, Adina'le," Ima says to me Thursday morning after Aba and Tovah have left. Her arm flaps. One day that will be me. "My aide can handle the class today, or I'll get a . . . I can't think of the word, but you know what I mean."

Impatience twists in my stomach. I am usually so gentle with my mother, but today her memory lapse makes me wince. "Substitute. And I'll be fine on my own." I tell myself the reason I don't want her to stay with me is that she loves teaching, and I don't want her to miss a single day of it. But the real reason is closer to this: every time she gropes for a word or jerks involuntarily, my ribs press together so tightly I worry they'll snap like twigs. And the next time she hallucinates—

Tick, tick, tick . . .

Huntington's turns my loving mother cold and monstrous and foreign. Crazy, some might say. You aren't supposed to see your parents in that kind of agony—something I cannot forgive God for.

I wonder what it will do to me.

I fall back asleep and at ten thirty wake up groggier than I was at six thirty. My hair is tangled and my mouth is stained pink from yesterday's Siren lipstick and mascara crumbs dot my cheeks, but I don't feel like showering or changing out of my pajamas.

Music has always brought me comfort. When Papa, Aba's father, passed away, I spent the entire month playing Prokofiev. After Ima was diagnosed, it was Bach. Now it is Debussy.

The prelude itself is not complex, but the challenge lies in its simplicity, how you convey the innocence of the pastoral girl. I will settle for nothing less than perfection. I practice for hours, until the pads of my fingers throb and my legs are stiff from standing, but I force myself to keep going.

Until it hits me: one day I won't be able to do this anymore. My hands will act out, and my fingers will misbehave, and my mind will forget. I stagger backward, tucking my viola into its case before I collapse onto my bed, holding my head in my hands. I stay like that, counting measures, counting beats and breaths.

Then I close the music book and run my thumbnail along the crease so I don't have to look at it, though I'm close to memorizing the prelude. Arjun would be pleased.

Arjun Bhakta, who prepares for snowstorms that never come, who knows my secret, who sent me away.

I lay my head back on my pillow, focusing on the way his hands gripped the arms of his chair, the way his back muscles flexed against his shirt, the way he growled my name. I slip my hand inside my underwear. In my mind he doesn't pull away. He wraps me in his arms and kisses me back. I unbutton his shirt and reach inside his corduroy pants, feeling him everywhere.

I wonder if he'd be gentle, andante, the way a slow piece of music swells to a powerful, intense climax. Or if he'd be fierce, prestissimo, crashing into me like he can't get close enough.

In this fantasy, he can be all those things.

♩ ♫♩

Tovah said we'd deal with it together. The night we learned about Ima's diagnosis, that's what she promised. Here are the times I have needed someone to *deal with it* with me:

The morning after we found out about Ima.

The day after that.

A week later, when I broke down in the middle school girls' bathroom and wiped my face with the too-rough toilet paper until it was red everywhere.

88

Two months after that when Ima screamed at Aba for burning a pot of rice.

A year after that when Ima hallucinated spiders crawling all over the kitchen floor and it scared me.

When Tovah decided she'd rather live abroad for a year instead of with our gloomy little family.

When I found the applications on her computer.

The moment I pressed delete.

The day we turned eighteen.

The morning we took the test.

A thousand times in between.

♪ ♫♪

Tovah used to be in orchestra too. She played violin for a year in fourth grade before declaring all the music we played boring. To convince her to stick with it, I dragged my viola into her room and gave her an impromptu concert, though back then all I could play were "Hot Cross Buns" and "Twinkle, Twinkle, Little Star."

Tovah made a face. "I'd rather play something you can actually sing along to. Like Aba's music." I detested Aba's music. It was so loud. It grated.

"You can sing along to 'Hot Cross Buns,'" I insisted, and I started the song again. *Hot cross buns. Hot cross buns. Something-something, something-something . . . hot cross buns!*

Tovah snorted. "Please don't sing, Adi," she said, and I was thankful when we traded those little-kid songs for pieces by classical composers. But Tovah quit anyway.

You try out so many hobbies when you're young, and you outgrow them the same way you outgrow overalls and sandboxes and baby teeth. Viola was something I could never outgrow. It was my power to create, to take risks, to be bold. I have never felt as natural as I do with my chin on my Primavera and a bow in my hand. The instrument and I, we fit.

♩ ♫♩

Sunday morning, someone knocks on my door. I called in sick to work this week, skipped youth symphony rehearsal, slept through Shabbat. I am a perfect Jew. I haven't touched electronics or money or done any kind of work. I rest, rest, rest.

I bolt upright in bed. "I'm . . ." *Not doing anything.* My viola's in its case. My battery-drained laptop is on my desk. My parents want me to talk to our rabbi—not happening—and we're supposed to go to family counseling "when I'm up to it," but I don't know when that will be. The longer I keep everything inside, the longer it doesn't exist. That logic is flawed, but I can't handle it any other way.

"Please." Tovah. When I don't reply, she interprets my silence as tacit approval and enters holding a stack of papers. We used to spend so much time in each other's rooms. Sometimes one of us dragged a sleeping bag across the hall for a "sleepover." We gossiped and watched bad movies and talked about all the things we wanted so badly we ached for them.

"I found some new information online," Tovah says. "I've been doing a lot of research about support groups and counseling. And there are these supplements some people take that can potentially slow the onset of—"

"I know how to use the Internet."

This is what Tovah does: She researches. She studies. The muscles in her jaw ripple. "I wanted to help." Before she turns to leave, she slides the papers onto my nightstand.

"Are you going somewhere?" I ask, noticing she's wearing a backpack.

"Oh. Yeah." She rocks back and forth on her feet. "Volunteering at the hospital, then probably studying at the library."

In other words: life as usual.

If our results were flipped, Tovah would have plenty of people to talk to, to stroke her hair and tell her *hakol yihyeh b'seder*. Lindsay would console her and the entire student council would organize a benefit for Huntington's research. They would collect a record-breaking amount of money and present one of those giant checks to a charity organization, and Tovah would be smiling in all the photos.

"Close the door behind you."

Once her footsteps fade, I allow myself a peek at her research.

NEW RESEARCH LEADS TO BETTER TREATMENT FOR HUNTINGTON'S DISEASE. . . .

HUNTINGTON'S PATIENTS: 10 TIPS TO KEEP YOUR BRAIN YOUNG. . . .

SOME INDIVIDUALS DEVELOP SYMPTOMS IN THEIR LATE-TEENAGE YEARS. . . .

I blink and read that section more closely.

Some individuals develop symptoms in their late-teenage years or early twenties. Huntington's may progress more quickly in teenagers.

I knew it was possible for symptoms to develop earlier than they did for Ima, and there is no way to predict when they'll start. It is rare, the article tells me, for symptoms to develop so young, but *rare* still means *possible*.

I take my laptop to bed and grope around for the power cord. I balance it on my thighs, its heat warming my always-cold skin. No patience for reading, I watch videos. Some patients twitch and jerk like Ima, speak slowly like Ima, though without her distinct Israeli accent. Each month she sheds part of herself as the disease chews her up from the inside out.

My future will unfold in every corner of this house, in the kitchen and in the living room and next to me at the dinner table. A hooded figure with a scythe creeping closer and closer and closer . . .

At first my symptoms will be so slight that no one will notice but me: involuntary twitches in my face and fingers, a wrong note on the viola. Forgetting names and conversations, losing coordination, trouble processing long pieces of music, irritability, depression. Then I'll struggle with my balance. I won't be able to stand still onstage. I'll have trouble walking and swallowing. I'll lose weight. Chorea—that's what they call the involuntary movements of someone with Huntington's—will get worse. At that point, I estimate, I'll have to give up viola. I might never

92

become a soloist. I might forget how to play entirely. Erase these past nine years of my life.

Near the end, I will lose my ability to speak. I won't be able to use the bathroom by myself. I will have to be tube-fed and I will no longer live among people I love, but in a nursing home, among the elderly with melting-plastic faces. There, surrounded by needles and beeping devices and suffocated by that thick, sour smell of hospital, I will waste away. No relief, just a slow progression into hell.

I've wondered about all this before, cried over it with my door shut and my music loud when I imagined losing my mother, but now there's an element of realness that cannot be avoided. Before, there was a chance my imaginings were simply that: imaginary. It was a coin flip. Heads or tails.

I shut my laptop. My viola's across the room, collecting dust bunnies. In the dark, its F-holes look like angry eyebrows, as though the instrument itself is disappointed in me. Although it's still early and my parents haven't gone to sleep yet, I can't bring myself to get up and play again.

Twelve

Tovah

EVERY PATIENT HAS MY SISTER'S FACE. MY MOTHER'S. When I landed this hospital volunteer spot, I felt victorious, though I only work a four-hour shift every other week. I wanted more hours, but so did all the other high school volunteers who want to become doctors.

Today four hours might as well be forty. It's my first shift since our results, and though I'm essentially a delivery girl—ferrying flower arrangements from the front desk to patients' rooms, ensuring patients have water and blankets—I can't concentrate.

"Can you deliver this to room 2420?" a nurse asks me from behind a person-size bouquet of roses. The tiny elderly woman is so happy to see it, her eyes well up.

I wonder who will bring flowers for Adina one day.

As I'm leaving the room, the tag outside the door informs me it's 2240, not 2420, meaning whoever's in 2420 is flowerless. I'm not about to steal the roses back, so I buy the nicest arrangement in the gift shop I can afford, scribble *We're all thinking of you. Get well soon* on the card, and present it to the man in the right room.

I'm relieved when my shift ends. When I pull out my phone in the lobby, I have three missed calls from Lindsay, which is odd because I can't remember the last time the two of us talked on the phone. I'm debating calling her back—I'm still annoyed with her for essentially ignoring me after the test results—when she calls again.

"Is everything okay?" I ask as I head into the hospital parking garage.

There's a long, shuddering breath on the end of the line. "No."

When she doesn't elaborate, I say, heart rate picking up speed, "You're going to have to give me more than that. Are you hurt? Is it something with Troy?"

"I'm at the Bartell's on Forty-Fifth," she says, "buying a pregnancy test. And I thought I could do it by myself, but I'm on the verge of a meltdown in the pregnancy test aisle, and did they have to put the pregnancy tests right next to the diapers?"

The words "pregnancy test" obliterate every other thought in my head. I unlock my car and jam the key in the ignition. "I can be there in ten minutes."

𝕏⟨𝕏⟩𝕏

Lindsay's sitting on the aisle floor, hood pulled up over her head.

"Linds." I sink down next to her and place what I hope is

95

a comforting hand on her shoulder. Obviously I knew Lindsay and Troy were having sex, but we all put condoms on bananas in health class. We learned about the pill and the patch and what our teacher called "outercourse." While I blushed through the entire sex-ed unit, I was glad no one simply told us "don't do it."

"Thanks for coming," she says. She sniffs but doesn't cry. "Can you pick one for me? I can't decide. There's too many."

She's right. Rows and rows of brightly colored boxes loom over us. "Probably not the kind that shows a smiley face if it's positive?" It's a horrible joke, but I'm not sure what else to say.

Fortunately, Lindsay's not offended. "No, probably not," she says, chewing back a smile. "Get two? To be sure?"

I grab the least pregnancy-is-a-beautiful-gift-looking ones and pull her to her feet and toward the front of the store. With her eyes cast downward, she hands a wad of bills to the red-smocked cashier. The impulse-buy section tempts me; I buy a few pieces of candy, because whatever the outcome of these tests, we're going to need the mood-boosting phenylethylamine chocolate provides.

We decide without words that I will drive us both to Lindsay's. I nibble a chocolate bar while we sit in traffic, though Lindsay just plays with the wrapper of the one I give her.

"Does Troy know about this?"

"No. I didn't want to tell him until I knew for sure," she says, and maybe it's the phenylethylamine, but it feels good to have something that, for now, is only mine and Lindsay's.

Lindsay flips on the lights in her dad's single-story condo. Her

96

parents divorced a few years ago, and she spends weekdays and every other weekend with her dad because her mom's busy with school. She worked twenty years as an accountant before realizing it was draining the enjoyment from her life. After the divorce, she adopted two cats and a guinea pig and went back to school to become a veterinary technician.

Lindsay has always wanted to do it right the first time: go to the right school, get the right degree, marry the right person. It's why she pushes herself with so many AP classes. However, she's not as certain about what she wants as Adina or Zack or Troy or I am, only that she'll figure it out once she gets to college. She likes most of her classes but doesn't seem to deeply love any singular thing.

In the bathroom, Lindsay crosses her legs on the rug and I lean my back against the cabinet next to her.

"How did this happen?" I say as calmly as I can.

Lindsay sighs. "We started having sex without a condom. A couple months ago."

"Without a condom?" I practically yell, and then get ahold of myself and lower my voice. "Sorry. But . . . without a condom?"

"We're the only people we've ever been with. And I'm on birth control." Twin pink spots appear on her cheeks. "We wanted to know what it would feel like. Without one."

My face is burning too. "What did it feel like?"

She digs a hand into her thick black hair and pulls it across her face. Hiding. "I don't know. Different. But then I missed my period. It's two weeks late, I think. I'm not great at keeping track." She yanks more of her hair across her face when I raise my eyebrows at her. "I know. I know. Believe me, I know. So I started googling things last night, and did you know pretty much any minor discomfort can be a pregnancy symptom? Mood swings. Fatigue. I was like, shit, I'm *always* tired." She laughs, and this gives me permission to join in.

I'm probably supposed to say something reassuring like, *I'm sure you're not pregnant!* But instead I say, "Let's do this," and I open one box and she opens the other, and I glance away while she pees on both sticks.

"And now we wait," she says, perching them on the sink edge.

Wait. Her words knife through my stomach. Lindsay will know right away if her life will change. I had to wait four years.

The next few minutes are quiet, except for the sound of Lindsay yanking at stray threads on the bath rug. Silences aren't supposed to be uncomfortable between close friends, but this one makes me itchy. Makes me wish I'd talked more in the weeks surrounding my own fateful test—if not to Lindsay, then to Adina, who clearly wanted to.

When her phone timer goes off, Lindsay snatches the two sticks and exhales deeply. "Negative. Thank God," she says. "I'm going to buy a jumbo box of condoms this weekend."

𝇕𝈀𝇕

We're lying on pillows on the floor in Lindsay's room, an empty pizza box between us. Lindsay painted her nails gray and I painted my toes a glittery blue while we quizzed each other on *Hamlet* for our AP Lit test next week. We have school off tomorrow, and it's been eons since I spent the night here. I'd forgotten she keeps a bottle of vodka (certified kosher, according to the label) hidden in her underwear drawer, which we drank shots of with our veggie pizza.

I've missed all this, as unremarkable as it is.

"Somehow, I thought senior year would be easier," Lindsay says. "But it's just as much work as ever. More, actually."

"It'll be worth it."

She examines a smudged gray nail and twists open the polish to touch it up. "Can you believe I applied to fifteen schools? A little excessive, but I have to get out of this gloomy place. California sounds nice. Or Florida, or Arizona . . . somewhere warm."

"'What made you decide to apply to our fine institution?' 'Well, I want to finally get a tan.'"

"Direct quote from my application essays."

High school graduation is an exodus. Most AP kids will be leaving Washington for universities with impressive names. I've always known Lindsay and I would end up at different schools in different states, and surely Adina and I will too.

Picturing Adina at conservatory chips at my heart. She'll be struggling with her result so far away from the rest of us. A harrowing thought slams into me: this might be my last year with my sister, who, despite everything she's done to me, was once my closest friend. If I haven't already lost her, I'm in the process of it.

Something on Lindsay's bookshelf catches my eye. Makes me forget Adina for an instant. That's the maximum amount of time I can ignore what's happened to us: a single instant.

"You still have that thing?" I ask as I get to my feet too fast, the vodka warping my surroundings, sloshing my brain around inside my head. I teeter over to the shelf and pull out a slim purple binder.

"I guess so?" Lindsay says, blowing on a nail as I sit back down and splay the binder between us. "I haven't thought about it in forever."

The first sheet of paper says ANTI-MAN CLUB in silver Sharpie bubble letters. The rest of the pages are filled with boys' names and, for lack of a better word, infractions. We passed the binder back and forth throughout middle school and the beginning of high school—right up until Lindsay started dating Troy and was no longer AM enough for the AMC. There are sixty-seven names on it, and it would be a creepy thing to own if either of us was ever on trial for murder.

Maybe a pregnancy scare and the Anti-Man Club will bring Lindsay and me back together.

Lindsay starts reading. "Number twelve, Oliver Kang, for trying to look up my skirt when I was wearing a thong. Number twenty-nine, Cole Hammond. He copied my answers on a test in freshman-year English, and Mr. Jacobs gave us both zeroes. Number thirty: Mr. Jacobs. I haven't forgiven any of them." She flips the page. "Hey, Zack's on here." She squints at number forty-one, which, sure enough, says *Zack Baker-Horowitz*. "We wrote 'Kelsey' next to his name. Do you have any idea what that means?"

"Yeah. Kelsey Rawlings." I grit my teeth, remembering. "She was the other sophomore class rep that year. Zack asked me about her. If I thought she'd be interested in him." The two of them dated for only a month, though.

"And you were jealous."

"Yes. Yes, I was." I peek at the list again. "I'm going to show him." In my altered mental state, it seems like a good idea.

Do you remember that list Lindsay and I made about all the guys we didn't like?

Zack's reply appears after a few minutes.

Yes. Troy and I always tried to steal that from you.

I snap a photo of number forty-one. **You're on it.**

"What's going on there? With you and Zack?" Lindsay asks, shutting the binder and settling back against her pillows. I groan. "What? You don't like him?"

Typically I never have the courage to rip Lindsay from Troy, even when I need her more than he does. Tonight I like having her to myself, even under these strange circumstances. After all, there's no one else I can talk to about this.

"No . . . I do." My mind is fuzzy and goopy, my synapses firing slower than usual. I throw back another vodka shot. It burns the back of my throat.

"What is it, then?"

There's nothing stopping me from acting on my feelings for Zack. That's part of the gift of this negative result.

"I'm . . . scared. Sometimes I start thinking about being with him, or kissing him, and then my mind inevitably jumps to sex." I whisper the last word. Why does it feel so weird to say out loud? "I feel like I'm fourteen that it still embarrasses me like this."

"Troy and I didn't have sex until we'd been together for a year."

"What was it like?" Lindsay never gave me details, and I was too shy to ask for them.

A dreamy look falls over her face. "It was nice, but awkward. We were in his car, and I kept thinking someone was going to drive by and see us."

"And it felt good?"

Cadavers don't scare me, but when it comes to sex, somehow my own living body does. When I'm running, I know exactly how to push myself. Sex would require relinquishing some of that control. Letting someone else in, both physically (ha) and emotionally. Leaping into an unknown that is all feeling and no logic. Someone touching my body and wondering if they're comparing me to my sister.

"I mean . . . You know what an orgasm feels like, right? Do you ever"—Lindsay laughs awkwardly—"um, do it yourself?"

My cheeks flame. While I know masturbation is one hundred percent normal, it's something I've never talked about with anyone. "Oh . . ." I say. "Sometimes?"

At some point it became something I do when I can't fall asleep right away. I've only thought about Zack once or twice. Most of the time I read and reread a sexy passage in a book.

"That's *good*!" Lindsay insists. "It's important to know what you like. I had to show Troy what felt good, and he eventually got the hang of it. And it's actually kind of great to tell someone what you want when you're that close."

"That does sound great. Being that close." I let out a long breath, my face probably still several shades of red, but truthfully, this conversation is extremely enlightening and more of a relief than anything else.

"It doesn't have to be scary. Okay, it's mildly terrifying to take your clothes off in front of someone for the first time. But I guarantee they're not looking at all the flaws you see when you look at yourself in the mirror. When you get to that point with someone, you're so caught up in them that none of that stuff matters."

"I doubt I'll be taking off my clothes in front of anyone anytime soon." I don't want my body to be embarrassing—I want to own it, the way Adina does. The way I'm learning Lindsay does.

"If and when you do, you know you can talk to me, right?"

"Yeah. Of course," I say, but I wonder where this offer to talk was when I was waiting for the results of the genetic test.

Lindsay slides her computer onto her lap and starts googling cat-eye makeup tutorials. She has a couple dozen windows minimized, AP study guides and college websites and financial aid information. My phone lights up with a text.

I was on the list because of Kelsey? Why?

Jealous. Also, it's entirely possible I'm drunk right now.

Reeeeaallly. So I could ask you all kinds of secrets right now and you'd be too drunk to keep them in?

I show this to Lindsay, who steals the phone and types,

My biggest secret is that I'm so hot for you. I yelp, steal it back, and write something a little more innocent.

zips lips *unlocks lips to drink more vodka* *rezips lips*
Why were you jealous of Kelsey?
¯_(ツ)_/¯
Drunk Tovah is very interesting.

"Linds, I have to ask you something." Then I force myself to be brave. After all, I've already talked about a number of things I never thought I'd talk about. "Is there any reason we haven't talked about the test? The one I took, I mean." As though it needs clarification.

Lindsay half frowns at me. "What do you mean? You never bring it up. I'm sorry. . . . I guess I don't know what I'm supposed to say."

"I don't know either. It was looming over me for so long, and now it's . . . not." But that's not entirely true. It's always going to be there, even if it never affects my body and mind.

"How's Adina handling it?"

"We've barely talked, so I honestly have no idea."

"I'm just so relieved you're okay," she says, emphasizing the *you're*. "It's horrible for her, but she's not going to get it for a long time, right? Decades or something?"

"Yeah. It's . . . a strange situation for all of us." I chew the inside of my cheek. Lindsay can say she feels sorry for Adina, but she barely knows my sister. Then again, neither do I.

Lindsay gives me a little hug, as though it makes up for her recent lack of involvement. "Hey. I know what'll cheer you up." She clicks to Netflix on her laptop. "Have you seen this show?

Everyone says it's amazing. Troy's already on episode four, so if we watch three tonight, I can catch up to him."

"Sure. Okay."

Whatever closeness I thought I'd regained with Lindsay tonight was fleeting, but instead of paying attention to the show or wondering how to fix our friendship, my mind turns to Adina.

I don't want to lose her, too.

Thirteen

Adina

FIRST CHAIR HAS BEEN GETTING COLD. I EARNED IT IN sixth grade, and the few who've dared challenge me since have lost. First chair is a message: *I am the best*, it says.

Violas are difficult to hear in an orchestra—difficult for the untrained ear to pick out our distinct sound—but if we were gone, you would absolutely notice. That is why becoming a soloist is so crucial. I need to be heard.

"Welcome back, Adina," the orchestra conductor, Mrs. Roberti, says as I enter the room. "Feeling better?"

I force a smile, turning my lips into a sideways bass clef. "Much."

Last night at dinner Aba asked if I was sure I was ready to go back to school. I'd been home for a week and a half, and he and Ima have let me skip Saturday synagogue services too. He said I could take a few more weeks, even a month off. He spoke delicately, like the volume of his words could break me. At least he wasn't badgering me about college again. It was a terrible thought, that I've swapped that horror for one that is much worse.

I glanced at Tovah, who smiled at something on her phone before hastily shoving it into her pocket. When her eyes caught mine, she looked guilty, like she'd been caught doing something she shouldn't have been: smiling, texting, generally feeling as though her world had not been turned upside down.

Spending another day at home would have been a hundred times more claustrophobic than the classroom. So here I am. Back.

We begin a Tchaikovsky piece I played a couple years ago with Arjun, but my bow isn't as fluid as it usually is, and my fingers stumble up and down my viola's neck. The orchestra devours my sounds as I fall further and further behind. Finally the bell rings, and I stow my sheet music in my case and take out my canvas lunch bag.

"That piece is so cool."

The voice belongs to Connor Mattingly: tall, reed-thin bassist. He eats lunch in the orchestra room sometimes, laughing too loudly with the other guy who plays double bass—dick inadequacy, I swear—and a girl violinist.

"Cool," I repeat. These people don't understand classical music the way I do. Knowing full well I am acting snippy, I continue: "Tchaikovsky composed some of the most popular music in existence, including *The Nutcracker*, *Swan Lake*, and the 1812 Overture, so yeah, I'd definitely call him *cool*."

Connor doesn't catch my sarcasm. Instead he grins, revealing a row of clear braces. "You know, since we all sit in here at lunch, you should eat with us. If you want to." His friends are already arranging chairs in a circle.

I shove my avocado and cheese sandwich back into my bag. "I'm not that hungry today." Without waiting for a reply, I scoop up my viola and leave the room.

The hallway is covered with posters for honor society, debate team, robotics club. Orange and black banners cheer, GO, JAGUARS! When I got to high school, I'd already committed my life to viola, and I imagine my single-mindedness made it difficult to make friends. What was the point of wasting time on something I might not enjoy, like a club or a sport? But what if I'd tried yearbook or soccer, or I'd grown close to the other kids in orchestra, and now I had friends to talk to about this? Now there are only a handful of people I can talk to, and all of them either don't want to talk or talk far too much. Or they don't appreciate Tchaikovsky.

I don't have an off-campus lunch pass, but our security's so lax I'm able to slip out the back entrance without anyone stopping me. I take the bus so Tovah can drive herself home later. I've never skipped school before, but I'm only missing fifth, sixth, and seventh. What do precalculus and physics and US Government matter to me now?

I get off the bus in Capitol Hill. Gray clouds press down on me, threatening rain. I hunch my shoulders and take long strides down Broadway, a street crammed with taquerias and art supply stores and boutiques and a couple sex toy shops. I duck into a coffee shop, order a latte, and take a seat near the window so I can watch the rain. The latte foam makes a leaf pattern. I take a sip, and the leaf is gone.

One day I won't be able to do this: drink coffee, get rained on, enjoy the classical music playing in the background of the coffee shop, play stupid games on my phone to pass the time.

There are an awful lot of things on the one-day-I-won't list. Mentally, I tear it into tiny pieces.

♩ ♫♩

When I get back on the bus, I reapply the Siren lipstick I tattooed onto my coffee mug and don't make eye contact with anyone. As kids, Tovah and I used to make up stories about the people we saw. We learned to ride the bus early, like most city kids, before the training wheels came off our bikes. She'd say, "Look at that guy with the ferret on a leash. He's totally training him to perform in the circus." And I'd point across the aisle and whisper, "That girl tapping her three-inch-long fingernails against the pole? She's growing them out to try to break a Guinness World Record."

The bus goes up, up, up that familiar hill. I have no idea what to expect at today's lesson, but Arjun did not cancel, so I guess it's still happening. It's pouring when I get off, soaking my hair and eyelashes, dripping down my nose. My coat is in my locker at school, keeping my books warm. I'm still early and I don't want to buzz up yet, so I lurk out front, lucking out when I catch a woman heading out of the building. I jam my boot in as the door is closing.

"I just moved in, and I'm such a scatterbrain. What's the

code again?" I flash a smile, hoping I sound genuine.

"One-nine-four-five," she says. "The year the complex was built."

"Right." I commit the numbers to memory. "Thank you."

"Sure," she says, her grin now matching my fake one. "Welcome to the building. The bottom dryer in the laundry room likes to eat socks."

I hear the music before I reach his floor. It's a viola sonata by Shostakovich, a twentieth-century Russian composer who finished this piece weeks before his death.

The music roots me in place, but on the inside I am in motion. Strings soar and fall, winding circles around my heart, tugging it this way and that. Behind his door, Arjun's slicing and sawing and plucking. The piece is so beautiful, I ache right along with it. It is hopeful, then hopeless, then flitting between the two as though it cannot make up its mind. I've never heard it played with this much melancholy before, and it makes me wonder if Shostakovich knew he was going to die. He was waiting for it to happen, and this was his way of expressing it.

When the song is over, I chance a few steps forward and ring the bell. Footsteps pad along the hardwood floor, and then Arjun throws the door open.

"Adina? We're not scheduled for another half hour." His hair is a little out of place, as though he's been exercising instead of playing Shostakovich. It is a burgundy sweater day.

"School got out early," I say. "No. That's a lie. I left early. I cut class."

"Oh."

"I don't have anywhere else to go. Or anyone else to talk to. Maybe we could . . . talk." It's only when I say it that I realize this is what I have been aching for: to talk to someone who isn't a doctor, who has no connection to my family, who is entirely on my side. Someone who cares for me and only me so much he cannot be objective about this miserable mess.

His statue face softens, dark eyes widening with an emotion I can't place. Sympathy? "Come inside."

If it is sympathy, I decide I don't mind. I prop my viola against the wall and lead him into his living room, not the studio. It is sparsely decorated, a geometric-patterned rug, simple shelves, no television. I sit down on the couch and unzip my boots so I don't track any mud onto the rug.

He takes a seat in an armchair on the other side of the room. It doesn't match the couch, but I like the incongruity. "Can't you talk to your family?"

"They all look at me differently now. It hasn't been that long, but it feels like everything's changed." I heave a sigh. "You're the only one I feel like I can talk to."

He straightens his posture, as though he is taking pride in my compliment. I didn't mean to flatter him, but I'm glad for his reaction regardless. "Really?" he says.

"You don't act like I'm fragile."

"You're not someone who should ever be considered fragile, I don't think."

I pick at my tights, tugging on one long thread. "I haven't

been able to play since I got the results. Not really. But I heard you playing just now, and I don't know, something happened to me. I've heard you play before, but this time . . . I didn't know the song could have so much sadness in it. I *felt* sad listening to it. That's exactly what music should do, right? That's what you teach us to do, play with enough emotion to make other people feel something? I know that whatever happens to me, I can't let myself get lazy. I can't stop playing."

"Thank you," he says, genuine. "I've never met anyone who feels music the way you do. I've always thought that one day I'll have nothing left to teach you."

"It's true. I'm sure I'll be better than you one day," I joke. "Maybe I should find another teacher to keep your ego intact."

This jolts him. "You haven't wanted to find another instructor, have you? Because of . . ." He can't finish the sentence.

"No. I only want you."

The words linger in the space between us. Perhaps I intended the double meaning, but I truly didn't come here to try to seduce him. I thought I'd tell him about my insomnia or the article Tovah found about Huntington's symptoms in teens. He gets up from the chair and sits on the couch next to me. I say nothing. The past few weeks, he has tried to put space between us, but now he is getting close to me on purpose.

The couch groans softly beneath his weight, and my skin sparks with electricity at his nearness. Many measures pass before he speaks again.

"I should be honest with you. I've been attracted to you for a while," he says. "You're so talented, and you're beautiful, and you're intelligent. And you're, well, I feel like I understand you, and you understand me. Sometimes I feel like a stranger in this country, and I think you do too."

All I can do is nod.

"But you are my student. I wasn't supposed to have those feelings for you. I needed some time to think, I guess. I didn't know that everything I was feeling wasn't . . . wrong."

Hearing him confess that feels like passing my hand through a flame without getting burned. This is proof my body is still powerful. It flips a switch, turns me from fawn to minx again.

"You can have all the feelings for me that you want. I won't tell anyone. We can keep it inside your apartment, and no one will ever know."

"Adina . . ."

I lick my lips, aware he is watching me. "I want you," I repeat, intentional this time. "You want me. Life is short. Why should we deny ourselves something that could feel really amazing?" I reach out a finger and stroke it across his wrist. "This isn't wrong, is it?"

There is a new energy between us. An inevitability. "No," he says. "It's not wrong."

"And this?" I place my palms on his chest, inch them toward his shoulders. His eyes flutter shut, but again, he doesn't stop me.

"This, I like," he says. He puts a hand on top of mine. We are only touching in innocent places, yet my heart finds a racehorse rhythm. His thumb strokes my knuckles, and I feel my cold skin start to heat up.

I lean in close, my lips a whisper from his. "This?"

His eyes flick open for an instant. "Yes," he says, and I trap the word between our lips.

Our first kiss tastes a hundred times better than my fantasies. There is no hesitation or uncertainty, only force and greed. He kisses the way he plays viola: hard and fast, leaving both of us breathless. I grip his collar. His hands are in my hair, clutching me close, and though my hair is damp and tangled from my walk in the rain, under his touch, it must be the softest thing in the world.

Suddenly I pull back.

"Adina, what is it?" His voice is hoarse, as though kissing me has drained all his energy and he has little left to speak. "Is everything okay?"

"You're not doing this because I'm sick," I say, my own voice quaking over the words. I want to be irresistible, not pitiable. "Or that I'm going to be sick . . . I don't know. I can't get the tenses right."

"I promise you, I'm not," he says, his fingers still winding through my waves. He takes a breath. "When you asked several weeks ago if I imagined us . . . *together* . . . the answer is yes."

I can't formulate a response, so I use my body instead of words. I climb onto his lap so I can kiss him with my whole body pressed against his, so I can feel between my legs exactly how badly he wants me. We kiss like that for a long time, long enough for me to memorize his every texture. His jawline, rough with the sketch of a beard. His mouth, slick and hot against my neck. His teeth, sharp as they tease my skin.

Desperate to feel even more of him, I peel off his sweater and unbutton his shirt. My hands explore the hair on his chest, something I find undeniably sexy about older guys. He runs his hands up my legs beneath my dress, fingers getting caught on the runs in my tights.

A buzzer rings, making us spring apart.

"Shit," he says, breathing hard. He coaxes a shirt button into the wrong hole, tries again. "Shit, shit, shit. That's my next student."

My lips pull into a smile. "I've never heard you swear before." His speech is usually so formal. I'm breathing hard too. I had no idea so much time had passed. A laugh bubbles up my throat as I realize I have painted his mouth with Siren red. I help him thumb it off.

"It's only because I'm genuinely frustrated that we have to put this on pause." On pause. Meaning we can hit play at some point. His brows furrow, and he continues: "What you said earlier, though, about keeping what happens between us inside this apartment? It has to stay that way, Adi. I can't risk any of my students—or their parents—finding out about this."

"I know," I say quickly as I slide off his lap, trying to ignore the flash of irritation that runs through me. My age has made me a secret before. A part of me hoped it would be different with Arjun, but I understand why it can't be.

I straighten my clothes and run my fingers through my hair. It doesn't matter where I have him because he is finally mine. Kissing him has delicious side effects: my face warm, my lips fried, my insides melted.

"I'll be back next week," I say as I zip my boots. "Or maybe next week is too far away?"

He pushes my hair away and kisses the back of my neck. Now that the way we both feel is obvious, touching is effortless. "Come over tomorrow."

"I have work." I can't afford to miss a shift. "After? I can be here around eight." I'll lie to my parents if I have to.

"Eight," he confirms, the word hot on my skin.

♪ ♫♪

No more procrastinating. When I get home, I round up the requirements for the conservatories on my list. What happened at Arjun's reinvigorated me, plucked me from days and days of gloom. But furthermore, if I somehow miss these deadlines, I will never forgive myself. Regardless of what else is going on in my life, I have been working toward conservatory for too long to give up on it. Tonight I will not think about Huntington's. I will think only in quarter notes and rests, alto clefs and codas.

I free my viola and open the video recording program on my laptop, giving the camera a half smile before I launch into my pre-audition pieces. Any time I am dissatisfied with the sound, I start over.

I'm in the middle of a flawless rendition when someone knocks on my door. "Adina? It's dinnertime."

"Aba!" I shout, frustration jumping my voice an octave. I punch the stop button. "I was recording. For my applications."

I can practically hear him recoil. "Sorry. I'll keep some warm for whenever you're ready."

Two hours later, I am finally pleased with my videos. My fingers are sore and my hands are cramping, but I shovel fettuccine into my mouth while I type out my essays. *Which musician, living or dead, would you like to collaborate with, and what might you produce together? How will you benefit from an education at our school? What is your most memorable experience with music?*

I climb into bed only after I've turned in every application, Debussy echoing in my ears.

Fourteen

Tovah

ABA PLAYS NIRVANA THE ENTIRE DRIVE. HIS FINGERS drum the wheel, his eyes occasionally catching mine in the rearview mirror. He smiles whenever this happens. We hum along as Kurt Cobain growls *we can plant a house, we can build a tree*, since neither of our voices compares to Kurt's scratchy, raw one.

Adi is asleep next to me and Ima is asleep next to Aba, but I can't nap during road trips. A couple hours of sleep isn't worth missing the scenery. The farther north we go, the shorter and stockier the buildings get. Streets are replaced with forests, strip malls with acres of farmland, cars with cows and horses.

Canada for Thanksgiving was my parents' idea. We'll trade turkey and cranberries for a long weekend of family time. A distraction from our sad reality. British Columbia doesn't look all that different from Washington. Same mountains and trees and gray skies. When I was small, I thought all countries had some defining feature. Ima's few photos of her life in Israel gave me visions of an exotic, sacred place. Synagogues with high ceilings and ornate architecture. Sandy beaches and ancient ruins.

I'm hoping, too, that the time away from home will give me a chance to talk to the sister I've spent years pushing away. It can take years for people to come to terms with a positive result, but regardless of where we end up in the fall, this is probably my last year living across the hall from Adina—and therefore, my last chance to make things right between us.

My phone vibrates in my pocket.

You around this weekend? Troy went with Lindsay to her grandparents' and I am BORED.

I'm in Canada.

Not helping my boredom.

I'll see what I can do.

I take a photo of someone walking a dog. I text it to Zack with the caption **CANADIAN DOG**. Then I do the same with a fire hydrant, a telephone pole, a plastic bag on the sidewalk. I'm not sure it's very entertaining, until Zack responds.

You're funny

When we reach the hotel, my parents retreat to one room, and Adina and I unpack our suitcases across the hall. I plug in my laptop and open an AP Bio lab report, but I can't concentrate. Adina's already swapping her dress and tights for pajamas. Taking her phone into bed with her, fingers flying across the screen.

I almost start talking to her half a dozen times, but my sister is a deer, and I don't want to frighten her away by being too forward. If I'm going to make progress, I have to be gentle.

Every so often, I hear her laughing, and it's so, so nice to hear that I don't ruin it by asking her what's so funny.

⋈⋈⋈

We pretend we're a normal American family on vacation. We tour gardens and historic churches and a museum devoted entirely to miniatures. In the car after the museum, Ima sighs deeply and says, "Matt, girls, I might have to call it a day." Her face is weary, and my heart pinches. I wonder if she notices how much other people stare at her near-constant jerking and twitching. If that adds to the weariness.

For the first time, I wonder if getting into Johns Hopkins will mean missing the last few good years with Ima. But Ima would hate for me to close myself off to an opportunity because of her.

"We can rest before dinner," Aba says.

"I might take a nap too." Adina looks up from her phone for what seems like the first time today. "Unless you need the room for anything, Tovah."

"Go ahead," I say too quickly. God, it's like I'm scared of her or something. She should be able to take all the naps she wants.

Aba and I spend the next few hours exploring the city. We meet Ima and Adina for dinner at a kosher restaurant that takes forever to find. We've only ever spent Thanksgiving with the Mizrahis or other friends of our parents. It's odd to share this one with strangers and waiters.

I'm used to people gawking at Ima in public, though in the past they stared at our family for other reasons. It's unusual to hear Hebrew spoken in Seattle; most people can't identify the language. I've been asked multiple times if I'm speaking German or Arabic or Russian, and when I say that it's actually Hebrew, I'm met with, "Isn't that a dead language?" It nearly went extinct thousands of years ago but was revived during the nineteenth century. Today more than nine million people speak Modern Israeli Hebrew. The guttural "chet" and "resh" sounds feel natural on my lips.

Once when Adina and I were little, we were in a restaurant with our parents, the two of us fighting about me quitting orchestra. Adina thought I hadn't given it a fair chance. We eventually grew so loud we were yelling at each other. "Die! Die!" Ima said to us over and over, which in Hebrew means "enough," but to all the nearby restaurant-goers, it appeared as though she was wishing death upon her children. Sheepishly, she explained to them that she was not, in fact, a murderous mother.

Tonight, though, the waiter's gaze lingers more on Adina than my mother, and for an entirely different reason. It's been this way with my sister and ninety percent of human males for a long time. His name tag says Beau. I comb my fingers through my short hair and eye the curls that crest Adina's shoulders.

After we order, I lean in to my sister and say, "Beau was checking you out." Trying to be conversational. Trying to talk to her the way I'd talk to Lindsay.

"Who?"

My stomach twists in annoyance. It was so obvious. "The waiter."

"Oh," she says, like she didn't even notice.

We recite a bracha before we eat, as always, and then my father raps on his water glass with a knife and clears his throat.

"Please don't make us talk about what we're thankful for," Adina says before Aba can say anything.

Aba frowns like that's exactly what he wanted to do.

"I'm thankful for something," I say, making eye contact with Aba, showing him I'm on his side, like always. He beams at me. "I'm thankful we didn't have to go to school yesterday."

"I'm thankful no one got carsick on the way up," Ima says.

"I'm thankful your ima convinced me to leave my laptop at home."

Adina lifts an eyebrow but doesn't say anything.

I keep it going. "I'm thankful for this salmon, which is delicious."

"That I'm awake to have dinner with my family."

"That one of my daughters appreciates Nirvana."

We all look to Adina. "Okay, okay," she says, shaking her head like she can't believe she's related to us. "Fine. I'm thankful only one of my parents forces us to listen to Nirvana."

It isn't very funny, but we laugh anyway.

At the end of the meal, when Beau clears the table, he says, "I hope you enjoyed everything this evening."

Adina looks up at him from beneath her lashes and smiles

with her heart-shaped mouth. "We did. Thank you for taking care of us." The way she says it, it sounds suggestive.

Two pink spots appear on his cheeks. "Anytime," he says.

A mix of envy and admiration surges through me. I can't help it. I wish I had one-tenth of that confidence.

⋉⟨⟩⟨⟩⋊

Back in our hotel room, Adina turns on the TV. I'm about to send Zack a photo with the caption **CANADIAN TV**, but I freeze when Adina gasps and says, "Remember this movie? Oh my God."

It's a mediocre romantic comedy from five years ago. A girl and guy are baristas at rival coffee shops, and the girl is a klutz but the guy finds her charming and the guy wasn't ready for marriage until he met her. The usual clichés. Adina and I are suckers for sappy, unintentionally hilarious movies.

"It's the part where they try to get each other to fuck up by ordering a really complicated cup of coffee!" I say. "Turn it up."

"The best part," Adi agrees, spiking the volume.

"Do you remember," I say, "when we got kicked out of *Mystic Harbor* for talking?" It was a tragedy romance with two attractive white people kissing on the movie poster.

"Yes! That was so unfair. Our commentary was more interesting than the movie. I can't believe—"

"—that the girl was actually her twin sister the entire time? I wish secret twin story lines would go away. There's no way that happens in real life as much as it does in movies."

My hand is still on my phone, but after a few minutes, I

123

relax back on the twin bed and prop my head up with a pillow. Maybe this is how we fix us: gradually, while watching a dumb movie.

During a commercial break, Adi says, "You want some candy from the vending machine?" An ad for a knife that can cut through granite plays onscreen.

"Get M&M's, if they have them."

When the door clicks shut, I grab my phone, which has been blinking next to me for the past fifteen minutes.

My favorite movie is playing at Rain City Cinema next Sunday. Ever been?

Rain City Cinema is a run-down but well-loved indie theater where audience participation, such as throwing things at the screen, is highly encouraged.

Yeah. Lindsay and I saw Rocky Horror there a few years ago.

I'm gonna kick myself if you say no again, but I guess I'm feeling lucky today. Want to come?

I ball my damp hands into fists and recall my conversation with Lindsay. Zack could be new and scary—but also thrilling.

Sure, that sounds fun.

Awsome, can't wait.

We make plans to have dinner beforehand, and even though he misspelled "awesome," I'm grinning when Adi returns with candy.

"What is it?" she asks.

"Nothing," I say quickly, shoving my phone on the bedside table. "Just the movie. What'd you get?"

She spreads her haul on the bed. I snatch the M&M's and she chooses a bag of jelly beans, both of which are kosher. They're the types of candy we used to get when we went to the movies together. More accurately: when we sneaked in candy from the drugstore next to the theater.

Adi in pajamas, her long hair in a messy ponytail, carefully picking out all the peach and pear jelly beans because those are her favorites, looks so innocent and childlike. It makes the reality of what will one day happen to her—to her body and her mind—seem more unjust.

She never wanted to know.

"Adina," I start gently, *gently*, because I have to acknowledge it if we're going to move forward. "I'm sorry. I'm sorry for forcing you to take the test. That should have been your own personal decision."

She chews loudly on a jelly bean. "I don't want to talk about it, Tovah." But she doesn't say it in a mean way, and when the movie ends and another one starts, we don't turn off the TV.

During the opening credits, after the actor's names flash onscreen, I say, "I love Camila Rivera's production design."

I watch Adi, waiting for her to grin. She does, remembering our game.

"Oh, yeah, and don't even get me started on Richard Potter's music supervising," she adds as his name pops up. "*Truly* top-notch."

We used to do this all the time: pretend we knew the crew the same way we'd know the actors.

"They got Yvonne St. James to do the casting? She's my favorite!"

We're both laughing now. The game reminds me that for most of our lives, we were inseparable. Our parents begged the school to put us in different third-grade classes because they thought it would be a good idea to get us out of our comfort zones. By the end of the first week, I'd made three new friends and Adi had cried twice. So back I went into her class, where I had an automatic partner for every classroom activity, group project, and presidential fitness test, which we both failed because we couldn't touch our toes with our fingertips.

After a while, we fall back into relative silence. We don't talk about college or boys or any of the things I talk about with Lindsay. Every commercial break, I want to interrogate her. *Who were you texting all day? How are your conservatory applications coming? When are you coming back to synagogue, and what do you do when you're not there? How are you doing with all this? Are you okay? Are you okay? Are you okay?*

But I don't. I keep the questions locked inside because even though we only open our mouths to make fun of a particularly cliché line of dialogue, Adina and I never have this anymore. In a few days we'll be back at home, but for now it's just me and her, and I let myself pretend this can last longer than tonight. That we can have this when our futures turn real again.

Winter

Fifteen

Adina

DECEMBER IS FOR DEAD THINGS. ONLY A FEW LEAVES cling to tree branches, and a raccoon corpse is pancaked on the side of the freeway. I read somewhere that more people die in December than any other month of the year.

I'm thinking about death as I sit across from Maureen, the genetic counselor, because even though her office is aiming for cheery, with its lavender walls and paintings of sunsets, death is everywhere. This is the place where I learned my life would change, and where, ostensibly, I will learn how to handle it.

"I'm glad you're here," Maureen says. Her chin-length blond hair frames her face, and she's dressed casually in a black sweater and dark jeans. There's a whole-note-shaped birthmark beneath her left eye.

"Really?" I came only because this is my chance to finally get answers to the questions Tovah's research sparked. My parents still want me to meet with our rabbi, and though I've reluctantly begun attending synagogue with them again every week, a religion I don't believe in won't give me the answers I need. An old man in a kippah cannot possibly understand what I am feeling.

"Sometimes people test positive and I never see them again," she says softly. "This is a good step, a huge one, even if you don't realize it."

"Oh." I tear at a loose thread on my tights. "Thanks. I think."

Maureen offers a sympathetic smile that scrunches up her birthmark, turns it into a whole rest and makes me wonder how much bad news she's given over her lifetime. "Tell me how you've been these past few weeks."

The past few weeks have been a seesaw of bad and good. Bad: everything this office represents. Good: everything with Arjun.

I settle for an answer somewhere in the middle. "I've been . . . okay."

"You're back at school, right? And you're still playing the viola?" she asks, and I nod. "Good. Like I said before, Adina, the majority of patients I see who test positive have been able to carry on with very regular lives. Most of the time, symptoms don't manifest until your forties."

I widen the hole in the knee of my tights. "Is there any way to know when symptoms will show up?"

"Unfortunately, that's the most challenging and frustrating part of getting tested so young. We have no way of knowing when symptoms will manifest for you. They started for your mother in her early forties. It might be the same for you, or it might not."

"I read online that sometimes people start showing symptoms much earlier than my mom did. Like . . . like in their twenties."

"It's unlikely that you'd exhibit symptoms that early."

"But it happens."

"Well. Yes. But it's also possible they don't show up until you're seventy or eighty," she says. "We'll be keeping a close eye on you. You know to tell us—me and Dr. Simon—if you start experiencing anything like what your mom went through, but each person is different. Your symptoms might not be the same as your mom's."

"So we each get our own special version of Huntington's."

"I suppose that's one way to think about it." For the remainder of the session, she talks about symptoms and youth organizations and support groups. But what I focus on is this: The next few times I drop something, the next time I lose my temper, it could be that I'm simply clumsy. It could be that I'm premenstrual. Or it could mean the end is beginning.

In the back of the bus on my way home from counseling, I compose a message to Arjun.

Can I come over tonight?

Part of me wanted to tell Tovah everything about Arjun when we were in Canada. He was the reason I was so calm on my family trip, after all. Tovah used to know everything I couldn't tell our parents, like when I borrowed Ima's razors and secretly started shaving when I turned eleven because I hated the dark fur covering my legs. There are a hundred reasons I can't tell her this, but above all else: she wouldn't understand.

Tovah apologized for guilting me into taking the test, and perhaps I can forgive her. Rationally, I know it is not her fault that I tested positive. Still, I cannot get rid of the feeling that I would be happier now if I didn't know.

But maybe Arjun would still be hiding his feelings for me.

At yesterday's lesson, during which no actual music was played, our mouths and hands rediscovered what they learned how to do the previous week. We haven't slept together yet; we haven't had enough time. It is inevitable, though, and I cannot wait.

I'm halfway between Maureen's office and home when he finally replies.

Teaching until 9.

Those three words land in a heavy pile in my stomach.

Tomorrow?

This week isn't good.

My hand tightens around the phone. What the hell does that mean? What makes this week bad? Is he having doubts about us?

He is the only person who doesn't treat me like I'm made of glass. I'll do anything to keep him from changing his mind.

Don't make me do all the things I want you to do to me all by myself. That sounds lonely. . . .

His response is quicker this time.

Come over next week after your showcase rehearsal.

132

I'll be done at 6. Will you cook dinner for me?

I'm testing him.

I can do that. And then maybe you can show me those things you do by yourself.

He aces it.

♪ ♫♪

I ride the bus for another hour, until long past sundown. These days it feels like I live on buses. On a mental map, I connect Seattle's neighborhoods: Fremont to Ballard to Loyal Heights to Crown Hill to Greenwood to Phinney Ridge and back to Wallingford. When I was little, the city was a blob that gradually became more defined, until I could read a map as well as a piece of sheet music.

Tonight is the first night of Chanukah, and though it is not as significant as Rosh Hashanah or Yom Kippur, I'd rather skip it.

It's past eight o'clock when I get home. In our window, the menorah is already lit, candles burning.

"Adi?" Ima calls from the living room. "Is that you?"

I freeze. "Hi, Ima." Quickly, I unlace my boots, slipping past the living room on my way to the staircase.

"Yalla. Come in here, please?"

Slowly, I back up, my muscles tensing. She's curled in a chair grading papers, a geography assignment with colored-pencil maps of the United States. On the couch is a half-finished knitting project.

"Chanukah sameach."

"Chanukah sameach. Where's everyone else?"

133

"Aba is studying Hebrew in his office, and Tovah is upstairs doing homework. How was your session?"

"Good, I guess."

"What did you think of Maureen?"

"I've seen her before, Ima."

"I know," she says. *But it's different now* is what I'm sure she means.

"You know I like her."

"She's very understanding. Very . . . knowledgeable," Ima says. "Adi, do you see that bag over there?" She points to a blue bag with gold Stars of David printed on it sitting on the dining room table. "Can you bring it to me? I know we haven't done Chanukah presents since you and Tovah were little kids, but I wanted you to have something."

I retrieve the bag and pull out a bracelet, a silver chain with blue spheres painted to look like eyeballs.

"It's the evil eye," Ima explains in her fifth-grade-teacher storytelling voice. "Do you know what it means?" I shake my head. "The evil eye was a malicious look thought to be powerful enough to inflict pain and suffering on whoever the person was glaring at. This eye here, it glares back to protect you from evil. This bracelet belonged to your savtah. My mother. She wore it all the time. Never took it off, in fact."

"Todah. It's beautiful." I fasten it around my wrist and give it a shake. I plan to wear it every day. "Did you get something for Tovah, too?"

"I only had this from my mother," she says. "But I didn't

want Tovah to feel left out, so I found a similar bracelet online and told her it was from her grandmother too. You won't mention it to her, right?"

"I won't." Before the test, this would have made me happy: another secret between Ima and me. But now I wish my mother hadn't given me something so special—because it makes me wonder whether she's doing it out of guilt. *You tested positive, but here, have a bracelet!*

"Good." Ima returns her attention to her papers. "You haven't been by the classroom lately."

"School and rehearsals have gotten really busy." Half true. She must know I've been avoiding her. "How are your kids?"

"Caleb and Amanda were holding hands during the movie I played this week."

"You mean Annabel?" Ima routinely forgets names like this.

"Oh. What did I say?"

"Amanda."

"I meant Annabel," she says, and she gives me a guilty look, because we both know the blanks in her memory are one of the many things I will inherit.

When I was little and hurt myself, Ima found a way to take away the pain. *Here, transfer it to me,* she'd say. And I'd hold out the knee I'd banged up or the elbow I'd smacked against the wall and she'd cup her fingers around it and say a made-up word like *shoomp!* Then she'd touch her hand to her own knee or elbow and screw her face up. *Ouch,* she'd say. *See? It worked. You're all better now.*

There's no way to make this disappear.

"Keep me company while I grade these?" she says. "Let's put on a movie. We haven't done that in a while, either."

"B'seder." Okay.

Ima doesn't ask if we should invite Tovah down, and I don't suggest it. I put on an old Audrey Hepburn movie and pull a textbook from my backpack, but the words swim in front of my eyes. I'm stitched into the fabric of the sofa, mesmerized by the sight of my mother. She has become someone always in motion, prone to wild jerks that used to be occasional twitches.

I watch, when she isn't looking, with more scrutiny than I ever have before.

♪ ♫♪

I can't sleep. The sheets are twisted around my ankles and my skin is damp with sweat. My period made an appearance earlier tonight, and my abdomen is all knotted up like it usually is on day one. Absently, I wonder how many more periods I'll have in my lifetime. If I'll ever hit menopause.

I peel myself out of bed and turn on my laptop. Again I watch the videos. Again I listen to the way people with Huntington's talk. My mother's sentences used to sound like songs. In the coming years, she'll stutter through both her Hebrew and English, and one day her rich voice will be gone.

I can't clear my mind for long before it traps me back in this place. This place where it loops over the reality that my mother is going to die, not of old age but in five or ten, or if we're lucky, fifteen years. It will be brutal and entirely unfair, watching her wither and waste away. And then it will happen to me.

Unless—unless I don't live that long.

Unless I make certain I never become my mother.

I sit completely still for a few minutes. An unfamiliar charged thrill zips through me.

But I couldn't. I couldn't do that. A strange sound gets caught in my throat—a laugh? Apparently, some half-asleep part of me finds this idea half-funny, though it is absolutely not. God, I must be delirious.

What if I could?

I smash the laptop shut, as though the screen had some kind of macabre instruction manual on it. The room is plunged into darkness again, and I hug the sheets tights around me and try to fall asleep. The possibilities, realistic or not, haunt me into the morning.

Sixteen
Tovah

ZACK SITS ACROSS FROM ME IN A COZY RESTAURANT that serves individual potpies. After I say a bracha, he regards me with a small smile.

"You always do that," he says. "It's interesting."

"For as long as I can remember," I say with a shrug. "Before eating, after eating, in the morning, in the evening . . ."

"I caught a few words, but not all of them."

"I could teach you."

"I'd like that," he says. "I've always wanted to learn more Hebrew."

"Well, you know 'tov' already, which means 'good.'"

"Yes. You're very tov."

I flush. I run through a few other common Hebrew phrases with him before changing the subject. "Tell me more about art school?"

"Art school." Zack leans back in his seat, flexing his arms above his head. "I'll go to whichever one will have me."

"And your moms, they're cool with it?"

"I had to convince Tess, but Mikaela is a free spirit. She thinks it should be illegal to throw away something you can compost." He half grins like he's about to tell me a secret and continues: "She even smokes pot."

I nearly choke on my water—I wasn't expecting to hear that. It's like learning your parents love a TV show you thought you discovered. "Do you smoke?"

"I did it with Mikaela once. She wanted me to do it in a 'safe environment.'" He air quotes this. "It was about as fun as you can imagine getting high with your mom would be. I got really hungry and we ordered way too many pizzas for the two of us to eat. Anyway, Mikaela's a sculptor. She's had a few pieces commissioned by the city, so she knows it's possible to make money as an artist. . . . It's just really fucking hard."

"Do you know what you want to do with your art? Mixed-media murals, or gallery shows, or what?"

He shrugs. "I'm not sure yet. I can't imagine not making art, so I have to see wherever it takes me."

As we eat, I try to ignore to seed of guilt in my stomach. There it is again: my inability to enjoy myself without thinking about my sister. Since Canada, there's been a strange, tentative peace between us. I don't want to lose that, but I also want to push past peace into something resembling friendship. I'm just not yet sure how.

Zack reaches across the table and touches my evil-eye brace-let, his index finger spinning one of the beads. Jewelry's always itched and scratched me, but this is a link to a family member I know so little about, so when Ima gave it to me for Chanukah, I vowed to wear it as much as possible.

"That's new," he says. A statement, not a question. This close, I can smell his ocean-salt cologne.

"So is your cologne."

His cheeks flush. "You got me there."

"This was my Israeli grandmother's, on my mother's side."

"Can't say the same about my cologne." He continues to map a path around the beads on my wrist with a fingertip. "Have you ever been to Israel?"

I shake my head. "I want to go, though. Someday. What about you?"

"Someday," he echoes, moving his hand away from mine. "When do you hear back from John Hopkins?"

"Johns Hopkins," I correct, because its founder's first name was Johns, not John. "Middle of December. A couple more weeks."

"*Johns* Hopkins," Zack says, emphasizing "Johns" with a teasing smile. "And then you're gonna be a doctor?"

"A surgeon."

He grins. "I like that you're ambitious. Couldn't get enough of Operation when you were a kid?"

"Please, like that game's realistic. I like knowing how and why the human body works, and how to fix it if something's wrong. Like, okay, do you know why we . . ." I grope for a way to finish the sentence. "Why we . . . blush?" I wrap my fingers around the cold water glass, then subtly bring them to my cheek. I've been doing it our entire dinner; I might as well acknowledge it.

"Is it like yawning? Once you start talking or thinking about it, you can't help it? Like you're blushing right now."

"It's involuntary, actually. It comes from our fight-or-flight response. When we're embarrassed, our bodies release adrenaline, which makes our hearts beat faster and our breathing quicken, and it also makes our blood vessels dilate. That makes more blood flow to them, causing our cheeks to turn red."

"Your blood vessels are so dilated right now."

I hide my face with my hand. "Sorry." I peek through a few fingers. "That probably sounded boring."

"No," he says. "That was interesting."

"Really?"

He reaches across the table to pull my hand from my face, and his mouth lifts into a smile as our eyes meet. I want to make him smile like that again and again. "Yes." Then the smile flattens, as though something's just occurred to him. "Has Troy seemed . . . weird to you lately?"

"Weird how?"

"I barely see him alone anymore. He and Lindsay are always together."

"I know!" It's strange to have someone vocalize an insecurity I'm still in denial about. "They're in love, I get it, but do they have to make the rest of us feel invisible?"

141

Zack blinks at me, and I realize how out of character the admission was for me.

"I mean, I love Lindsay," I backtrack. "But I feel . . . abandoned sometimes." Even during her pregnancy scare, she was allowed to have a crisis, but I wasn't.

"Same. Last weekend Troy bailed on me at the last minute."

"That must have been the same time Lindsay bailed on me last minute. And sometimes," I continue, really getting going now that I finally have someone to talk to about this, "I think it's going to be just us, and then Troy shows up. Or y—" I break off, realize I'm about to insult him.

"Or me?" he fills in.

"Not that I mind," I say quickly. "Things change, I guess."

"Well, then," he says, his smile sad but hopeful, "it's a good thing we started hanging out."

Outside the restaurant, Zack grabs my elbow. "We need to make one more stop," he says, steering me in the opposite direction of the theater.

He leads me into a convenience store, which is empty except for a few kids pumping fake cheese onto nachos. I assume he'll buy some candy for the movie, but instead he grabs a box of plastic spoons.

"You'll see," he says when I quirk an eyebrow at him.

We hurry down the block toward the cinema, marquee lettering spelling out CULT HIT "THE ROOM"—ONE NIGHT ONLY!

"Haven't heard of it," I say.

"The thing I need to tell you about it," Zack says, looking sheepish, "actually, the thing I probably should have told you before is that it's regarded as one of the worst films of all time."

"Then the thing I need to tell you is that I love shitty movies," I say, and he laughs.

"Seeing *The Room* for the first time is a special experience. You're gonna love it, I swear."

And I do. The dialogue is forced and awkward. Plot points completely disappear. The acting is on par with my third-grade class's production of *Cats*. Then there are the spoons.

"Do you see all the framed pictures of spoons in the apartment?" Zack says into my ear. "They're those pictures that come in the frame when you buy it. The ones you're supposed to take out."

Whenever one of the framed spoon pictures comes into view, we hurl plastic spoons at the screen along with the rest of the audience. It's the most fun I've had in weeks. Months.

"Oh—sorry," I whisper when I reach into the box to grab a spoon at the same time Zack does. Our fingers tangle, but I don't pull back. Neither does he.

My heart jumps into my throat. His thumb rubs against mine, back and forth and back and forth until the movie blurs because this tiny movement is dizzying. Tentatively, I run my index finger along the knobs of his knuckles, dipping into the valleys in between. Learning his skin. When I peer up at his face, he's smiling in the dark.

We don't stop holding hands until the credits roll.

"Was that not the best cinematic experience of your life?" Zack asks as we file out into the night with the rest of the audience.

It was, for a number of reasons.

"It was incredible. The acting! The writing! The cinematography!" *The feel of your hand in mine.* I want to grab his hand now, but before I can become brave enough, he kneels and plucks a damp scrap of white paper from the sidewalk.

"Something for your mundane mixed-media project?"

He nods and shows me the faded supermarket receipt.

```
Ginger ale
Cold care tea
Cough drops
Beer
```

"Sometimes you get gems like these." He tucks it into his pocket. "I love this guy. He was sick as hell, but he still wanted to get drunk."

"I can't wait to see what you do with it." I zip up my hoodie as Zack loops a scarf around his neck. "Do you want a ride home?"

Zack doesn't drive; he confessed earlier when I saw him get off the bus that he's failed his test three times, and his moms won't let him take it again until he logs fifteen more practice hours.

"I don't mind taking the bus."

"I want to drive you."

He grins. "Excellent. I kind of want you to drive me," he

says, and we spend the drive quoting the movie and brainstorming sequels.

"Why haven't we done this before?" he asks when I put the car in park in his driveway. His house has an herb garden in the front yard and a chicken coop in the back.

"Hung out? We have."

"Not alone. We obviously get along, but I think you avoid me."

"I don't avoid you," I insist.

"You do," he says, but he doesn't sound offended. "When you texted me a few weeks ago, I don't know if it was because you were drunk with Lindsay or what, but I'm glad you did."

"I—I am too," I manage, my tongue feeling three sizes too large for my mouth.

"Your blood vessels are dilating again." He grins, showing off that space between his front teeth. "Laila tov, Tov," he says, wishing me good night in Hebrew before getting out of the car and tapping the hood a couple times. I'm beginning to love my name.

I let out a deep breath, collecting myself before putting the car in reverse. Zack's presence is big and overwhelming, and I can't get enough of it. But I have only a few moments before guilt sours my joy.

Every good thing that happens to me from now until the end of my life will be tainted by Adina. It's a selfish thought, but that doesn't make it any less true. For years I thought I'd never get to experience any of what I felt tonight, but the reality is that I have so many chances to date. So many possibilities.

Maybe that's what I should be feeling guilty about.

Seventeen

Adina

I SHOULD FEEL GUILTY ABOUT EAVESDROPPING AT showcase rehearsal, but I don't. In fact, I wish everyone would whisper so I wouldn't have to hear their conversations.

"You're totally getting into Juilliard," says one girl to another as she tunes her violin. "Is it okay if I hate you a little?"

"Shut up. I doubt I'll even get an audition."

"You will. I'll be lucky if I get into Cornish."

Hattie Woo plays violin in the youth symphony, and Meena Liebeskind plays viola. We traded hellos when I came in, but we are not tied together by the strings we decided long ago to devote our lives to. Conservatory spots are limited, and we must fight for them.

"Have you gotten any auditions yet, Adina?" Meena asks me.

They are so conceited, I decide to lie. "Yes."

Hattie shakes her head, her long black braid whipping back

and forth. "She's lying. None of the schools have started auditions yet."

I get to my feet, unintentionally aiming my bow at her. "Are you sure about that?" I challenge, and Hattie shrinks back, questioning whether she believes me.

The greenroom is nothing special, a few couches and chairs, a long mirror smudged with makeup, a wall of photos of past conductors and principal musicians. It's not at all like the grand symphony itself, with its chandeliers and deep red seats and balconies stacked toward the sky.

Later tonight, Arjun is cooking me dinner, which makes what is happening between us feel more real. Arjun and rehearsal are the only things keeping my mind from straying back to where it wandered a few nights ago. Because of Ima, I have been forced to think about death more than most people my age, but I'd never considered ending my life as a solution to anything. I've tried to dismiss the terrifying spark of an idea: I was tired. I was distraught after talking to Ima. I was depressed after watching those videos. I've shut it in a drawer and locked it away between folds of my brain, but it's still *there*. I cannot unthink it.

"Adina Siegel?" a small man dressed all in black calls from the greenroom entrance. Boris Bialik, whom I auditioned for to earn this spot. I give him a weak smile and wave, the evil-eye bracelet winking at him from my wrist. "Pleasure to see you again."

From his clipped tone, it sounds as though seeing me again is more of a hassle than a pleasure. He is sour because I skipped rehearsal after my test results.

"Thank you," I say, getting to my feet and making sure my posture is straight. "I've been looking forward to this show."

"We invite luminaries from conservatories across the country to this showcase," Boris Bialik says. "You could very well be playing for your future professors. Commitment is crucial."

I feel my face flush, like I am being challenged to prove myself. "I certainly hope so. I have never been more committed to anything than viola."

He peeks at his watch, which is studded with diamonds. "Laurel is waiting for you."

Thanking him, I head toward the stage, my muscles wound tighter than the tuning pegs on my viola. I've had strict teachers and conductors and music directors, but his words have put me on edge.

Laurel's handshake is a tight, quick squeeze. Everyone in the showcase is under twenty-five, and she looks to be around exactly that age. It is my first time rehearsing with a pianist.

"Boris gives all the newbies a rough time," she says. "Don't worry. You'll be fine."

I let out a breath, allow myself to relax a little. "Good to know. Thanks."

Laurel positions herself on the cushion behind the baby grand and opens her sheet music. "This piece is one of my favorites of Debussy's. Should we see how it goes?"

I tuck my viola under my chin and stretch out the fingers on my left hand one by one. They are a little stiff, but I'm sure they'll warm up. The first time I performed on this stage with the youth symphony, I couldn't believe how much larger it was compared to the middle and high school auditoriums I'd played on in the past. This is my first time standing on it—the way Arjun has me do during lessons. When I'm onstage with an orchestra, I'm seated in front, other musicians surrounding me. I am not the star. In a couple weeks these empty seats will be filled with people watching me, expecting me to create something brilliant.

Laurel is skilled, but not too showy. She knows exactly how to highlight the viola, because that is exactly what this piece is about. Soft, sweet notes pour from my instrument, and the beauty of it lifts my spirit. *Très calme et doucement expressif.* I can do this. I pull the song tight around me, shutting out everything wrong and bad.

But then my finger slips.

I have the piece memorized, but suddenly I have to think hard about what comes next, as though the notes are not imprinted in my muscles, trapped in my fingerprints. *No.* I can't let the song get away from me—but it's already drifting, my memory fuzzing, my fingers lost. I stumble over an entire measure, then skip two more, and Laurel trips over her keys to catch up to me.

The piano stops, and that's when I realize my chest is tight and my throat is dry and I'm sucking in deep lungfuls of air.

"Adina?" Laurel says. "Adina, are you all right?"

I put a hand to my chest, my heart banging against my palm. "Yes. I got a little light-headed, I guess."

Maureen's words come back to me. *We'll be keeping a close eye on you*. There's no way I'm exhibiting symptoms this early. I'm just anxious. That has to be it.

"Do you need the music?" Laurel asks.

"This never happens. I swear I know the song." I don't have the time to be anything less than perfect.

"Being up here does things to people sometimes. It's no problem at all. Why don't you get some water, and then we'll pick it back up whenever you're ready?"

"Water would be good," I mumble. In the wings of the stage, Boris Bialik has his arms folded across his chest.

Hattie and Meena are waiting in the greenroom as I hold a paper cup beneath a water cooler. "Stage fright?" Hattie asks.

"That's a shame," Meena says.

I simply nod, hoping with my whole heart that's all it is.

♩ ♫♪

Arjun refills our wineglasses with garnet-colored liquid and joins me back at his dining table. Rachmaninoff streams from his top-of-the-line speaker system, and I'm woozy from the wine, the kitchen blurred around the edges. The speakers are, undoubtedly, the most expensive thing in this room. It's an old apartment. Later, I'll tell him he should ask his manager about getting the stove fixed so more than one of the burners work.

When Arjun asked how I played, I lied that it went well and hoped he wouldn't notice the heat on my cheeks. Lately I have been dreaming in Debussy; I cannot believe I needed the sheet music to finish the piece. That can't happen on New Year's Eve.

"That was incredible." I gesture to my empty plate. He made an eggplant curry so spicy it made my eyes water. "Thank you."

"I don't cook for people much," he says. "Don't usually have the time. Or the space to have a lot of people over. I'm glad you enjoyed it."

"Do you always cook vegetarian? I don't mind at all. I'm just curious."

"Sometimes. I grew up vegetarian, but I cheat now that I'm in the States. You keep kosher, right?"

"My family does, but I don't. I stopped when my mom—you know. It didn't seem important anymore."

He nods, and when he turns his upper body to me, I close the space between our chairs and rest my head on his chest, listening to his heartbeat. Tonight he is wearing fitted jeans, a gray long-sleeved thermal, and plain white socks, so much more casual than when we meet for lessons. I prefer him the other way, with his starched collars and wool sweaters and argyle socks. But if this is what he wears when no one else is around, I wonder what it means that he's dressed this way for me.

Here at his kitchen table, on a night I don't have a lesson, I feel like his girlfriend. And I realize . . . I *want* to be his girlfriend. I want to hold hands on the city bus and try new restaurants. I want to go to a coffee shop and drink lattes and kiss the foam off each other's lips. I want to walk around his apartment in nothing but my underwear and one of his collared shirts.

I want. Two simple words that contain every note of every song I've played for him, every second I've lain awake at night imagining us together. I want, I want, I want. Why shouldn't I be allowed to have?

"Do you want to go out somewhere?" I ask. "We could go to a jazz club, or a movie, or go for a walk around Capitol Hill. . . ."

"You know we can't." Gently, he pushes my head off his chest so he can start clearing the table.

"What, every single one of your students is hanging out at the jazz club on a school night?" I wince as I say it. Arjun turns toward the kitchen sink, doesn't look at me. "I'm sorry." I scramble to smooth things out between us. "Hey, could you teach me something in Hindi? You speak it, right?"

"Yes, but not everyone in India does. The official language of Gujarat, where I grew up, is Gujarati. That's what I speak with my family."

"Teach me something in Gujarati."

He thinks for a moment and at last turns to face me, a smile on his lips. "Tu sundar che," he says. "You are beautiful."

My shoulders relax. We are okay again. "Do you want to learn some Hebrew?"

"I think I know a little. Shalom, kvetch, schlep . . ."

Those words in his voice make me laugh so hard I nearly choke on my wine. "'Kvetch' and 'schlep' are Yiddish. 'Shalom' is Hebrew. It means 'hello,' or 'peace.' You can say, 'hi, how are you'—shalom, ma shlomech?" He repeats it. "Tov," I say. My sister's sometimes-nickname. "Good."

He returns to the dishes, and again I feel the need to drag him back to me. Sometimes it's as though he's playing a mental tug-of-war, weighing whether he wants me here or not.

Maybe he feels sorry for you, taunts a small and horrible voice in the back of my mind.

I shove it away as I get to my feet and explore his kitchen a bit, since I've never really been in here. A flyer for the New Year's Eve showcase is stuck to his fridge with a magnet with a dentist's sparkling face and phone number on it. Probably free. Curious, I open the refrigerator, not quite sure what I am expecting to find but surprised by what greets me. Leftover ingredients from tonight's dinner, but not much else: some butter, a third of a tomato, a jar of something called achar.

"Whoa, your milk is seriously expired," I say with a laugh.

"I guess I eat a lot of takeout," he says sheepishly, and it makes me jealous. I suppose when you live alone, you can fill your fridge with whatever you want.

"Do you want to toss this out?"

"I'll get it later."

I close the fridge and lean against the counter next to him. "What was it like, growing up in India? In Gujarat?"

A few moments of quiet pass before he speaks. "I was born in Ahmedabad. That's the largest city in Gujarat. Have I told you about all the stray dogs there?" When I shake my head, he dries his hands on a towel and continues: "There are so many. They're so, so skinny, and some of them, you can see their ribs jutting out. Every morning on my walk to school, I'd buy a mango off a street vendor, slice it up with a pocketknife, and feed it to the dogs. One dog used to follow me all the way to school most days, and he'd be there when I got out. Like he was waiting for me. My parents wouldn't let us have a dog, so I pretended he was mine."

I picture a young Arjun feeding a dog a mango. "That sounds adorable." I hook my fingers through the belt loops on his jeans. When I kiss him, I bite down lightly on his bottom lip. It makes him groan deep in his throat. Hopefully he has forgotten my suggestion to venture out into the world. I don't need that. He is right here.

"Sometimes I forget you're in high school," he says. "You don't seem eighteen at all."

"Maybe you're stunted," I suggest.

"That must be it. I'm stunted, or you're wise beyond your years." Then a strange expression comes over his face. "You're eighteen," he repeats.

"I believe we've established this a number of times."

"Are you . . . ? I mean, have you . . . ?"

"Have I what?" I tease, though I'm fairly certain I know where this is going.

"Have you had sex before?" And there it is. The words glide out so easily. I always think *sleep with*, though I've never actually slept the entire night next to a guy. "It doesn't matter to me either way. I just want to know."

"Yes," I tell him. Eitan was the first, but he wasn't the only. Last year at work, a college guy named Pat, a drummer in a shitty punk band, asked me out, and I saw an opportunity to get back the power I'd craved since Eitan left. We didn't exactly date, but we slept together for a few months, until he quit the music shop to spend a semester in Argentina. He was the second guy to leave me for someplace else, but I wasn't heartbroken. That time I was smarter. I had told myself it was only physical between us, that we were only together for the time we spent in his room with the door locked, a sock on the knob, his roommate sexiled.

Trying to be coy, I stare up at Arjun from beneath my lashes and pass the question back. "Have you?"

His eyes crinkle at the edges, and he tells me yes, though not condescendingly.

"Good. Glad we got that out of the way." I pick at my tights, imagining them on the floor of his bedroom. All of a sudden, I'm nervous. I'm not inexperienced, but he has surely done this many more times than I have. I want my performance to impress and astound. In that way, I suppose, it isn't too different from what I did onstage at the symphony hall earlier today.

"You know, I haven't heard you play in a while," I say, stalling for time.

"You mean, since you eavesdropped on me?" He quirks an eyebrow in jest, and I try to look apologetic. "I'll play if you will."

"A duet?" If I play flawlessly tonight, perhaps it'll cancel out my performance this afternoon.

"Why not?"

I follow him into the studio, where he sets up two music stands, takes out his own viola, and pages through a book. We find a Mozart piece that starts languidly. The first few minutes,

I try not to watch him. As the concerto builds, I allow myself a peek. He's sawing back and forth on his viola like he's about to break it.

His gaze is full of an energy I've never seen before. It's raw and rich and makes me feel alive, something I've desperately needed to feel lately. By the end of the concerto, we're both breathing hard. I have more than canceled out my rehearsal.

"Another?" I ask, and he shakes his head no. He sets down his viola and grabs mine, too, and then he's kissing me with more fierceness than ever before.

"Bedroom," he says, and together we stumble out of the studio and down the hall.

His closet door is slightly ajar, exposing a few crisp collared shirts. Books are stacked on a neat black shelf, and a thick one on his night table has a bookmark stuck inside. I had fantasies of undoing his buttons one by one, but tonight his shirt has none, so I tug it easily over his head. His body is lean, not too muscled—skinnier than I thought he would be, but I don't mind. I press my hands all over his chest, as though trying to convince myself he is real and this is happening. It is. Oh my God, it *is*.

Suddenly he pauses, clasps my hands in his. "You're sure about this?"

And though I have wanted this for so long, I appreciate the question. "One hundred percent."

He unzips my dress, the fabric slipping away from my skin. Dips his hand into the waistband of my tights. Groaning into his ear, I place my hand over his and guide one, two fingers inside so he can feel how desperate I am for him. I can't keep standing like this for much longer.

"You said you imagined this before," he says. "Is this what you pictured?"

"Pretty close," I manage between breaths. "Is it what you pictured?"

"Almost." He backs me up until I'm on his bed, on top of his navy sheets, and then he strips off my tights, cups my hips, and puts his head between my legs. I clutch at the sheets, at his hair. I am putty.

"Come back," I whisper-whine, because I want him to see my face when he makes me fall apart. He laughs at my request, this deep and sexy sound octaves lower than his regular laugh. I drag him up to me, pulling off his pants and boxers, and at last take in all of him. All mine. He reaches into a bedside table drawer and tears open a foil packet, and then there is no going back—we will be two entirely different people to each other from this night on.

He has amplified my senses. I hear the symphony of his breathing, in-out, in-out inoutinoutinoutinout. I taste the salt on his skin, the sweetness from the wine on his tongue. I feel his hair between my fingers. I have never been with someone who cares that it is good for me, too. Someone who isn't in a rush to send me away. He is more aggressive than the others, which makes me feel like he needs me more than I could have possibly imagined. All this is not happening because he pities me. There's too much emotion, too much raw need. Still, I want to hear him say it.

"Tell me you want me," I say next to his ear.

"I've always wanted you," he says with a ragged breath, and maybe I really am made of glass, because I shatter.

Eighteen
Tovah

"THIS PLACE HASN'T CHANGED AT ALL," ADINA SAYS AS we get our skates. Size eight for me, six and a half for her. When we were younger, I teased her about her baby feet. She whined that I was being mean, but I think she secretly loved her dainty shoe size.

After much convincing that she could afford to take a break from her relentless practicing—which at home she does only with her door closed—she agreed to come to Great Skate with me as long as I wouldn't mention Huntington's disease. I can do that. Our fragile peace is a sheet of ice over a newly frozen pond. Easily breakable.

Adi sniffs the skate before putting it on her foot. "It smells like someone peed in this."

"They spray them with antifungal . . . spray," I offer, and she heaves a dramatic sigh.

"And did they have to cover the whole place in Christmas decorations?"

There's a tree in one corner, stockings mounted on the walls, and a cardboard cutout Santa you can take a picture with.

"You want to put up a menorah? Scatter a few dreidels around?" I'm being facetious. It bothers me too, the assumption this time of year that everyone celebrates Christmas. That it's an "American holiday" that means exactly nothing to my American family. As a kid, I couldn't stand it when people said "Merry Christmas" instead of "Happy Holidays." It's easy to be inclusive, and yet most people just don't care.

"That's not the point," Adina says, huffing as we step onto the rink.

Truthfully, I'm on edge too. It's the first day of winter break, and I haven't heard from Johns Hopkins. My obsessive e-mail checking got my phone confiscated in AP Calculus last week. A few classmates stifled giggles—Tovah Siegel had never had anything confiscated before.

Clearly out of practice and uncertain on her skates, Adina clings to the walls. I skate backward in front of her as she pushes off, gliding a few feet on her own.

"You got it!" I tell her, and for a brief moment a real grin flashes across her face. She's proud of herself.

Then she skids and the smile vanishes and her face scrunches back up like she's concentrating very, very hard.

This is the magic of roller-skating: take anyone who has an

atom of confidence and watch them struggle. Even Zack, who most of the time exudes bravery, wobbled on his skates on my birthday. I haven't seen him outside of school since our movie date, and he's visiting family in Portland over winter break. Every day this past week, though, he sat next to me at lunch. He always sits with our group, but suddenly it felt deliberate, the way he chose the chair closest to mine and sometimes knocked my foot with his and one time draped his arm across the back of my chair.

"What's this music?" Adina asks, pulling me out of my Zack trance.

"Something from the eighties. Duran Duran, I think? It's kind of charmingly bad, right?"

"More like grating, obnoxious, and lacking in creativity."

I set my jaw. She doesn't have to insult everything.

"Look," I say because it can't just be Great Skate bothering Adina, "I know things have been hard for you and you don't have a lot of people to talk to. . . ."

She drags her toe to stop abruptly. "You said we wouldn't talk about it."

I phrased it wrong. "I know. I know. I was wondering if you wanted to hang out with Lindsay and me sometime. Maybe with Zack and Troy, too?"

"Zack," Adina repeats.

"Yeah. Zack. Troy's friend."

"The way you said his name." She smirks. "Is he maybe not just Troy's friend?"

I stare down at my battered skates. "We're . . . hanging out."

"So you're letting yourself date."

"What?" A flash of panic, as though I've been found out.

"You haven't dated anyone before, and now you are. It doesn't seem like a coincidence that you started doing it right after we took the test."

"It's . . . not," I say flatly. There's no point lying about it. "It's not a coincidence. And I thought you didn't want to talk about—"

"I don't!" she says, her voice rising. Cracking—along with our tentative peace. "But that's the thing. It infects every fucking part of our lives. It's impossible to have a conversation without it."

"I'm going to take a break," I say, because if I stay here, I'm going to lash out at her, and I can't let that happen. I skate off the rink without looking back at her. Let her fall and rip her tights. Let her look ridiculous. So far this night has confirmed what happened at the hotel was a fluke: something to do because we had nothing else to do.

I slump into a chair near where we stowed our shoes and pull out my phone, hoping for a text from Zack.

Instead, there's an e-mail from Johns Hopkins University.

My lungs tighten. It's about to happen. After all these years, it's *finally* about to happen. *When I got into Johns Hopkins*, I'll tell people, *I was at Great Skate watching a bunch of little kids skate to "The Safety Dance."* We'll all laugh about it.

Forcing out a deep breath, I open the e-mail.

> Dear Tovah,
>
> We have completed our initial review of your
> application and have decided to hold it for
> further consideration in March. Please do not be
> discouraged by this. We had a record number of
> applicants this year, and the majority of students
> who applied early decision were deferred. . . .

I read it again.

Deferred. The word is foreign. Not part of my vocabulary. I hold it in the center of my tongue. Taste it. Deferred. Right now all it means is "not accepted."

Over and over I read the e-mail, as though I'm expecting it to tell me something different on my twenty-ninth time through it. The words blur and my thumb smudges the phone screen because of all the scrolling I'm doing and something deep in my chest winds itself into a tight, tight ball.

My phone blinks with a new message, and I half believe it's another e-mail from Johns Hopkins telling me they made a mistake, that they're proud to welcome me into next year's freshman class and they're so sorry for the confusion. But it's spam. Sexy singles in my area want to meet me.

I've molded myself into exactly the kind of person Johns Hopkins should want, and I don't understand what it means that they haven't given me a yes or no yet. I've always planned ahead—but the problem now is that I suddenly can't think past today. My mind spins with too many questions I can't answer. What happens next and what do I do and there is still a sliver of a chance, but what if I wait and wait and wait and they reject me in the spring anyway and early decision was binding and I haven't applied anywhere else but now I need to and, and, and . . .

Two child-size skates appear in my line of vision, and I follow them up to my sister's face.

"What's going on?" she asks, pointing to my phone. "Is it something with Ima?"

"No." I shove the phone back into my pocket.

"Then what is it?"

Maybe if I rip it off fast, it won't hurt. "I got deferred from Johns Hopkins." I grit my teeth. It sounds even worse out loud.

"Oh." Adina furrows her brows. "What does that mean, exactly?"

"It means I didn't get in early decision. My application's been moved to the pool with everyone else who applied regular decision." I wince, steeling myself for another verbal attack.

Instead my sister's expression softens. "I'm sorry," she says, and the genuineness in her voice surprises me. Then again, she knows how much this school means to me. She understands passion. Ambition. "Do you want to go home and wallow about it?"

Maybe she's being kind because of what she did to sabotage me sophomore year. Maybe she realizes this could be her fault.

I push those thoughts away. We're getting along: that's more important right now.

"A little, yeah. Is that okay?"

"God, yes. We can get ice cream on the way home and find a shitty movie to watch. I think *Mystic Harbor* is on Netflix."

The tension in my chest eases slightly. My sister is back, for now.

We stop at the organic market near our house and spend way too much on three flavors of ice cream, hot fudge, and a jar of maraschino cherries. When we get home, I kiss my fingers and touch the mezuzah, but Adina doesn't. I wonder if she forgot.

We rearrange the pillows on my bed and position my laptop on the edge of my desk. My bed isn't big, but our bodies don't touch, like there's an invisible line down the middle neither of us is ready to cross yet.

"The rink was pretty bad," I admit between bites of mint chocolate chip, "down to the Christmas decorations."

"Thank you." She aims her spoon at my laptop screen. "I forgot how much I love this movie. What is it about bad movies that makes them so much better than good movies?"

"It's more fun to talk about how shitty something is than about how good it is," I say, making a mental note to introduce her to *The Room* later.

Halfway into the movie, my attention wanders, flicking between the screen and my phone. On Facebook, Emma Martinez from student council and Henry Zukowski from AP Bio and Raleigh Jones from AP Calculus are celebrating early acceptances to Brown, Swarthmore, Wesleyan. Jealousy turns me manic. I open my essay, wondering if there's any way I submitted the wrong version, or if my recommendation letters weren't as glowing as they could have been, or if something was missing from my résumé. . . .

"Are you on your phone?" Adi asks.

I scan my essay. "Maybe I had some typos on my application essay? Or I somehow sent the wrong file? Maybe there was a mistake."

I need a reason. A *why*. I need this to make as much sense as aerobic respiration or photosynthesis. Was I deferred because of that B-plus in Introduction to Drawing, the only flaw on my record? Because I took six AP classes this year, not seven, though my non-AP is student council, and don't schools want to see leadership experience? Because my application didn't stand out enough?

Because of what Adina did?

Adina smashes down the pause button, freezing the *Mystic Harbor* actors before their first passionate, rain-soaked kiss. "What the hell, Tovah?"

"I'm sorry," I say automatically. Her words stir up fresh guilt. My problems are not in the same country as hers and Ima's. They're not on the same map. Does that make them less valid? At any given time there are millions of people legitimately suffering in the world; my privileged problems pale in comparison. I know that. But my sister is suffering right next to me. I can't reconcile all these feelings. "I'm just trying to understand what happened."

166

She hops off the bed. Doesn't tidy up the messy blankets. "I felt bad for you at the rink, really, but you're being ridiculous. You expected to get in, and you can't accept that you still probably will; you just have to wait a little longer? I'm *so* sorry you don't get everything you want exactly when you want it. Poor Tovah."

I did expect to get in early. But I also worked really fucking hard for it.

I scramble to my feet too, and it's then that I notice a chocolate ice cream splotch staining the pillow Adina was lounging on. "I hope you're planning to clean that up later."

"Sure," Adina says with a snort, tossing her curls over one shoulder. "I'll add it to my list of priorities along with deciding whether I want to start any experimental medications and wondering when I won't be able to pick up the viola anymore."

There goes our peace, and I'm falling through the ice.

"So that's how it's going to go," I say. "You win every argument from here until the end of our lives?"

"Until the end of mine, at least."

I gnash my teeth. "I'm allowed to be upset too. Everything I've done these past few years has been for that school."

"Lucky for you," she says as she heads for the door, "you still have plenty of choices. You could get rejected from every school in the country, and you'd still have more options than I do."

"It's not like you don't have choices," I snap. The rage bubbling inside me feels even better than the warmth I felt holding hands with Zack. "You want to talk about moping? You've been moping ever since we got the results, and you don't seem to realize that you have options too. Counseling, support groups, experimental meds. This sucks for you, it really fucking sucks, but do you think Ima spent all her time acting the way you do?"

"You don't know how Ima feels," Adina fires back.

"I don't. You're right." Because I'm not part of the special club they have. I march over to where she's standing in my doorway and try to edge her out. "I'm going to bed, so I can lie awake all night thinking about my choices."

Adina puts her palm on the door, shoving back against it to hold it open. "Shut up! God, sometimes it's like you don't even care about Ima. If it's not about school, it's not on your radar."

"Is that seriously what you think?" This is why I can't let the guilt fully take over. When she says things like this, it's clear she doesn't understand me at all. I worry about our mother too. Sometimes it's too much to be in the same room with her for long.

"It's not what I think. It's the truth."

I heave all my weight on the door, as though if I can *just—close—it*, then I can shut out everything she's saying, too. But Adina sticks her foot inside.

"What are you doing?" I say, voice climbing to a shriek as I bounce the door against her foot, trying to get her to move. "Get out of my room!"

We're ten-year-olds throwing tantrums.

"I'm not done talking to you!" Her face is red and her eyes are slits. "You never let me finish a conversation with you."

"This is a conversation? Really? I thought it was you telling me everything I'm doing wrong." I heave my back against the door, crushing her in the space between it and the frame.

Footsteps pound up the stairs, and Ima marches down the hall toward us. "What the hell is going on in here?" she asks, following it up with a string of Hebrew curse words.

I step back from the door, freeing Adina, who's still pushing on it so hard that she stumbles.

"It's nothing," she says quickly.

"Do you have any idea how late it is? Do you? Or are you both so . . . so self-absorbed that you didn't think some people in this house, on this block, are trying to sleep right now?" Her words are razor-sharp. She kicks my door. Hard. "This is unacceptable behavior from both of you."

I shrink deeper into my room, Ima's words snipping several inches off my height. This is one of her mood swings. This isn't her. Still, part of me thinks we deserved it. We've disturbed our mother with our venom for each other.

"Ani miztaeret," Adina apologizes, and I echo her.

Ima crosses her arms over her chest. "Both of you . . . you . . . you need to figure this shit out. You can't scream at each other like children."

As Ima turns to head back downstairs, Adina races to her room and shuts the door, leaving me with a poisonous mix of rage and guilt and shame. There's nothing like hearing your mother swear at you. It makes me wonder what her classroom is like these days. What happens if she loses her temper in front of those kids?

Her words echo in my head even as I close my own door and melt into bed, my cheek on the ice-cream-stained pillow.

The last time Ima was this furious with me, I was nine. Adi had borrowed, then broken, a rock tumbler that I'd gotten for our birthday. I went to Ima's room and through my tears I said, "I hate her. I hate Adi."

Ima yanked my wrist a little too hard.

"Ouch!"

"You don't hate Adi," she said. "Do you know what that word means? 'Hate'?"

"It means I don't like her. I don't want her to be my sister anymore."

Ima shook her head and sat me down on her bed. And then she told me all about what hate means to the Jews. About the Holocaust.

I spent the next few years consumed by Holocaust literature. Consumed by trying to find a *why* somewhere in all that history, heartbroken when I couldn't. You can spend lifetimes searching tragedies for reasons why.

It was after that conversation with Ima that I realized two things, one about my religion and one about my sister. Being Jewish, being half Israeli—that would always make us—me— different. Not just in a please-say-Happy-Holidays-not-Merry-Christmas kind of way. It went deeper than that. It was a connection to something more. Centuries of suffering and hardship and being told we didn't belong.

Over the next couple years, I began my own Torah study,

and everything took on new meaning: my bat mitzvah, keeping kosher, observing Shabbat.

The second thing I realized was that I didn't hate Adina. She might frustrate and infuriate me, embarrass and humiliate me, but I didn't hate her. I never could.

But tonight I came close.

nineteen

Adina

TONIGHT ONSTAGE, EVERYONE WILL BE WATCHING ME.

"How are you feeling?" Arjun asks backstage at the symphony hall. He is wearing a dark-gray suit and a pale-yellow tie I cannot wait to unknot later.

"Nervous."

"That's normal. It's good to be a little nervous."

I exhale, a tornado gust of wind. "How about a lot nervous?"

"You'll be fantastic, Adina. I have no doubts." He drops his voice. "Slight change of plans after the show. I've been invited to a New Year's Eve party at Boris Bialik's house. The performers are welcome, too, and he asked me to extend the invitation to you."

I scan the hall, make sure it's empty. My family's already seated. "I was looking forward to being alone with you." That was the plan we made during winter break, when I divided my time between practicing in my room, sleeping with—no, having sex with—Arjun at his apartment, and selling guitar picks and bow rosin at Muse and Music. I cannot kiss him at midnight in a room full of people.

"We'll get a chance. I promise." His eyes follow the lines of my body, from my emerald dress's sweetheart neckline, to the dip at my waist, to the flare at my hips. The pumps I borrowed from Ima pinch my feet, but I imagine her looking glamorous in them, going somewhere people would notice her for all the right reasons, and that makes them hurt a little less. I'm wearing the evil-eye bracelet, my only jewelry. My hair is braided and twisted on top of my head so it looks like a crown, held in place by a thousand bobby pins and a gallon of hairspray. The finishing touch: Siren on my lips.

"I hope so." I bring my hands to the knot of his tie. To anyone walking by, it would look like I'm adjusting it. Instead, I give it a sharp tug.

"Tonight," he promises, his hand lingering on my lower back for only a second before he joins the audience.

My set is the last one before intermission, so I remain backstage for the first hour of the showcase, listening to the strings and the applause. Representatives from top conservatories are in the audience. After my mistake during rehearsal, I have something to prove to all of them.

I take my place behind the curtains until someone calls my name, and I lead Laurel the pianist onstage.

Lights temporarily blind me, and I teeter in my heels, but

once I blink the bright spots away, I take in the sheer grandness of the symphony hall. It is a sold-out show. I can barely see past the first few rows, but everyone is dressed up. Tonight I am on my own for the first time. Solo. Exactly where I am meant to be.

I straighten my spine. My legs stop trembling, and suddenly I am stable. Then I take a deep breath and drag my bow across the strings.

♪ ♫♪

"Spectacular," Boris Bialik says in the lobby after the show. He pumps my hand up and down. "What a marvelous performance, Adina."

"Thank you," I manage to say. My heart is still racing. I knew I played great, but I had what felt like an out-of-body experience while I was up there. Nothing existed but the music and me.

"Will I see you at the party this evening?" Boris asks. "I would love to chat more about your future in music."

A hand cups my shoulder. "She'll be there. Thank you, Mr. Bialik."

"Mr. Bhakta, you were right. She is a delight. Such emotion, such raw talent. And, if you'll excuse me, Adina, such beauty."

Heat rushes to my cheeks as Arjun's hand ever so slightly presses tighter on my shoulder.

"Thank you very much," I say, but the comment, which in the past might have made me glow, irks me tonight. Does my beauty somehow make me more talented? More worthy of being onstage, because I am nice to look at?

"If you'll excuse us," Arjun says, steering me away, "her parents are waiting."

"Absolutely."

I push out a deep breath when Boris is out of earshot. "This is a little overwhelming."

"Get used to it," Arjun says. "You were the highlight of the show. Your parents have been waiting to congratulate you."

When I become a soloist, I will always be the highlight of the show. I will be the entire show. So I square my shoulders and lift my head higher. One day I will grow accustomed to this attention, but tonight, combined with Arjun next to me, it's almost too much.

They're in a corner of the lobby, Tovah in a loose-fitting gray sack of a dress, Ima in floral-patterned silk, Aba in a suit. Ima's arm is linked through his.

"So beautiful, Adina'le," Ima says, patting my arm. She hugs me and says in Hebrew into my ear, "I'm so proud of you."

I stiffen at her touch. The way she yelled at Tovah and me a few nights ago is still fresh. "Todah, Ima," I say before I pull away.

Tovah looks up from her phone. Our parents have never let her skip a performance, the same way my presence was always required at her Science Olympiad competitions in middle school.

"Nice job," she says flatly, like it would kill her to be legitimately happy for me.

"You looked very natural up there," Aba says. I wonder if he still thinks my music is a waste of time or if my result has erased his wish for me to go to a state school.

Ima tells Arjun, "We can tell working with you has made such a tremendous difference."

"Adina is gifted. It's a real pleasure to work with her."

"Will we see you at home tonight?" Aba asks me.

I shake my head. "There's a party for the performers at the director's place. I was hoping I could go?"

Asking permission in front of Arjun makes me feel like a child, but fortunately Aba smiles and says, "Have fun. Home by twelve thirty, okay?"

"Matt," Ima says. "It's Thanksgiving."

We all go quiet. Tovah's gaze flicks to Arjun, as though trying to ascertain whether he knows what this means, and Arjun is looking at me as though waiting for permission to react. I'd like to melt into the floor, turn my skin into carpet.

"It's New Year's Eve," I say. "Not Thanksgiving."

Ima blinks. "Memory lapse. New Year's Eve. Of course. No later than two, okay?"

"Okay," I grit out.

As they turn to walk away, Ima stumbles, low-heeled shoe catching a knot in the carpet. Before Aba can catch her, she topples into a pyramid of empty wineglasses on a nearby table. They crash to the carpet, shattering.

I rush over, Arjun following close behind.

"I'm fine. I'm fine," she says, swearing in Hebrew under her breath. Aba and Tovah pick glass shards out of her long skirt. Other concertgoers are crowding around, asking if she is okay. Ima's face turns tomato.

I grind my own heels deep into the carpet, making sure I am steady.

"Can I get you anything?" Arjun asks my mother. "Water, a chair? Do you need to sit down?"

"No, thank you. I'm just . . . clumsy."

Arjun signals one of the ushers to help clean up the glass. Still strangers are staring. Some shake their heads, embarrassed maybe.

The horrible truth is that I'm embarrassed too.

♪ ♫♪

The penthouse party is like something I've only seen in old movies. Someone is playing a jazz tune on the piano, twinkling lights shine down on us, and a chocolate fountain bubbles in the kitchen. Everyone here is so much older than I am; even their laughs sound more sophisticated than the laughs I hear at school. I pinch a bacon-wrapped scallop off a tray and eat it in one bite. It is small but decadent. I take another.

As soon as we arrived, some of Arjun's musician friends swept him away, leaving me alone to mingle with the appetizers. I assume he'll return to my side at some point, but he's spoken to at least a dozen people so far, and while I haven't let him out of my sight, he hasn't once glanced my way or attempted to find me. I suppose these are his people, and he is obligated to make the rounds. Still, it's hard not to feel envious when I see him clink his glass with a group of friends in cheers, or wildly shake a woman's hand, or laugh when a man claps him on the shoulder and then reels him in for a hug.

A couple professors, music writers, and Seattle Symphony members introduce themselves to me, eager to talk about their schools or the future of classical music. Once the last one ambles toward the chocolate fountain, someone squeezes my arm.

"I loved playing for you," Laurel says. "You got over that stage fright after all. You were a different person up there. So much energy!"

"Thank you for the accompaniment," I say, but my eyes are still on Arjun, who's in the middle of telling an animated story to a group of symphony members. I can't hear what he's saying, but he waves his hands like he's conducting an orchestra.

She sips from her glass of wine, and I curse my childish sparkling cider. "I hear you're applying to conservatory."

"Yes," I say, and list the schools I applied to.

"That's fabulous. I went to Berklee, and I loved it." As she talks about her college experience, I only half listen. On the other side of the room, Arjun is finally alone.

A man taps a fork against a glass to get everyone to quiet down, and a pianist begins "Auld Lang Syne." A few people start singing along.

"Excuse me," I say to Laurel. With everyone distracted, I manage to pull Arjun inside the bedroom people have used to stash their coats and bags and scarves.

"What are you doing?" he asks when I lock the door behind us. The room has a king bed and a large window with a view of the Space Needle, where fireworks have already started to glitter the night sky.

178

"You've barely glanced at me all night. You said we'd have a chance to be alone."

"There were a lot of people here I had to talk to." He glances at his watch. "It's almost midnight. Everyone's going to be up on the roof."

"Exactly." I pull his face down and slant my mouth against his. His stubble tickles. I run my lips back and forth across it a few times. My skin might be red in the morning, but I won't care; at least it will remind me of him. He is a man and not a boy, not like the children tearing through the halls at school.

I need to show him he's mine. Even surrounded by so many people who want to talk to me about my "future in music," I am his, too. I hold my palm against the front of his suit pants, feeling his erection. He groans deep in his throat. I love that sound. Lowering myself onto my knees, I unbuckle his thin black belt and unzip his pants.

"Adi," he growls as I take him into my mouth. We have had sex, and he has put his mouth on every part of me, but we have not yet done this. It's always felt so intimate to me. His fingers grab at my coiled hair, the slight pain telling me he wants this so desperately that he cannot control himself.

He is mine. I am his. None of those people out there can change that.

Outside they are counting down. *Ten, nine, eight, seven . . .*

But I can barely hear them. I focus on Arjun's breathing. I'm using my hands now too, my hands and my mouth, my knees pressed hard into the carpet.

Finally, he lets himself go, his hands flying up to brace himself against the wall. I swallow and get to my feet, continuing to watch him. It takes a few more moments for his breathing to return to normal, and once it does, he zips his pants and hugs me close.

"Happy New Year," I whisper.

"Happy New Year, Adina. That was . . . a surprise."

"A good one?"

He gives me a strange look. "Yes. Of course."

We stand there in silence for a while as the party sounds get louder. Through my pantyhose, my knees are wrinkled by the carpet. Peering at myself in a gilded wall mirror, I repin my hair as best I can. Arjun's reflection looks uncomfortable, like he doesn't know quite what to do with himself.

He scratches at his elbow. "Do you want to go up to the roof?" he asks. "We'd probably have a better view of the fireworks up there."

I don't want to share him, and I can't understand why he wants to rejoin the rest of the party after what we've done. But the rest of the night, he'll be thinking about this, so I agree. I sift through the coats and bags on the bed to find my silver clutch and, unclasping it, I check my phone.

Six missed calls and two voice mails, all from Tovah. *Shit. Shit.*

My hands are shaking so badly, it takes a few tries for me to find the right keys.

"What is it?" Arjun asks, but I can't answer.

"Adina, it's Ima," Tovah's recorded voice says. "She was in the bathroom and . . . and she fell again. We're taking her to the ER right now. Call me. Please. Or just come to the hospital." She gives the cross streets and then hangs up. The next voice mail is her saying they're at the hospital and "pick up, pick up, why the hell are you not answering your phone?"

I drop the phone from my ear.

"Adi, what's wrong?"

Ignoring him, I push a trembling index finger to Tovah's name. Five rings. She doesn't answer.

"Adina?"

"It's my mom. She fell, and she's in the hospital."

Arjun's face completely changes. "I'll drive you," he says, fishing my coat from the pile. I want to be able to appreciate that he knows which one is mine, but I can't dwell on the insignificance of that now.

Everyone else is so distracted by New Year's festivities that we're able to slip out of the party unnoticed. Arjun pulls a ticket from his inside jacket pocket and hands it to the valet, and soon we're on the freeway, pushing eighty miles per hour. We don't talk. When he pulls up to the hospital, I lean over to hug him. Cling to him, really.

"She'll be okay," he says. He traces the braids in my hair. Some of my bobby pins have fallen out, possibly making a Hansel-and-Gretel trail from the symphony hall to the party to the hospital. Then he pulls back, pats my shoulder. "Let me know if you need anything?"

"Okay." What I need is for him to come inside with me, hold my hand in the hospital elevator.

Instead, I get out of the car and into the cold, and he drives away, leaving me aching for more things than I can count.

♪ ♫♪

She smacked her head on the side of the bathtub. They needed to use staples to close her up. I can't even imagine the gruesomeness of it all, can't let myself wonder if there is red staining the rug in my parents' bathroom.

"She lost her balance," Aba explains. He, Tovah, and I are in the waiting room. Ima is sleeping; they pumped her body full of drugs that will lessen the pain. She doesn't have a concussion, thank God, and the CAT scan didn't show any bleeding in her brain. Still, the doctors wanted to keep her overnight for observation, and we'll have to monitor her closely for the next couple weeks.

My eyes burn, threatening to spill over. Tovah stares out the windows at the slowly brightening sky. None of us says much. We try to sleep as best we can, but I cannot relax with the terrible smell of hospital and a coughing man in the corner and a quietly weeping family across the room. The waiting room chair digs grooves in my spine and neck. My performance clothes are stiff, and Ima's too-tight heels are numbing my toes. I haven't brushed my teeth and my throat is dry and my lips are raw from rubbing off my lipstick.

Around seven in the morning of a brand-new year, a doctor tells us we can see her, but she's drowsy and "might still be a little out of it." When I get to my feet, I almost lose my balance, forgetting I'm still in heels. The doctor guides us down the hall, past rooms and rooms of sick, sick people.

A bandage is wrapped around Ima's head and a needle is threaded through the veins in the crook of her elbow. I am sure Tovah could explain what all this is, but it is easier not to know. My mother is broken: that is what is happening.

"Ima," I croak. I squeeze her other hand, the one without a needle in it. Her skin is tissue paper, her veins the brightest blue.

"This is a sign." Aba strokes her hair. "You can't keep working if this continues to happen. It isn't safe for you, Simcha."

And she agrees. My strong mother agrees with my father telling her what to do for maybe the first time. "I think you're right," she says. "I . . . don't have the focus. I want to be able . . . to give it my full attention. . . ."

"Shh," Aba says. "Don't talk too much right now. Save your energy."

A grapefruit-size lump forms in my throat, but I can't swallow it away. Looking at my mother, I am slammed with a tidal wave of fear. This is going to be me.

Slipping in the bathroom.

Banging my head on a bathtub.

Wrapped in a hospital bedsheet.

Dying.

Dying.

Dying.

I draw my hand away from Ima's. She wasn't holding on very tightly anyway. I press it against my chest, like it'll help me

183

breathe easier, but it doesn't. This is my life. In twenty years or sixteen or twelve or eight or five. The timeline is indefinite, but the result is inevitable.

"I'll be right—" The last word gets stuck behind my teeth. I push out of the hospital room, but it's claustrophobic in the lobby, too. That hospital smell chokes me. I'm getting sicker breathing it in.

Elevator. I punch the button once, twice, three times, but then someone wheels an oxygen tank next to me and I can't get inside that metal box with actual living death. Stairs. *Click, click, clomp* go my mother's heels. I trip, twisting my ankle. *Shit.* I land on concrete, grabbing my ankle, massaging it with my fingertips. Have to keep going. Have to get out of here.

"Honey, are you okay?" a nurse at the main station asks as I limp through the first-floor lobby, but I don't slow down to answer.

Finally, I make it outside. The air out here is morning-cold but fresh, and I get a few more blocks away from the hospital before I tear off my shoes and the sidewalk chews through my pantyhose.

Breathe. I'm breathing now.

My ankle will turn violet tomorrow.

I stop on a residential neighborhood street, dropping my hands to my knees. Has it really been only twelve hours since the show? In the distance, the hospital becomes a rectangle, then a dot. The sun is peeking up behind the trees, a sign that the world has continued to spin all the way into a new year. A year Ima has begun with staples in her head and needles in her veins.

It will only get worse from here, and that is something I am certain I cannot live with.

Shivering in my dress and ruined pantyhose, I start walking again, sidewalk square by sidewalk square, block by block. One by one I yank the remaining pins from my hair, waves stretching onto my shoulders and down my back. I left my clutch back at the hospital, but my phone's surely dead now anyway. Useless. Don't need it.

Slowly, I allow myself back into the dark place in the depths of my mind, unlocking what I hid there. Only today it doesn't sound quite as dark. It sounds like relief. Like a solution.

Almost like a cure.

Robe-wrapped people open front doors to collect their morning papers and stare at the strange girl in a green dress limping purposefully down the block. I smile at them, wishing I could tell them I am okay. They don't need to worry about me.

While I don't know when my symptoms will begin, I cannot let the disease have power over me even now. I cannot mope through the remaining years of my life, waiting to become my mother. The waiting and the worrying will drive me mad. I'm sure of it.

Everything I've wanted—getting into conservatory, becoming a soloist, traveling to places I've only visited in my mind, a real relationship with Arjun, even growing close to my stranger-sister again—is still possible, even with my shortened timeline. It isn't the trajectory I imagined weeks ago, months ago, years ago, but it is the best option I have. The only option, really. If I plan correctly, if my determination becomes an obsession, then I can fit everything in.

The alternative would be to allow the disease to gnaw away everything that makes me Adina. I am scared of HD; I'm not too proud to admit that. I am scared of what it will do to me. How it will warp me. Aba and Tovah will suffer from it too. They will watch Ima die, and then they will watch me.

A car honks and a dog barks and I make a vow to myself. The best solution would be to spare everyone the additional agony and do it on my terms: quickly, painlessly, peacefully, once I've accomplished everything I have ever dreamed of. So as soon as my symptoms appear, that is what I will do.

In the meantime, I can have my beautiful life.

And then, when it stops being beautiful, I will end it.

Twenty

Tovah

I'M TOO OLD FOR BALLOON ANIMALS, BUT THAT DOESN'T
stop me from asking the clown at our school carnival to make
me a DNA double helix.

"A what?" he asks.

"A double helix. It looks like . . ." I slice my hand through
the air to mimic the spiral shape, and the clown lifts his red-
painted eyebrows in confusion. "Never mind, here." I show him
an image on my phone, and after several minutes of stretching
and twisting and tying, he presents me with my slightly mis-
shapen balloon double helix.

Joke's on me, though, because now I have to carry it around
the rest of the night.

The January carnival is a welcome distraction from Ima's
deteriorating health. She was released from the hospital when

we went back to school earlier this week, and while her head wound will heal, she's not returning to work.

I wait for Lindsay, who's at the ring toss booth next to me. We had to rip tickets for a while until a couple freshmen took over our shifts. In exchange, we got handfuls of free tokens. Being on student council means half my time spent at any event is not devoted to enjoying it. I've gone to Homecoming and Tolo all four years of high school not to dance, but to serve refreshments and check coats.

"Tovah? Tovah Siegel?" A guy in the ring toss line is calling my name. He smiles, revealing clear braces.

"Hi?"

"I'm Connor," he says. "You're, uh, you're Adina's sister, right?"

"Her twin, yeah. We're fraternal," I feel compelled to add, and he nods like of course this makes sense now.

"I'm in orchestra with her," he says. "I play the double bass."

"Okay . . ."

His cheeks turn beet. "What's her deal? Like, is she seeing anyone?"

"I don't think so."

"Cool. Thanks," he says before he moves up in the line.

There are probably a dozen lust-sick Connors roaming the school at any given time. Adina knows exactly how guys like Connor, guys like that waiter in Canada, look at her, and she loves it. She hasn't mentioned any specific guys to me since we were preparing for our b'not mitzvah and we both had crushes on David Rosenberg, the first boy our age to grow facial hair. If she returns the affections of any of the multiple guys who ogle her, she keeps it a secret.

Lindsay wags a stuffed tiger prize in my face. "Rawr," she says. "What next? I wouldn't mind throwing a pie at Mr. Bianchi." She eyes the Pie the Teacher booth, which has been tonight's most popular game.

"Food?" I say, my mind still on Connor and my sister and how that pairing, I'm sure, will never happen. He's too uncertain of himself.

She makes the tiger nod. "Sure."

I follow her to the concessions, dragging my double helix behind me.

"Are you doing okay?" Lindsay asks as we get in line for cotton candy. "With . . . everything?"

I can sense her discomfort with the question. She's not quite making eye contact, and her mouth is bent in a pity smile. A for effort.

"Honestly, it's been rough lately," I admit. "My mom had a bad fall over winter break, and she's going to have to retire from her job earlier that we thought she would."

"That's awful."

"And my sister's . . ." I trail off, unsure how to explain what's happening with Adina. We've barely talked since my deferral. Before I've begun to formulate a response, Lindsay waves her tiger at someone behind me. Troy descends on us, carrying a stack of three cakes.

"I'm really good at the cake walk," he explains.

Lindsay nudges his shoulder, and he clambers to keep the cake on top from falling. "You can't be good at the cake walk."

"'Course you can. It's all a matter of statistics." Troy lifts the plastic off the top cake, and Lindsay dips her index finger into the chocolate frosting.

"I take it back," she says, licking it off. "You are *great* at the cake walk."

"Hey, Tovah," Troy says, as though just realizing I'm here too. "Zack's working on something in the art room, but he said he'd stop by later."

"Oh. Okay. That's great. I mean, he can do what he wants."

I expect them to tease me about my poorly hidden feelings for Zack, but they're no longer listening. Lindsay flicks the brim of Troy's Mariners baseball cap. "You don't have to wear this all the time. No one cares that you're prematurely balding."

"I care," he says as she steals the hat and puts it on her head. "Thief!" He places the cakes on the floor, but before he can snatch his hat back, Lindsay darts out of the way, running a circle around me. Turning me into an inanimate object.

Troy catches Lindsay. Starts tickling her. She howls with laughter that grates against my eardrums.

"Do you guys even care that I'm here?"

It bursts out of me. The adoring couple freezes and turns around.

"What are you talking about?" Lindsay says, brows slashed with concern. "Of course I care."

I shake my head quickly. "Whatever. It's fine."

"It's obviously not fine. What's going on? What are you talking about?

"I guess what I'm starting to realize is you're not really here for me when things are hard. Even though I was there for you when you—" I break off because Lindsay's eyes are the size of petri dishes and it's clear her pregnancy scare is something Troy still doesn't know about. It's not my secret to tell.

"You've honestly given me no indication anything is weird between us. You hardly ever talk about Adina or about Huntington's. How am I supposed to know it's bothering you?"

"You could ask."

"Did I not ask you how things are going three minutes ago?"

I twist my shoe into the gym floor. "No, you did. Forget I said anything." Then I mutter: "Really, pat yourself on the back for awkwardly asking me how things are going one fucking time in the past several months."

"What?" Lindsay steps closer to me, though with her height, she's hardly intimidating. "I cannot believe you're calling me out like this. In public."

Troy coughs. "Should I, uh, go?"

"No," Lindsay says, and she and I remain still, gazes locked, until a fourth voice breaks through.

"Everything okay?" It's Zack, standing a couple feet away.

I step out of line, and Lindsay gestures for Troy to stay in line with her. That's one thing she's good at: leaving me alone.

"How much of that did you hear?" I ask Zack, embarrassed by my outburst. I don't have outbursts. I'm the calm, collected twin.

He glances at Lindsay and Troy as though making sure they're out of earshot. "Enough to know you said what's on my mind a lot of the time."

I pump my fist half-heartedly. "Bonus friend revolt."

Zack cups my shoulder with one hand and gently steers me away from concessions. "What is that thing?"

"Oh." I hold out my balloon "animal." "I asked the clown to make me a DNA double helix."

"Amazing," he says, but he's looking at me, not the balloon. "Have you made the rounds?"

"A few times. You can only toss so many rings onto bowling pins."

He holds up a key ring, dangles it from one finger. "Then you won't mind if we go somewhere else? I've got special after-hours art room privileges, and I want to show you what I'm working on."

I can't follow him out of the gym fast enough.

The art room has low ceilings and long gray tables and a kiln toward the back. Paintings and sketches and engravings hang from every wall space. I've haven't been in here since Introduction to Drawing freshman year.

"This is my happy place," Zack says, and tonight it's mine, too. When he's in a room with me, he completely fills the space, giving it a new kind of energy. His hair is spilling into his eyes, and I find myself wondering what it would feel like to touch.

If it would be soft or coarse. If he'd like it if I ran my hands through it.

"I like it."

A canvas board and paint palette wait at the table where Zack must have been working. Since all the chairs are stacked in the back of the room, I hop onto the table, my legs dangling off it.

Next to me, Zack leans a hip against the table. "We don't have to talk about Lindsay and Troy."

"I'd prefer not to."

"You doing okay about Johns Hopkins?"

"From one sore subject to another."

He turns his mouth into a guilty scrunch. "Sorry, I didn't mean—"

"No, it's okay. Thanks for asking. I'm managing. I applied to other schools over break and barely made the deadlines. Obviously I'm still hoping I get in. But I guess I could really end up . . . anywhere." It's impossible, though, to imagine myself anywhere except Baltimore. I release the tension in my jaw. "Let's talk about something else. Let's talk about this." I gesture to the canvas, which is half-covered with price tags and candy wrappers and even a math test marked with a fat red C-plus—all objects I'm sure Zack has found.

"Before you ask," he says, "it actually does mean something."

"Yeah?"

He plants one palm on the table, right next to my thigh. His thumb brushes against my jeans. Then his eyes trap mine and he says in a serious voice, "It's about passing AP Studio Art."

"Ha, ha." I examine it. "It's looking a little . . . sparse."

"You wanna add anything?"

"Wouldn't that be cheating?"

Zack sweeps his thumb back and forth across my outer thigh. If this single finger scorches my entire body, I can only imagine both his hands would explode me. "I won't tell."

I consider the colors, then dip the paintbrush into cobalt and streak it onto the canvas, forming the Hebrew letters chet and yud.

חי

"I'm not very good at this."

"I like it, Tov," he says.

He moves closer so that his entire right hip is pressed against my leg. I swallow hard. Forget exploding: I might be made of sparks. There's something in me that some days is stronger than the guilt, and it's this: the flippy feeling I get whenever I'm around Zack. I could get addicted to that flippy feeling. Overdose on it.

"Of course you'd paint something in Hebrew."

"Do you know what it means? I mean, I know you're not as Jewish as I am, but . . ."

He squints at it. "Ah, fuck. They're gonna un–bar mitzvah me."

"Maybe I shouldn't tell you."

"Why, is it dirty?"

"No!" I swipe the brush across his cheek—to punish him? Flirt with him? Both?—and pull back, covering my mouth with my other hand to hide my laughter. "I am," I say through my giggles, "so sorry."

He's grinning too. "You are not. But it's fine, because"—he dips his middle finger into violet, then dabs it onto my cheek—"I'm going to get you back."

"You've started a war, you know that?" I ask, smearing canary yellow on his chin.

Soon there's emerald on the tip of my nose. Persimmon along his eyebrow. He drags garnet red along my collarbone, and the combination of his touch and the coldness of the paint makes me inhale deeply, closing my eyes.

When I open them, he's staring at me, daring me to make the next move. This time I paint him with my mouth, and he cups my face with rainbow fingers and kisses me back.

My body's electrified: neurotransmitters shooting off in every direction, oxytocin—the hormone associated with social bonding—levels rising. That's all science I can understand, but what's new to me is the labored sound of his breathing, the sounds he makes deep in his throat. I'm doing that to him. I'm making that happen.

When we break apart, I'm breathing hard too, like now that I can suck back in oxygen, it isn't enough. Isn't as good as whatever Zack was giving me.

"Hi," I say, which feels like it fits. I'm saying hi to a new version of him and who he is to me now.

"Hi." The way he's looking at me, his eyes unblinking, lips slightly parted—it's not the way he was looking at me before. I'm someone new too.

"That was . . ." It was so many things, but I don't have the right vocabulary to describe any of them. "Good. So good."

"This between us is going to be good." His thumbs skate along my cheekbones. "Your blood vessels are so dilated. Beneath all the paint, I mean."

I press my lips back to his, suddenly starving for him. I wrap my legs around him and pull him closer, until his body is up against mine. We kiss harder now, until all of a sudden he laughs against my mouth.

"What is it?" I ask, worried I've done something wrong, like used too much tongue or not enough, and how are you supposed to know what the proper amount of tongue is? My pulse is positively manic, and already I miss his closeness.

"Your face," he says. "I'm so sorry. You looked so beautiful tonight, and I ruined it."

My heart thrills at the word "beautiful." "We're even. I ruined yours, too."

"You never did tell me what this means." He gestures to the canvas.

"Chai. It means 'life.'"

"Chai. Right. I like it." He exhales, a happy, satisfied little sound. "Can you imagine going back to the gym after this?"

"We're not going back to the gym. We're living in here from now on. We'll use the kiln for warmth, and we'll eat chalk and we'll sleep wrapped in butcher paper."

He wraps his arms around me and kisses my hair. "Mm. Sounds perfect."

If this is what I've been waiting for four years to do, maybe it was worth it. Everything else in my life has veered off course: Lindsay, college, my family. Right now my mind has one solitary thought, and it is *Zack, Zack, Zack,* humming from my fingerprints to the tips of my toes. My body can, in fact, do some incredible things. This is me not planning, not stressing, not obsessing about getting everything right. This is me doing something entirely because I want it. Because it feels fucking fantastic.

It brings me more relief than I've felt in months.

Twenty-one

Adina

RELIEF. I HAVE NEVER FELT ANYTHING LIKE IT. IT SINGS through me, replacing my blood with liquid gold. It skips across the strings of my viola during my hours-long practice sessions, at Arjun's apartment and in my room and at the symphony. It drums next to my heart, *pound-pound-pounding* a new rhythm. *Re-LIEF, re-LIEF, re-LIEF.*

This new life begins with figuring out what I have missed out on.

While the carnival is not my usual scene, I am curious about it. My sister will be here, and as vicious as we've been to each other, part of me aches to reconcile with her. I cannot fathom the idea of living out the rest of my life, however much of it I have left, with a sister who cannot stand the sight of me. The way I lashed out at her after she was deferred from Johns Hopkins— that cannot happen again. I miss our sleepovers and bus stories.

I miss the person who once knew me better than anyone else.

If I am going to have any peace, I need my family to be whole. I am a sister learning to forgive, to forget.

The gym is packed with sweaty teenage bodies, filled with so much noise that I'd think this was a group of little kids, not people who are nearly adults. A guy on the football team or basketball team elbows me as he aims a rubber ball at a stack of cans. He does not apologize. Rubbing my arm, I disappear farther into the crowd.

Tovah's friend Lindsay is sitting on the gym bleachers, splitting an entire cake with her boyfriend. I hold up my hand in a half wave. "Hey." They don't look up. I clear my throat and project: "Hey, have you seen Tovah?"

Lindsay's face crinkles when she sees me. Of course Tovah would have told her both of our results. Still, it makes me feel exposed.

"I haven't seen her in hour or so. She disappeared somewhere with Zack."

"Oh. Well, thanks," I say.

"Do you—" Lindsay breaks off, as though reconsidering what she's about to say. "Do you, um, want to hang out with us? We have cake. Troy's really good at the cake walk."

With a mouthful of frosting, Troy adds, "I won three cakes."

It's a pity invitation. "I'm waiting for a friend," I lie, and the relief on her face is palpable.

Relief. Relief. Relief.

Why, exactly, did I think this was a good idea? No one goes

to a school carnival alone. I am not a school carnival kind of person.

I press through the crowd, my stomach tangled like one of Ima's never-finished projects. I don't want a balloon animal. I don't want to throw a thing at another thing. I don't want to win any of these meaningless prizes.

I burst into the hall, whipping my head in the direction of laughter and footsteps coming from the art wing. Tovah and Zack are making their way toward the gym. At first I think their faces are bleeding, but as they get closer, I see that they're actually covered in paint. His arm is around her shoulders, holding her close.

The most jarring thing about this picture, though, is the obvious happiness smeared all over Tovah's face.

"Adina?" she says in between giggles. She sounds drunk. Drunk on joy, perhaps, drunk on male attention. Her hair's slicked back with lime paint.

This uninhibited public display of affection is what I cannot have with Arjun, and it makes my stomach twinge with envy.

"Hey, I'm Zack," he says, because the two of us have never spoken.

"Hi." Even looking at Zack feels as though I am intruding on something personal, private.

"Can I talk to you?" I ask, indicating that I don't want Zack as an audience member. He gets the hint and backs up, giving us some space.

"What are you doing here?" Tovah asks when he's out of earshot, raising an orange-blue eyebrow.

Humiliating myself. "I, um. Thought we could hang out here. At the carnival."

She blurts out a toneless laugh. "Seriously? And do what, listen to you complain about how lame it is, like at Great Skate? Judge me for even more things you don't understand? Yeah, no thanks."

She spins back around and falls into step with Zack again. As they head back into the gym, snippets of their conversation mix with the insipid carnival music: "Everyone's gonna laugh at us" and "I don't care; you look adorable."

The gym doors bang shut, and I am so stunned I stagger backward until I'm against the cold metal of a locker, then let myself collapse to the floor, shaking.

She could at least wait until I'm gone—from this carnival and later, from this earth—to parade her Technicolor life in front of me.

I was wrong. Tovah will bring me zero relief. If she and I grow close again, she will be a constant reminder of everything I am missing out on. It's because we are twins that it will hurt so much, seeing her experience things that I cannot, knowing I am so close to them but unable to grasp them. I will watch her graduate college and become a surgeon and fix people and get married and maybe have children. I will watch her plan an entire fucking future without worrying about an impending death. I will watch her mull over choice after choice after choice.

Maybe life is better without her.

♪ ♪♪ᵕ

I've never liked my English class. I don't mind reading, but all our assigned books are written by dead privileged white men. I can't stomach how my privileged white Hemingway-worshipping teacher, Mr. Bianchi, touts their supposed literary genius.

So I simply stop going. Instead I spend second period in the empty orchestra room, or in the library, or in the abandoned east stairwell. A couple days I even skip first period and sleep late. There's no need to spend my precious hours reading about the heroic struggles of white males. And sometimes no need to waste brain space with special right triangles or Newton's Laws of Motion either.

It is my first small rebellion in what is sure to be a long list of rebellions.

♪ ♪♪ᵕ

I drag a box cutter over my index finger as I'm opening a new shipment of sheet music at work. It is an accident. I think.

My manager, Oscar, glances over my shoulder. "Adina, you okay? I'll get the first aid kit." He returns with a small white box, from which he produces a Band-Aid. "No more sharp objects for you."

"It slipped." Did it? Suddenly I'm not sure. I am never clumsy. I've never even nicked my legs while shaving.

Red beads spill out of the slit in my skin. I stare at my finger, wondering what my relief will feel like. Maybe it will hurt, this

202

small cut multiplied by one thousand. Maybe it will feel like nothing. I likely have several years or more to ponder how I'll do it. Whatever method I choose, it's better than what awaits my mother. I need to control it. I cannot simply succumb to genetics or the universe or God or whatever is out there. Nothing poetic like that.

Next year I'll have to help pay for school, and for my plane tickets if—*when*—I hear back about auditions, so I've taken extra shifts at Muse and Music. I have spent the rest of my time perfecting the pieces I'll play. My calluses get married and have babies with nearby calluses. A turtleneck sweaterdress hides the pink viola hickey on my neck. An audition will make all this worth it. Conservatory and life in a new city are the only steps for me if I want to go professional. It has always been my goal, but now it has become a requirement.

Oscar banishes me to the cash register, and since it's a slow afternoon, I spend it refreshing my e-mail. Hattie Woo from youth symphony was already rejected from Juilliard, so sad, and Meena Liebeskind is starting to consider music programs at *state schools*.

"Excuse me," someone says, and I glance up from the register. The man looks vaguely familiar. "I'm sure what's on your phone is really important, but I need to return something."

I shove my phone underneath the register. "I'm sorry about that. What can I help you with?"

He holds up a viola case and hands me a receipt. "I think you sold this to us. It was for our daughter, but she lost interest pretty quickly. Said it was boring."

Foolish girl. Guess she wasn't as much of a natural as her parents thought. "Since it's been more than thirty days, we can only buy it back on consignment."

"She barely played it. Is that the best you can do?"

"I'm afraid so," I say, a ribbon of irrational satisfaction threatening to pull my mouth into an unprofessional smile. He cannot simply demand what he wants and expect me to give it to him. Everyone wants to think they are an exception. He grumbles while I take out the consignment forms for him to sign.

After my shift, I message Arjun. **On my way over. Can't wait to see you**. Then I text Ima that I am doing homework at a friend's house, though I skipped another few classes this week and, to be honest, am not entirely sure what my homework is. Lying to my parents has become easy, perhaps because they want so desperately to believe I am not lonely. My positive result has made me a social butterfly.

What I have realized is this: The relationships I've had were not about love. They weren't even relationships. Whatever they were, they were about need, about want. *A pretty girl like you should have a boyfriend*, Tamar Mizrahi said. As though there is something about being pretty that makes you deserving of love. If there is, I haven't gotten there yet. To love.

That is what I need from Arjun: a declaration, a commitment.

He doesn't text back right away, but that's okay. Sometimes it takes him a while to reply, but he has two dozen students to keep track of, and maybe he's getting his apartment ready for me tonight, planning something special. After all, I did something special: I bought him a set of viola strings with my employee discount. The good kind, the kind he probably wouldn't splurge on for himself.

It is a mystery to me when lust turns to love, when sex turns into a relationship. If a relationship means playing duets and cooking together and teaching each other words in other languages, then maybe that is exactly what Arjun and I have. Maybe love is what comes next.

Arjun could love me, I'm sure of it, and that night I make sure of it twice.

♩ ♫♩

At Ima's retirement party, Tovah and I sit in her classroom chairs made for ten-year-old bodies. It is probably the last time I will sit in a chair like this.

Next to me, Tovah grinds her teeth.

"Can you stop?" I ask. "Do you have any idea how annoying that is?"

"No. I can't."

Some of Ima's former students are here. "Mrs. S was the best teacher I've ever had," says a twentysomething guy speaking in front of the room. "I hated math, but she wouldn't give up until I got my multiplication tables right. And now . . . I'm getting a PhD in math!" He holds up his hands and wiggles his fingers. "I don't count on my fingers anymore, Mrs. S!"

Finally, Ima gets up to make a speech. Her aide, Jackie, who's already taken over her classroom, gives her shoulder a pat. Ima grips the edge of the podium, but when her body shakes, she sinks back down in her chair.

"This is a little . . . difficult . . . for me to do," she says. The bandage is off, thank God, but she still doesn't look like herself. She staggers and slurs her speech and needs Aba's help getting dressed in the morning. "I love teaching. I didn't have a big family growing up, and teaching is like having a huge family. I'm going to miss this so much, but I need this time to spend with my family. My husband . . . Mark . . . and my two talented, intelligent, beautiful girls."

Matt. My father's name is Matt, not Mark.

The speech ends and kids' parents start distributing slices of the WE LOVE YOU, MRS. S cake. Ima gets the first piece, which she promptly chokes on. Aba thumps on her back, and her mouth drops open to reveal a chewed-up yellow mass that gets all over her chin and blouse.

I push out my chair, the legs squealing across the linoleum, and race for the door. My boot hitches on the threshold, and I stumble into the hall, righting myself before I fall. Panic flares through me. Clumsy again? I vow to be even more careful. It was stupid of me not to pay attention to where I was going.

Self-portraits cover the bulletin board outside the classroom. Distorted eyeballs and noses and wacky hair and skin colored green and blue. My mother's distorted too, though not yet quite as alien as these drawings. She will continue to become less and less familiar to me. I dig for good memories: when she chattered

206

at five times her normal speed and volume with Tamar and her other Israeli friends or sang songs in Hebrew to herself as she cooked shakshuka or showed me my first movie with Gregory Peck, whom she admitted was her first crush.

I want that old Ima back so desperately that even the calloused pads of my fingers ache. One day she won't even know who I am. She spent eighteen hours in labor before Tovah and I decided we were ready for the world. Tovah first, and then an emergency C-section for me, since I was a miniature contortionist. She has the scars to prove it. How can someone forget all that?

Part of me, a dreadful part, hopes Ima isn't lucid enough when I start to show symptoms. She might be in a home then, eating meals through a tube. Someone—Aba? Tovah?—will tell her what I've done and she will be too far gone to react.

How were your students? I used to ask my mother. What will I ask her now?

Kids . . .

Even if I get married someday, if I have time for it, I will never have kids of my own. I couldn't pass on my fifty–fifty chance to someone else. I've never allowed myself to ponder whether I want them. Sometimes I think I could be a good parent to a musical child. But more likely, I would be a terrible, selfish mother, too absorbed in my own life to be responsible for another human being.

Still, I would have been grateful for the chance to consider it.

None of that matters now, I remind myself. There is no room for doubt in my beautiful new life.

My phone lights up with an e-mail, and the words on the screen change everything. They make me forget about babies and the impossibility of my stomach growing big.

I have an audition at the Manhattan School of Music in March.

Inside my chest, a tiny orchestra bursts to life with "Spring," the sunniest of Vivaldi's *Four Seasons*. I read the e-mail over and over, making sure it's true. The orchestra plays louder and louder and louder and *yes*, I want to shout. *Yes*.

When I glide back into the classroom, I watch the threshold to make sure I don't trip. But my sunny mood storms over when I nearly run into Tovah, who is being fawned over by our old fourth-grade teacher.

"Such a remarkable future," Mrs. Augustine says. "I always knew you were headed for something big."

I am headed for something big too, I want to interrupt to say.

"You couldn't have known back then," Tovah says, blushing.

"I can always tell which students are going to be successful." As though she can take some credit for Tovah's achievements. "You were always so serious about your schoolwork. So focused. You'll be an excellent surgeon."

Tovah turns an even deeper red. "Thank you."

Perhaps no matter how happy I am, Tovah will always be happier.

The two of them hug, and Tovah spies me watching her. She stares hard at me, like she wants to say something acidic, but stays silent. I don't say anything either. Instead I get a piece of cake, find a lone tiny chair in the back of the classroom, and welcome the darkness in my mind. The darkness and I are close these days.

Tovah tried, with her promise of forgiveness back in Canada, but she will never understand. We may be twins, but some things cannot be shared. We can share some percentage of our DNA. We can share hair color and body types and an affinity for stupid movies. But this is mine alone.

Our results weren't fair. It's a childish thought, sure, but it's how I feel. I widened the rift between us when I deleted her applications, but she is the one who never got over it. She is the one who wanted to leave our family, who pushed me away, who forced me to learn about a bleak future I wish had remained a mystery.

And yet: she is the happy one. Lately she has been smiling more, acquiring experiences she previously shied away from. Living, while half the Siegels are dying.

I cannot enjoy the rest of my life with this sister in it. I am convinced of that now.

I finish my cake. I want another piece, but the kids have left only crumbs. They're on a sugar high that makes them race, tumble, dance around the classroom. Ima watches them with a slightly distant, glazed look in her eyes. Tovah is grinning at her phone.

My relief turns to rage. Time to amend my plan. Instead of letting my sister back in, I will cut her out and make her suffer, steal as much of her happiness for myself as I can.

Truly, I am doing her a favor. I am doing all of them a favor. My death will be less of a tragedy for Tovah if during my life I am full of spite. My cruelty will be at its core a selfless act, and my parents will pity me too much to punish me. I am a girl without consequences. A girl untethered.

Vengeance. That is what sings through me now.

Twenty-Two

Tovah

JANUARY SLIPS INTO FEBRUARY. I GIVE AWAY MY HOSPITAL shifts because I can't bear to be that close to death. I struggle to fall asleep, and when I do, I have these nightmares. A surgical mask is stretched across my face, so tight I can barely breathe. Someone's sliced open on the operating table in front of me, a different faceless person every night. I always make mistakes. I snip a vital artery. Jab a scalpel into a heart. I have to tell waiting, weeping family members that I've failed. I never fix anyone.

"You've been ignoring me," Lindsay says one day after seventh period. Her legs are so short she has to jog to catch up with me. "Tov! Slow down."

I pause as we enter the senior hallway. Since the carnival, we haven't had any conversations that last longer than the few minutes in between classes. She spends lunch with Troy, and I spend it with my homework or with next week's Torah portion or with Zack.

"I'm not ignoring you," I say, which of course isn't true.

She scrunches up her face, as though this conversation causes her physical pain. "I don't want to fight."

Lockers open and shut along with the regular end-of-day chaos. Since my attempts at heart-to-hearts have failed, I guess I can pretend we're best friends for a few more months. Until graduation. And whatever happens after that.

"Do you want to forget about it?" I ask, and her face softens.

"That would be so great if we could. I'm going to plan something fun for us. Okay?"

"Sure," I say, but I'm no longer looking at her because something else has caught my attention. My sister's at my locker down the hall—talking to Zack. "Message me later?" I say to Lindsay before she heads for her locker on the other side of the hall, and I quicken my stride.

Adina and Zack aren't friends. They met at the carnival, when I blew her off because I was convinced she'd act like her usual storm cloud self if we hung out together. Naturally, I felt guilty afterward—when do I not feel guilty when Adina is involved? Sometimes I wonder if I'm allowed to get mad at her or if, like she said when we fought, she wins every argument we ever have.

I can't read Zack's face or hear the conversation, but he grins when he spots me. "Hey. I was waiting for you," he says. "My art teacher was telling me about this photography exhibit that's all pictures taken underneath microscopes. Wanna check it out this weekend?"

"Yeah, sure," I say, but I'm looking at Adina. "What are you doing here?"

"I saw Zack by your locker and decided to say hi." Adina stares up at Zack from beneath her lashes. She does this thing with her cherry-red lips: she keeps them slightly parted, like a rosebud about to bloom.

"People probably tell you this all the time, but—"

"We don't look like sisters, let alone twins. I know," I say, because he's right. I've heard it a hundred times.

He shakes his head, messy hair dipping down below his eyebrows. He probably needs a haircut. I hope he doesn't get one until I've had a chance to run my hands through it a dozen more times. "I was actually gonna say that I can see the resemblance. A little bit. And your voices sound exactly the same."

"Really?" Adina and I say at the same time. Then Adina says, "Tovah hasn't said that much about you, but I'm sure that doesn't mean anything. She hasn't dated before, so she's probably not used to it. She's always been the innocent one."

I bite down hard on the inside of my cheek.

"I'm pretty innocent too," Zack says.

Adina touches his shoulder. Playful. A possessiveness I didn't know I was capable of flares through me. "I'm sure you could be corrupted."

"No one is corrupting anyone," I say as I turn my locker combination, missing the third number three times in a row.

213

Zack laughs. Like he thinks she's making a joke. "I don't know. I've had all the lectures about peer pressure."

"They only lecture us because they don't want us to have any fun." Then Adina faces me, her tone sugary sweet and mock soothing. "Tovah, it's okay. I'm sure you could figure out what to do with Zack in one of your biology textbooks. Maybe you can find a step-by-step guide."

At this I finally get my combination, yanking the door open so hard it smacks the metal locker next to it. My face is on fire. I can't speak. The inside of my locker—and the spine of a fucking biology textbook, of course—is the only safe place to look. Is Zack imagining the two of us together? I like to think I'd be able to figure out what to do. That we'd be able to figure it out together.

"I should, uh, actually go before I miss my bus," Zack says. "Tov, I'll text you later?" and without glancing at him, I mumble, "Okay."

"And I have viola." She peers inside my locker. Taps the metal door a couple times. "Study up, okay?"

Somehow, her boots sound featherlight as she strides down the hall with Zack, leaving me alone and feeling about as small as an atom.

Nirvana's blasting from Aba's downstairs office when I get home. I pocket my keys and knock on his door. He keeps an old record player in his office because he insists music sounds better on vinyl, and we used to listen in here together all the time. A live version of "On a Plain," his favorite song, pulls at something deep inside me. The lyrics ache, and Kurt Cobain's voice is so resigned, so matter-of-fact.

"Aba?" I knock again. "Aba? Are you okay?" I twist the knob and, realizing the door isn't locked, push it open. He's in an armchair, a handkerchief pressed against his eyes.

The sight of him pins me in the doorway. Pushes thoughts of Adina and Zack far, far away.

"Tov." My name. Good. Both. He blots at his face and gets up, running a hand over the beard that's grown in over the past week. "Is the music bothering you?"

"Nirvana could never bother me," I say in Hebrew. He isn't making eye contact with me. Probably embarrassed I caught him. "Could I listen with you for a little while?"

"Of course." He gestures for me to sit down in his chair. I shake my head and instead lean against the windowsill. Sometimes I wonder if his newfound commitment to Hebrew study is because he thinks it'll help him stay closer to Ima, or if he just needs a distraction. But I'd never have the courage to ask him that, and I don't want to know the answer.

"Don't tell your mother about this," he says, and then switches to English. "I don't know how to say any of this in Hebrew. I'm trying to be strong. I am. But it's hard sometimes. You and I, we have to take care of them. Your mom and Adina. You know that, right?"

"I know." My voice is tiny. I want to melt into the windowsill.

Become a constellation in the night sky. Escape.

Ima recently started a new antipsychotic to help suppress the jerking and twitching and writhing she can't control, and she sees both a speech pathologist and an occupational therapist. In her spare time, which she now has too much of, she knits scarves to fill all our closets.

"It's a lot to deal with sometimes. I'm fine. I really am. I don't want your mom getting worried." He's speaking quickly. "I don't want you getting worried, or Adina . . ."

"I know," I repeat. "Don't worry. I won't say anything."

We've always had secrets. One time we took a day trip to Aberdeen, where Kurt Cobain had lived, and bought a Nirvana demo tape for more than a hundred dollars. *Don't tell your mother*, Aba said. Adina and Ima could have their old movies and stale classical music. We had grunge.

"Can you tell me again about the show you went to?" I ask as the song switches to "Something in the Way."

"How many times have I told you that story?"

"Several dozen." But I don't care. I want him to think about something happy.

He closes his eyes, as though trying to retrieve the memory. "It was a small venue, but the energy in there was immense. The guitar was crunchy and the feedback squealed, but no one cared. Cobain was so *raw*. That's really the best word I can think of to describe it. Raw. I doubt any of us there could hear the next day. The guys were so young, too. Not much older than I was. And they had such long hair. I didn't cut my hair for two years after

216

that because I wanted to be just like them. Eventually my mom had to force me into a barbershop."

I laugh. "You realize the ticket you gave me is probably worth a few hundred dollars, right?"

"Easily. But I couldn't ever sell it." He smiles. "When you have kids, you hope they'll like some of the same things you do, but of course you want them to be their own people too. I like to think you and your sister have a little of both: your own passions, and some of mine and your mom's, too."

"I guess we do." I try to picture a future in which I introduce Nirvana to a child of mine. It's too blurry, too distant.

"It's a shame you and Adi aren't closer," he continues. "When we learned we were having twins, your mom was so excited. Because she doesn't have siblings, she thought you two would each have an automatic best friend. But I suppose these things wax and wane. Neither of us can understand what your sister's going through, and I know she'll reach out when she needs you, and she *will* need you, Tov."

"Yeah. Maybe," I say, but I can't imagine the girl who so shamelessly embarrassed me in front of my boyfriend reaching out to me about anything.

"I can still remember bringing you two home from the hospital. How your mom and I set you down in the cribs and just stared at each other, like, *what do we do now?*" He laughs, but it's a sad, hollow laugh. Nostalgic Aba is a little too much for me to handle. "Hard to believe those little babies are eighteen now. This time next year, you'll probably be flying home to visit us on break."

217

"If I get in," I add quickly, stomach clenching. It's still just out of reach, no matter how badly some days I want to grab it and hold it tight. Erase some uncertainty from my life. "I'll be at least thirty by the time I actually start working as a surgeon." *Thirty*. What will be happening to Adina when I'm thirty, when I've finished med school and internship and residency? What about my mother?

"It'll be worth it."

I take in my father's khaki pants and practical Eddie Bauer button-down. His eyes are half-closed, his knuckles tapping out the bass line on his desk. I used to love looking at old pictures of Aba, who in his twenties rocked a shaggy beard and chin-length hair and plaid flannel shirts. In those pictures, he looks so cool. He doesn't look like someone's dad. Sometimes when I'm doing homework at my desk, I glance up at the Nirvana ticket on my wall and try to picture him at a show, screaming every lyric, lost in a mosh pit.

After her stint in the Israeli army, Ima moved to the Pacific Northwest for college. She and Aba went to the same small liberal arts school, and they met at a Jewish Student Association–sponsored Purim party, which some non-Jews call the Jewish Halloween, though the only thing it has in common with the American holiday is that we wear costumes. Really, it commemorates Queen Esther of Persia, who in biblical times foiled a plot to exterminate the Jewish people.

Aba showed up to the party as Adam and Eve—he toted around a Barbie doll with strategically placed leaves—and

Ima was dressed in all black as Charlie Chaplin. She stayed silent and in character the entire night, but she scribbled her number on a napkin, and when Aba called her the next morning, he was thrilled to hear her voice for the first time. They talked for two hours.

When he tells the story, it sounds like he fell in love with her during that first phone call.

If I get into Johns Hopkins, I won't be leaving behind just Ima and Adina. Somehow I've never thought about what my departure would mean for Aba. He always seems so solid, so *we'll get through anything*. This crack in his armor makes me wonder if he thinks we might not.

"I've always preferred live albums," Aba says. "They're a bit of a surprise, because the song never sounds the way it does in your head. Never the way it's perfectly recorded, you know? Cobain doesn't quite hit the note, or the solo gets extended. . . ."

"I know what you mean," I say, but I'm not really listening to the crunchy chords. Maybe my diagnosis wasn't the lucky one. In my life I'll have to watch my mother die, and then my sister. At the very end, Aba and I will take care of them. And when they're gone, we'll have to somehow take care of each other.

I have to live with this forever too.

The last song on the record ends and the audience starts clapping. After the applause fades, I get up, move the needle, and start the album over.

Twenty-Three

Adina

THE GUY I LOST MY VIRGINITY TO IS SITTING ACROSS the coffee table from me, dipping a celery stick into hummus, acting like this isn't one of the most uncomfortable moments of his life.

Eitan looks good. Better, even, than before, with suntanned skin and hair past his ears and more freckles than I remember. I haven't seen him in two years, and he's here for a few weeks visiting his parents. The Mizrahis live east of Seattle on Mercer Island, in a house a story larger and filled with more expensive things than ours. A tabby cat named Kugel pushes his pink nose into my knee, and I brush my fingers through his fur. He purrs as he figure-eights around my legs.

"Eitan has something exciting to share," Tamar says, scooping up Kugel and placing him on her lap. I frown. I wanted to keep petting him.

"I guess I'll come right out and say it, then. I'm engaged!" Eitan says, looking anywhere but at me as Ima wraps him in a hug.

"I remember when you were in diapers," she says. "And now old enough to be married?" His cheeks redden, but he's still smiling. "I can't believe it."

Aba pats his shoulder. "Mazel tov."

It takes me too long to react in a socially acceptable way. Someone I dated—*slept with*—is now engaged. It makes me feel at once both ancient and infantile.

"That's great," I say, but everyone else is talking so loudly that my words dissolve in the air.

"Tell us about her," Ima urges. "Is she Israeli?"

"American. She grew up in Dallas. She's teaching English over there too. Her name is Sarah." He pronounces it the Hebrew way, though, *Suh-rah* instead of *Sair-uh*. A slight difference, but I hear it. "I have some pictures," he continues, pulling out his phone and tapping the screen a few times. Sarah has blond waves and a small forehead and too many teeth for her mouth.

"Is that the Dead Sea?" Tovah asks, pointing to a photo of the two of them in bathing suits, covered with mud.

"Yep. You have to go to Israel, Tovah. You too, Adina." He adds this almost as an afterthought. "It's incredible. All the history. The culture. The food. I feel like I really belong there, you know?"

The phone gets passed to Ima. "He yafa me'od. She's beautiful. When is the wedding?"

221

"Next fall. We're thinking it'll be back in the States."

"Is she Israeli?" Ima asks.

Eitan pauses. "No," he says slowly. "She's from Dallas." What he doesn't say is: *You just asked me that. Don't you remember?*

"I can't wait," Ima says, not noticing the awkward silence in the room. She lifts my hand from my tights. "Adina'le, leave them alone."

I steal a sliver of red pepper so my fingers have something less destructive to do.

We spend dinner learning more about *Suh-rah* and Eitan's work in Israel, and Tovah talks about school and everyone expresses sympathy yet hope about her deferral, and when prompted, I tell everyone I have been invited to a total of three auditions, all on the East Coast, and we've booked plane tickets for the first week of March. Ima was supposed to go with me, and even though I insisted I could go alone, it is Aba who is taking time off work to accompany me.

After a while, as the two sets of parents fill and refill their glasses of wine—except for Ima, who cannot drink alcohol with her medications—I wander back to the living room, carrying my own glass. Through the bay window, Seattle glows in the distance.

"Can I sit here?" Eitan's in the doorway. His presence is tremendous. I don't remember him being quite this tall.

"It's your house."

He takes a seat on the couch opposite me, putting plenty of space between us. I'm sweating, and I hope to God I'm not blushing. I haven't been alone with him in two years, and that time, I wasn't wearing anything at all. Tonight my dress feels too tight, too hot, not enough of a shield.

"Look," he says, "I don't want things to be . . . strange between us."

"They're not," I lie quickly.

"You've barely looked at me twice tonight."

"Same with you."

He waits a few beats, then says, "Okay. You're right." He drags his index finger up the stem of his wineglass. "How . . . are you?"

"I guess you heard from your mom."

He nods, reaches for my shoulder as though to comfort me, but I stare at his hand as if it is an alien claw, and he draws it away before he can touch me.

I say, "I'd rather not talk about it."

"Sure. I understand."

Rest-two-three-four, rest-two-three-four. I check my phone for a message from Arjun, but there's nothing to rescue me from this conversation.

"Sarah sounds nice." I pronounce it *Sair-uh*.

"She is."

A different cat, an albino with red eyes, stalks into the room and rubs up against Eitan's socks. He strokes down the cat's spine, up its tail. Aba is allergic to any animals you'd want to keep as a pet, so we've never had them. But I love cats. I love their sleek coats and dainty paws. When I live on my own, I will get a cat.

It might even keep me company in my final days.

"Hello there, Tobias," Eitan says to the cat. "Are you . . . ? Are you seeing anyone?" he asks me.

"Yes. I am." What I want is say is that I'm seeing someone older, and he understands me much better than Eitan ever did. I want to win at the ex game.

"Oh? What's he like?"

"Adina, you're seeing someone?" My mother enters the living room and takes a seat on the couch across from us, Tamar following behind.

When I glance up, though, it's Tovah I lock eyes with. She's lingering in the hall, back arched against the wall. I can't read her face.

My hand buried in the cat's fur, I turn back to the mothers. "It's nothing official, so I didn't want to say anything. . . ."

Ima tightens her knitted shawl around her shoulders. "You could have told me." Because of course I tell her everything. Or I used to, before I came home from the doctor's appointment that changed all our lives.

Before she gave me her disease, an accusation I know is illogical yet I cannot help thinking sometimes.

"Don't you know enough about my life?" I fire at her, too ferocious. A kitten with her claws out. "We have plenty of other things in common."

The silence that follows makes me wish I could spool those words back into my mouth.

"Ima, you know I didn't mean that."

"I understand," she says. "You're going through a lot."

Her stung expression is the only thing that makes me waver about my plan. Some days I'm not sure whether I want to distance myself from her so my death is less tragic, or cling to her while I still can. I usually land somewhere in the middle, unable to make a choice.

"I have to go to the bathroom," I announce, because I cannot bear another moment of indecision. In my hurry to get up, I knock over Tamar's wineglass, spilling bloodred liquid onto the expensive carpet and scaring the cat, who dashes out of the room. "Oh my God! I'm so, so sorry."

I reach for a napkin, but Eitan holds his arm against mine to stop me. The sudden heat of sweater against sweater freezes me in place. The touch is so casual, as though we've never unbuttoned each other's clothes and pressed our bodies together. When you've done that with someone, when they have seen you at your most vulnerable, a simple touch never means the same thing.

"It'll wash out. Club soda and salt. I'll grab some," Eitan says, although I am thinking about how I did the same thing this morning, splashed orange juice all over the kitchen table.

This was how it started for Ima. Basic acts of clumsiness that, when strung together, made a disease.

I race out of the living room, down the hall past Tovah, who is leaning against the wall, smiling at her phone. I open my mouth to say something to her, then close it. I have bigger things to worry about right now.

Bypassing the bathroom, I head farther down the hall to Eitan's childhood bedroom. Where everything started. A couple suitcases on the floor, a simple bookshelf, a sloppily made bed. I have to grab on to the wall to hold myself upright. The memories are dizzying, yanking me back in time. I can smell his body spray and sweat, hear the Mozart—so predictable—playing in the background.

I imagine Eitan and perfect *Suh-rah* having sex. I bet they always come at exactly the same moment, and afterward I bet they cry about how fucking beautiful it was.

Part of me wonders what the hell was wrong with him. What kind of eighteen-year-old sleeps with a freshman in high school? *Do I look fourteen to you?* I had asked him.

The last time we slept together in this room, on this bed, I wasn't fourteen. I was sixteen, and he was home for winter break. We messed around for a couple weeks; then he went back to college, got his degree early, and moved to Israel.

I check my phone again. Nothing from Arjun. Staring down my twin in the mirror on the back of the door, I run a hand through my hair, use a fingertip to brush away a mascara crumb. This dress fits all wrong; I was right: too low in the front, my bra straps visible through the fabric.

I've never thought to demand more than the physical from guys, and now I can't think why. I trace the curves of my body. This can't be all I have to offer.

The door swings open, and I jump back.

"Adina?"

Eitan enters, making me shrink back. His childhood bedroom is too small for him now, definitely too small for both of us.

"I wanted to grab an Israeli newspaper from my suitcase," he says. "To show your mom. What are you doing in here?"

He should not make me this fucking nervous. I take a deep breath, collect myself. Summon the power I usually have around guys. "Wanted to see if your room looks the same."

He takes a few steps toward me, and I inch back, as though if he gets too close, he might pounce. Tear me open with his claws. He reaches for his suitcase. "I really need to get this for your mom. She wants to see it."

I cut my eyes at him, straighten my spine, make myself as big as possible. "I'm curious. Does your fiancée know about me? Does she know how old I was?" I drag the words over his skin like they are sandpaper.

Eitan crosses his arms over his chest. "You should get out of my room now."

He should be terrified of me, and one look at his face confirms that he is, a little bit. My power, restored. I hope I never have to see him again.

On my way back to the living room, I check Arjun's flight info on my phone. He was at a professional conference in Philadelphia this week, and he was supposed to get back to Seattle tonight. His plane wasn't delayed and he must be home by now, so I send an innocent text: *How was your trip?*

Arjun will love me the way Eitan couldn't. I don't have time for anything less.

♪ ♫♪

He hasn't replied. It's three in the morning, and he was supposed to be home hours ago. What if he got in a car accident on the way home? Since I can't sleep, I crawl out of bed and check the local news, the police blotter. There are no mentions of a sexy viola teacher perishing in a fiery crash.

I try to rationalize Arjun's silence. His plane must have arrived late, and he was tired, and he didn't want to wake me up. Philadelphia is three hours ahead. So it's really six in the morning for him. He didn't forget. He's just tired.

Repeating those words eases my anxiety only an infinitesimal amount. If I could see him now, I'd brew some tea, ask questions about his trip, stay up all night talking. Relationship things. I toss and turn for another couple hours, scripting conversations in my head.

I will be too tired for first period tomorrow, so I turn off my alarm. On days I skip school entirely, I ride the bus around Seattle, pick up shifts at Muse and Music, practice viola. Sometimes my mother doesn't realize it's a weekday and I should be in class. Other times I am able to convince her we're off for the day or I am not feeling well enough to go.

Having half convinced myself everything will be fine and I'll hear from him in the morning, I take my phone with me into the bathroom. I grab the nail scissors and start trimming my nails; I have to keep them short for viola, considering I'll be auditioning soon. I make sure my hands are steady. No shaking. I was so calm a week ago, and now I'm not.

Drastic mood shifts: one of Ima's first symptoms.

It makes me wonder if it will soon be time to set my plan in motion, a thought that fills me with a cocktail of adrenaline and terror.

As I wash the white half-moons down the drain, I get an idea. The only pain I've ever felt has been accidental. Tripping on the sidewalk, stubbing my toe, slashing my finger with a box cutter. What would it feel like to hurt on purpose?

I pull down my pajama pants so my thighs are exposed and aim the scissors at my skin. I need to prepare myself for what is going to happen.

For an early death.

A death that might be pain or infinite peace or nothing at all.

At first I poke at my right thigh with the metal point. *I'm too cowardly*, I think, until finally I grit my teeth and dig the metal into my skin. A whimper catches in my throat as I drag the small scissors across my thigh. The blade is sharp and it goes in much deeper than I thought it would, much deeper than I thought I'd be able to stomach. Red comes to the surface, and though I'm biting the inside of my cheek because it *hurts*, it feels like something else. . . .

Like a release. Like relief.

Someone knocks on the door, startling me, and the scissors drop to the floor.

"Adina?" Tovah.

"I'm in here!"

My phone lights up on the counter.

Jet-lagged. Sorry.

I have been balancing a grand piano on my shoulders, buckling beneath its weight, and with these words I can finally stand upright. I breathe out a sigh mixed with a laugh that takes with it all the tension in my body.

I need to see you. I can't wait until my lesson. I delete it, then type, **I miss you so much.** Delete that. **I want to see you** is what I finally decide on.

Tomorrow evening?

Yes, I text back, remembering how good it feels to breathe deeply when my chest isn't knotted up like one of my mother's balls of yarn. We can still make this work. I have time.

Tovah bangs on the door. "I need deodorant. I'm going for a run."

The blood has formed a thin river across my thigh. I clean the scissors and return them to the drawer.

"I'm still in here." Here she is again, acting selfish: She is the only one who matters. Her run is so important. She cannot always get what she wants, even if it is something as simple as deodorant.

"It's four in the morning. What are you even doing in there?" She smacks the door again. "Come on. Are you five years old right now?"

"Yes." I take my time searching for a Band-Aid, smoothing it across my broken skin. Through the transparent bandage, the red of my blood spreads. I add another Band-Aid.

"Can you just hand me the deodorant? I swear, I won't look at . . . whatever it is you're doing."

230

"In a minute." I pull my pajamas back up and sink to the floor, rereading Arjun's texts.

"Are you . . . okay in there?" Tovah asks.

I groan. Embarrassing. "God. Yes. I'm fine," I say, and finally open the door.

Tovah and I pass each other in the hall. I refuse to meet her eyes, as though, even though it is impossible, she knows what I was doing in there.

Twenty-four
Tovah

OVER AND OVER, WE FAIL MISERABLY AT STARTING A campfire.

"This is probably an embarrassing time to mention I was a Boy Scout," Zack says. "Though I never did earn my fire-safety badge."

"Not helping," Troy says as Lindsay holds up her phone so all of us can see the how-to YouTube video. "We should arrange the logs in a triangle shape, like this. . . ."

The four of us spent the day trekking through old-growth forests, and though Zack and I have had plenty of alone time, I haven't yet figured out how to talk to him about what Adina said after school the other day. On one hike, Zack pulled me against a tree, leaned in, and whispered into my ear: "Sleeping next to you tonight is gonna be amazing." That helped me feel significantly better about it all.

Eventually, we borrow a lighter from some nearby campers and get a small fire going. The smoky-wood smell fills the air around us. As the sky turns bruised, then black, we cook hot dogs on skewers and drizzle mustard onto them.

"Anyone know any good ghost stories?" Zack asks, licking mustard off his hot dog before it drips onto his hand.

"No ghost stories, please," Lindsay says. "I'd like to sleep tonight, thank you very much."

Troy flicks a pebble onto the fire. "I should have brought my guitar."

"You can't play guitar."

"Yes, I can!"

"You know four chords."

"And that's all you need to play a punk-rock song."

I scoot closer to Zack. "I have an idea. My sister and I used to play this game on long car trips when we were bored. Each person says one sentence, and the goal is to make them into a story."

"Let's do it," Zack says, and we try our hardest to turn the story scary, but Lindsay foils our plans every time it gets creepy.

"It was a dark and stormy night," Troy begins.

"The wind rustled through the trees," I say.

"It sounded like the screams of children," Zack adds.

Lindsay glares at us. "Suddenly, the sky opened up and it started raining gumballs!"

We tell stories until the fires in the distance start going out. Around midnight, Troy pours water on our pit, and Lindsay gently tugs my elbow so she can speak into my ear.

"I don't know about you," she whispers as the guys watch the flames die, "but we only brought one sleeping bag."

My stomach plummets to my toes for more than a few reasons, one of them being that Lindsay and I aren't close enough to joke like that anymore. She and Troy disappear into their tent, leaving me with Zack and two sleeping bags and an entire night alone.

We change into pajamas separately, first me and then him, and when he opens the tent to let me back in, he's wearing sweatpants and a long-sleeved thermal tee. We zip the tent closed and use our phone screens to guide us into our separate sleeping bags. My heart rate must be well over one hundred bpm. Does he think we're going to have sex? Was "camping" code for "sex," like Lindsay insinuated?

Virginity is a strange thing to lose. It seems like something you should gain instead: intimacy with another person, a closeness you've never had with anyone else. I don't know if I'm ready for it quite yet. There are too many other things between kissing and sex we haven't done.

His sleeping bag rustles as he changes position, propping himself up with one elbow. "Tell me a secret," he says. Outside, crickets chirp. If we have crickets in the city, I never hear them. "Something I don't know about you."

"Hmm." I think about it for a moment. "I cheated on a test in fourth grade."

He holds a hand to his mouth in mock horror, which makes me laugh. "Tovah Siegel. No."

"It was a reading test on a classic book I thought was boring, about a girl who was stranded on an island. I only read half of it and figured I'd be fine for the test. But I had no idea how to respond to most of the questions, so I looked at the girl's paper next to me. I learned my lesson, though."

"You got caught?"

"No, or it wouldn't be a secret. The guilt tore me up. I purposely failed the next test to make up for it. What about you?"

"Well . . . I'm a mutant."

"What?"

"I have four toes on my left foot."

"No. Seriously?"

"Your grin is kinda scaring me."

I try my best to bite it back. "The human body is fascinating. Think of all the ways we can get screwed up. It's a miracle more of us aren't mutants. Like you."

"Right. You could've consumed Adina in the womb or something, right?"

"I guess so."

"I used to freak other kids out when I was little. Some kids made fun of me, but Troy told everyone that my missing toe was a mutation and I was actually one of the X-Men, and that shut them up. And my big toe's really giant. It's like it ate the missing toe."

"That's not a real secret," I accuse. "I mean, it's interesting, but I want something deeper."

"Fine." He's quiet for a moment, then: "I hang out with you

and Troy and Lindsay, and I don't feel as smart as you guys. He doesn't always act like it, but dude's a genius. Aced his SAT, straight As, the whole thing."

"Zack. You're smart."

He shrugs. "My grades would disagree with you. And I'm sure my texts are full of grammatical errors you're too nice to point out."

"There are a lot of ways to be smart," I say, though I probably wouldn't have considered Zack's art intelligent before this year. "It's not all about grammar or tests. Your art, for example, that's smart. I can tell how much thought you put into it, even when you claim it doesn't mean anything."

"What I'm trying to say is, you never make me feel that way. Like I'm not smart enough to be with you, even though you're a genius too. And I really appreciate it." Our fingers find one another between our sleeping bags, and his thumb rubs mine, dragging another confession from me.

"I have another secret," I say, and though it isn't something I've intentionally hidden, it all comes out: Huntington's. Ima. Adina. "Sometimes I feel like I can't even be sad about it because the guilt is so overpowering."

He grips my hand tighter. "I can understand that. Your sister, she's intense."

"We haven't been in a good place for a long time."

"I could sorta tell."

"I've always felt upstaged by her. She was a viola prodigy, and she's always been so comfortable in her skin. Until middle school, I felt like the invisible twin, I guess." I sigh. "She was flirting with you at school the other day."

"I'm with you," he says simply, as though that cancels out whatever Adina's intentions were.

"Still. She knows how to charm people when she wants to."

Zack points to himself. "Not charmed. You, on the other hand . . ." His mouth tilts into a grin.

I want to smile back, but: "All those things she told you—she was right. I'm innocent and inexperienced." Truths are spilling out of me tonight, fears and insecurities and secrets. It feels good to finally be honest with someone.

"I am too. I haven't done anything, really. I've done . . . more with you than with anyone else."

"Oh," I say, grinning into the dark as the crickets fill the silence between us. Urging us on.

"We could corrupt each other," Zack suggests. He reaches out and draws a line down the curve of my leg through the sleeping bag. Hip to knee. I shiver. "Cold?"

"I've never been camping. I didn't expect it to be so freezing."

"Nighttime can be a little rough." He pauses. "You can, uh, come in here with me if you want to." The tremor in his voice is so endearing that it practically pulls me from my sleeping bag.

"I really want to."

With a little maneuvering, he adjusts the bag so we can both fit inside. I'm about to say that I don't think there's enough room for both of us, but I *want* us to be that close, sleeping pressed up against each other. I slide my feet down the length of the bag and align my body with his. He zips us up, and though I was right, there isn't enough space, I don't want any space between us.

We start kissing, and the night and general aloneness help our hands find each other's skin quickly. I'm not worried about whether my chest is too big or whether he's comparing me to my sister. He wants *me*. It's difficult to separate what our bodies do from how our bodies feel, the clinical from the intimate. What's happening between us is so much more than a chemical reaction, so for a while, I turn off my brain. We push against each other with our pajamas on, fingers and lips and discovery, and it's all new and wonderful, like we're the only two people who've figured out how to feel this way together, how to push our bodies off a cliff.

Once our breathing slows down again, I burrow even closer into him, face pressed into the hollow of his neck, which is always warm and always smells like a mix of soap and paint and, tonight, campfire ashes.

"I've been thinking a lot about us and what's gonna happen next year," he says. "I know we just started going out a couple months ago, but there's a good chance I'll end up on the East Coast in the fall too. That's where most of my art schools are. And I know you'll get into Johns Hopkins, and you'll be in Baltimore, so . . ."

Swallowing around the knot in my throat, I echo him: "I'll be in Baltimore. Maybe."

"Long-distance would be tough, but we won't be that far away. We could see each other every weekend."

238

He's combing my hair, his fingers so light, and I can tell in those touches that he's imagining us there together, bundled up in our winter coats, sipping cocoa, strolling mitten-in-mitten through campuses with bright red trees.

For a while I don't say anything.

"Tov?" he says. "What do you think?"

"I think . . ." I have to force the words out. "I think seeing each other every weekend sounds amazing."

He kisses my forehead. Whispers, "And we can fall asleep like this more often."

This feels too good, imagining our imaginary future. The logical side of my brain tells me this could all fall apart based on one admissions decision. But logic isn't warm and solid, and it doesn't have its arms wrapped around me. It scares me how deeply, how *much* I feel when I'm with Zack. There's too much of it, and I can't contain it, and one day it'll burst out of me like a solid ray of light.

⋈⋈⋈

Adina is packing as I'm unpacking. She leaves for her audition trip tonight: New York, Boston, and Baltimore. Peabody, one of the schools Adina is auditioning at, is part of Johns Hopkins, though on a separate campus. My parents encouraged me to tag along, but I couldn't bear it. Not with my future still so uncertain.

Adina's door is half-open, which I interpret as an invitation. Quickly, before I can change my mind, I drop my duffel on my bed, snatch a box from my closet, and knock on her door.

"Come in."

"Excited for your trip?" I ask, on such a high from camping that I bounce inside her room like I'm human sunshine.

She folds a sweater into a suitcase, then turns to me. Her grin is sunshine too. Real. Thank God. "I can't wait."

"I, um, got you something." I hold out the box. "For your auditions."

She arches a brow but accepts the gift. Unwraps it. "Tovah . . ." She picks up the container of Larica rosin. It's top-of-the-line; I looked it up.

I bought it a few weeks ago, but after she humiliated me in front of Zack, I wasn't sure I was going to give it to her. But I'm able to forgive, and after the camping trip I know my sister isn't a threat. Zack wants only me, all of me. The expression on her face makes me feel like I've finally done something right when it comes to the two of us.

"I want your auditions to go well."

"Thank you."

"It's funny," I say, dipping a toe into the seemingly calm waters between us, "we're both dating people for the first time."

"What?" Adina sounds startled.

"What you said at the Mizrahis'. You're dating someone, but it's not official or anything? I won't tell Ima and Aba, if you're worried about them making a big deal about it or something."

"You don't know him."

"Was it . . . Connor?"

"Who?"

"He's in your orchestra class."

"Oh. The bassist. We've exchanged maybe five sentences ever."

"He asked me about you."

"He did? When?"

"A while ago. I guess I forgot."

"He's pretty forgettable. Why would he ask you about me?"

"I don't *know*, Adina. I told him I didn't think you were seeing anyone."

"Well. I am. And it's definitely not him." She opens her underwear drawer and carefully zips a few lacy underwire bras into a lingerie bag. My bras look like I'm going to the gym. I need new bras.

"Kind of fancy for an audition trip."

"I like to look good."

"Who's going to be seeing your bra?"

Her eyes knife into slits. "Maybe I'm wearing them for myself, not for anyone else. Kind of antifeminist for you to think I could only wear a sexy bra for a guy."

I clench my teeth. "You're right. Pack all the sexy underwear you want." I go back to my original line of questioning. "Can you at least tell me what your boyfriend is like?" *Has he seen you in those bras?* "Is he Jewish?" If I sound desperate, it's because I am. I ache to talk to someone about the things I can't—and don't want to—share with Lindsay.

"No. He's not Jewish." She sighs contentedly, and for a second I think she'll actually spill some details. "He's . . . different."

Different. Okay. I push out a breath. Maybe I was wrong to think she'd confide in me. Maybe nothing should surprise me about Adina at this point. Someone could tell me she spends her spare time reading to the elderly and my response, probably, would be, "Sure, that sounds like something she'd do, I guess," if only because *nothing* sounds like something she'd do anymore.

"Different how?" I chance.

She slams a dresser drawer shut. Edges me toward the door. "I don't ask you about your boyfriend, okay?"

"No, you just embarrass me in front of him." The words slip out, and I grit my teeth hard. "I'm sorry. I didn't mean that. It's just, whoever he is, he's your first boyfriend. I guess I thought we'd talk about those things."

Adina laughs hard. Cruel. Before she shuts the door in my face, she says, "He's not my first."

Twenty-five

Adina

MY LAST STOP IS BALTIMORE. THE RIDE FROM MANHATTAN is six hours long, and the steady, rhythmic *click* of the train on the track nearly lulls me to sleep.

I have not spent much alone time with my father . . . well, ever. Most of our conversations this trip have been stilted, staccato. It irks me to see him praying over his food in public. *How can you still do that?* I want to ask.

I shift in the train seat and scroll through my phone. Arjun hasn't answered my last few messages. Lately his replies have been a mere couple words, and I've initiated almost every conversation. I send another casual text. **How was your day?**

Aba orders us coffee from the train café. When he takes a sip, he sucks in his cheeks and says, "Not as good as the coffee at home. How can you bear to leave that behind?"

He's trying to make a joke, but we don't share a sense of

humor. If Tovah were here, she'd find a way to make him laugh, but I just give a weak smile before adding sugar to my own cup.

"Aba . . . do you still think going to conservatory is a bad idea?"

He takes another sip of his subpar coffee before responding. "I don't know what to say. You know I wanted you to apply elsewhere so you could get a more well-rounded education."

"You didn't think I'd be successful."

"That's not it. No parent wants their child to fail. Of course I think you're talented, Adi, but things happen. I wanted you to have options, that's all. But now, if this is what you want . . ."

Because I am dying, I can do whatever I want.

Even Aba knows it.

"It is."

"I understand this is difficult for you. The most difficult thing you've ever had to deal with. If there were a way to make it so you never had to go through what your mother's going through, a way for me to switch places with you . . . well, I'd do it in a heartbeat." He sighs. "I won't pretend I understand how you're feeling. I can only know what it's been like for your mother. And on the outside, she handles it well. As well as anyone can. Better, even."

His candor renders me speechless. He's never spoken like this to me, not about Ima.

"Aba," I start when I find my words, but I can tell he's not done.

"I don't want you to think you don't have time, Adina."

I shiver. Of course he doesn't know my plan, but his words hit dangerously close to it.

"Ima is forty-six. She was diagnosed when she was forty-two. You're *eighteen*." He slides into the seat next to me, grabbing my hand, holding it tightly. His hand, which sprouts black hairs and weird speckled spots, is starting to wrinkle, his skin forming dozens of miniature accordions. "You can do everything you want to do."

And in a way, this feels like Aba is giving me permission.

"I love you, Aba," I say in a voice barely above a whisper, unable to remember the last time I said this to him.

He smiles. "Ani ohev otach."

When I am gone, perhaps Aba will be sad for a while. He will mourn the loss of a daughter he never really knew, but that is far better than the alternative: forcing him to watch me wither after watching his wife. That is too much for one person to endure. I want to believe he knows that deep down.

♩ ♫♩

Margarine sunlight slants through the windows of the small studio. Two women and one man, all smartly dressed, sit in chairs in front of a music stand. I prepared four pieces, including "Girl with the Flaxen Hair," and rosined my viola with the Larica Tovah gave me. My auditions in Manhattan and Boston went flawlessly, and I don't expect this one to be any different.

"Welcome, Adina," says a woman with sleek blond hair and a slight Eastern European accent. "I am Vera Mitrovic, head of viola here at Peabody." She stands to greet me, and we shake hands.

"A pleasure to meet you," I say. "You have no idea how much I've been looking forward to this."

Her mouth curves into a smile. "Have you ever been to Baltimore?"

"First time."

"And?" She says it expectantly, as though there is a right answer.

"I love it." I am not sucking up. Not entirely, at least. I love the architecture, the cobblestone streets, the row houses. Mount Vernon, the neighborhood home to Peabody, is more historic and artsy than anything I've seen in Seattle. Before my audition, I took touristy photos of the Washington Monument and sent them to Arjun. (He did not reply.)

"That is what I like to hear." The other two professors introduce themselves as Angela Romar and Donovan Green, and then I set up my viola and launch into my prelude.

This is when it all becomes real. I could live here. This could be my studio. I know from my research that Professor Mitrovic played in the New York Philharmonic for twenty years. I can only imagine what I'd be able to learn from her.

When I'm done, I exhale a long breath that trembles on its way out. I never get a substantial amount of air until I finish playing. This was my final audition, and I'm convinced it was the best of the three.

"Thank you, Adina," Professor Mitrovic says.

"Thank you for the opportunity." I turn to place my viola in its case, but my sore fingers lose their grip. The instrument slips from my hand, plunging straight to the wood floor. It lands with a painful smack, and the professors gasp.

I am frozen for a split second, but I recover it quickly, running my hands over it and making sure it's okay. My index finger finds a crack near its base, and my heart cracks right along with it. I imagine mahogany blood pooling on the floor beneath me. I got this Primavera viola as a bat mitzvah gift, and I've always been *so careful* with it.

"Everything all right?" Professor Romar asks, but she looks severe, like I have somehow offended her.

"Fine," I squeak, hugging my case to my chest as I race out of the audition room, my boots skidding on the floor. My feet have a traitorous route all their own.

♩ ♫♪

Aba is meeting up with an old friend who lives in Baltimore, so I have the entire afternoon to myself before we fly back early tomorrow morning. I get on a bus called the Circulator, curiosity pulling me several miles north to Johns Hopkins. My sister has devoted her entire high school life to this place; it must be pretty spectacular.

The route is a study in contradictions. One block is urban, with big buildings and trendy cafés, and the next is full of row houses and yards littered with junk. In Seattle, each neighborhood feels like its own bubble, but here everything runs together.

The campus is not quite as striking as Peabody, a place so beautiful it hosts weddings. Johns Hopkins looks like a textbook college campus: brick buildings and sprawling quad and students slouching beneath the weight of heavy backpacks.

If the past several years had unfolded in a parallel universe, Tovah might be here with me. We would try the hole-in-the-wall restaurants, be tourists at the historical sites, go to the Baltimore Symphony Orchestra at the Meyerhoff or the Maryland Science Center.

So far I have exacted only small revenges: embarrassing her in front of her boyfriend, taking the car when she needs it, sneaking into her room and resorting the assignments in her intricate color-coded filing system. I am saving up for a grand finale, though, something that will certainly destroy her. I am a crescendo; I will get louder and louder until I am nothing but noise and destruction.

When I'm done, she will have no choice but to despise me. And when I'm gone, she won't miss me.

No sadness. No tears. She can have the spotlight to herself, the way she always wanted.

For a second, I waver. Deep in my soul, I wish I could have her back, that we had never been broken apart. One thing she wouldn't understand, though, is my plan for when my symptoms show up. In Judaism, some people regard suicide as akin to murder. Tovah and I have never talked about it, but then, we've never had a reason to. She has never had a reason to feel sad, to fear for her life. If she had tested positive, she'd go to med school and find a fucking cure.

Even if I wanted to, there is no point in making amends. Why should she reconcile with a girl who is as good as dead? We cannot erase what we've done. I cannot go backward, only forward.

"Excuse me. Are you part of the tour?" asks a girl in a blue Johns Hopkins sweatshirt.

I stare at the group of eager kids and their parents that I've accidentally fallen into step with. "Yes," I say. "I am part of the tour," and I spend the next hour listening to the guide talk about the history and the architecture and the professors and the research opportunities and Johns Hopkins's world-class reputation. I can understand why Tovah has devoted the past four years of her life to this place.

When the tour ends, I navigate back to the nearest bus stop. If anyone wondered why a prospective Johns Hopkins student was carrying around a viola, they said nothing.

This bus ride, though, I cannot focus on the scenery outside. I keep hearing this sound, like a D-minor chord, and I can't figure out where it's coming from. I'm not listening to music—perhaps someone disconnected their headphones?

As we're stuck in traffic, the sound intensifies. I jump from my seat, knocking my viola case to the floor.

"Are you all right?" asks a woman next to me.

"Don't you hear that?" I ask, twisting my face and clutching my ears tighter. While I love minor chords, this sound, it's agony.

"Hear what?"

"That noise? It sounds . . . like a minor chord?"

"I don't hear anything," she says, eyeing me like I have lost my mind. Everyone else on the bus is unfazed, swiping at their phones or reading books or chatting animatedly with their friends.

It's suddenly clear only I can hear the minor chord.

The same way my mother hears imaginary dogs barking.

I sit back on the hard seat and cross my legs. The sound follows me back onto the street, making me even more confused. If no one else can hear it, and it's only happening inside my head . . .

Though I've been pondering death for months, the idea of my plan becoming reality sooner than I previously anticipated is enough to make me cold all over. I still haven't determined how I will end my life. I thought I had more time. I *need* more time—not just to plan, but to fit everything in. Achieve what I have always dreamed of: me on a stage and a captive audience.

In my mind I do some quick calculations. Perhaps I could audition for a symphony while I'm still in school. I could still become a soloist—maybe, hopefully—but how many tours will I go on? How many sold-out Carnegie Hall performances?

I hurry back to the hotel room and snap open my viola case, the minor chord still ringing in my ears. I trace my fingers over the scar, and then I start playing. It doesn't sound the same. I lock it back in its case so I don't have to look at how I've damaged it.

Arjun hasn't replied to any of my messages, so I send another few.

What are you up to?

Did you get my last text?

Hey, not sure if my phone is working. Text me back if you get this.

Then I wait and wait and wait.

Aba isn't back yet, so I start a shower to wash the day off me. I do what I always do in showers now: plant my feet firmly so I don't lose my balance.

With a fingertip, I trace the jagged pink-white scar on my thigh, remembering how it soothed me to dig the blade into my skin. Sometimes I ache to feel a little of that pain again.

Twenty-six

Tovah

I NEVER THOUGHT I'D BE THE TYPE OF PERSON TO GET senioritis, but I've been wrong about a lot this year. Second semester in student council means decorating prom posters and ordering crowns for prom royalty. I'm grateful for the mindless break from the rest of my classes.

I squeeze down on a tube of gold puffy paint as Lindsay and Emma Martinez, the student council president, chatter about prom.

"We're definitely getting a limo," Emma says.

"We'll probably get a hotel room." Lindsay blows on the paint, waiting for it to dry. "Not sure about a limo yet."

I concentrate on the W at the end of PROM TIX ON SALE NOW, but I screw it up and dribble gold all over the poster. With Adi and Aba on the East Coast, I've felt off this whole week. The house is half-empty, and I've cooked dinner for Ima and me most nights, usually something easy like stir-fry or spaghetti. The hard part is sitting across from her at the table with two empty chairs next to us.

It makes me wonder how it'll feel when she's gone.

"That looks great," says Ms. Greenwald as she circles the room. "Keep up the good work, you three."

I'm sure Zack would find some way to make this poster cool. I slip my phone out of my pocket to text him a photo of my artistic masterpiece—Ms. Greenwald doesn't care if we're on our phones as long as the work gets done—but before I can, I see something: the e-mail I've been waiting months for.

I push myself to my feet so quickly my knees pop.

"Be right back," I tell Lindsay and Emma, hoping they don't notice the tremor in my voice. "Bathroom."

Ms. Greenwald nods at me as I head out the door, teacher-speak for *I trust you not to abuse your bathroom privileges.*

My wobbly legs carry me down the hall to an empty bathroom. My fingers are so clumsy I miss my phone password a few times before I can read the e-mail.

Dear Tovah, it begins again. Like we're on a first-name basis. Like we're friends. *The admissions committee has completed its review of your application, and we are so sorry to tell you that we are unable to offer you admission to Johns Hopkins.*

The *so* is what gets me. Johns Hopkins is *so* sorry.

My phone lands on the linoleum with a soft *thwick.*

I press my hands against the porcelain sink. "*So* sorry," I tell my reflection.

Then I feel it. Deep inside my chest cavity, next to my stomach, this twist that makes me bend over, my head between my arms as I stare down at the sink drain. At the swirls of hair trapped inside it. The makeup smeared on the sides.

My heart slams against my rib cage over and over and over like it's trying to escape, and my vision blurs. I push the heels of my hands into my eye sockets, willing the tears not to start. I push so hard that when I take my hands away, there are spots in my vision. I'm shaking so badly, my breathing ragged.

They didn't even wait-list me. They absolutely, positively, definitively do not want me.

My first-semester grades were flawless and my additional letters of recommendation emphasized how good a fit I'd be for Johns Hopkins. But that wasn't enough. None of it was.

One, two, three, four deep breaths, the way Coach makes us do during track warm-ups sometimes.

Then I'm out the door, blinking back tears and sprinting down the hall and into the parking lot. I've never skipped before. Even though I pass a few teachers, no one stops me. It's like I've accumulated all this good-kid cred by being Tovah Siegel these past four years, and no one cares that a second-semester senior is about to skip the last twenty minutes of seventh period.

Fleetingly, I wonder what else I'd be able to get away with.

Where are you?
I have your backpack.
ARE YOU OK???

On my way up to my room, I type back something about my period, and Lindsay replies with a frowny-face emoji.

"Tov?" It's Ima, calling from downstairs. Faintly, her knitting needles *clack-clack-clack*. She knits slower than she used to. She has to give her fingers so many breaks. "Can you help me with something?"

I sigh and tromp down the stairs. "What is it?"

She places the needles next to her on the couch. "Are you all right, Tovah'le? You look a little . . . frizzled? Is that the right word?"

Ima's frown is deep, the wrinkles like parentheses on each side of her mouth. Depression is hitting her harder now that she's home all day, though Aba's been trying to work from home one or two days a week so he can keep her company and be there if she needs anything. This week, though, she's been all alone.

"You mean frazzled." My correction's much harsher than I intend it to be. "No, I'm fine. Just a long day. What do you need?" I hope she can't hear the impatience in my voice.

"The yarn." She picks up a skein of purple wool and crushes it in her hand. "There's a knot, and I can't"—tug—"seem"—tug—"to untie it." She curses in Hebrew. Hurls the ball of yarn across the room. Rage clenches her teeth and fists, reddens her cheeks.

As calmly as I can, I retrieve the yarn. It takes me a couple minutes, but I finally undo the knot.

"Todah," she says, the anger fading. Sometimes the mood swings last an instant, making her capable of going from zero to fury at any time. "Do you want to sit for a while? You can knit something for yourself, if you want. Remember, you tried it once when you were little? You made a few scarves."

No. That was Adina. She taught Adina how to knit, but not me.

One day, will she be unable to tell us apart?

"I have to do something upstairs," I tell her.

When I reach my room, I rummage through all my desk drawers, tossing trinkets and dull pencils and loose papers on the carpet. Finally I find it: *Gray's Anatomy*, the classic anatomy textbook. Cliché, but anyone interested in medicine has to have a copy. Aba gave it to me when I returned home from the Johns Hopkins summer program. I stare at the glossy cover, the well-worn pages with intricate drawings of the human body.

Then I yank the cover by the corner and rip it off. Fuck you, *Gray's Anatomy*.

I flip to a diagram of the four chambers of the heart, two atria, two ventricles. I tear it into halves. Into quarters. Into eighths. Broken heart, so sad.

The next page I land on is a grayscale rendering of the brain. I break apart the hemispheres. I shred the cerebellum, killing this person's balance and coordination, occipital lobe, rendering this person blind, and temporal lobe, making them forget it ever happened.

Losing Johns Hopkins must be my punishment for testing negative. It's how I can repay this cosmic debt I owe. It's the universe telling me luck doesn't exist, after all. I'm lucky and unlucky all at once.

It's the only way I can rationalize it.

I sever heads. I amputate limbs. I castrate men. I turn it all into confetti, and then into dust. When I finish, there are more books. Old lab reports I saved because I got As. Endless certificates of achievement and participation. All of them, dust.

The Nirvana ticket is the only thing I can't bear to destroy. Kurt Cobain didn't betray me. Nirvana made me no promises they couldn't keep. I put on "Lithium" and blast it, growling along off-key.

I am acting like Adina: ruled by my emotions. We haven't ever been that different, after all.

Adina. I've tried so hard with her, even when it felt impossible to do so. Maybe it's because of Adina, though, that I didn't get in.

My life has been eighteen years of alphabet soup, AP and SAT and GPA meant to lead me to JHU. The best biology education, then the best medical school, best residency . . .

Since I decided this was my path, people have always told me I'd make such a good doctor, a skilled surgeon. Everyone said they knew, *they knew* I'd get in. How can I tell my parents? My teachers? Zack, who once said he liked how ambitious I am? Am I still ambitious if I've failed?

Paper fuzz covers my clothes and floor like a thin dusting of snow. My room's a disaster zone, nothing left to take apart. Still, adrenaline surges through me, so back downstairs I go, taking the steps three at a time.

"I'm going for a run!" I shout to Ima before bolting outside.

I zip my hoodie all the way up and tie it under my chin. I forgot my special bra, but there's no going back now. The air bites at my ears, turning them numb. The reason is because—

Doesn't matter, doesn't matter, doesn't matter.

My legs carry me eleven miles north. Nearly a half marathon. Track started a few weeks ago, and I push myself harder than I ever do at practice. I run on sidewalks and through parks and parking lots. The sky darkens and the temperature drops, my clothes damp with perspiration. I have to keep going. Running used to be my time to think about the future without distraction, but today I understand why everyone uses it to clear their heads. The only thing in mine is the thump of my feet on cement, the pulse of my heart in my ears.

I don't know what will happen if stop.

But I do stop at a gas station in Shoreline, when my feet are screaming and my throat is dry. My family doesn't use disposable bottles because they're bad for the environment, but right now nothing sounds better than crunching plastic in my fist as cold water streams down my throat.

After I pay, I head outside and chug it all in nearly one gulp. I suck the last drops of it, the sides of the bottle caving in.

And then it all comes back up.

I fall to the pavement, my knees smacking the cement. I heave again, my stomach twisted and my throat raw.

"Are you all right?" asks a woman filling up her hatchback. "Should I call an ambulance?"

I wipe my mouth with the sleeve of my hoodie. Slowly get to my feet. "I'm fine. Thanks." Then I'm on my aching feet again, limping to the nearest bus stop a couple blocks away. It takes me three buses and almost two hours to get home.

Ima's standing outside my inside-out room, gaping at the paper snowstorm I left behind.

"Tovah'le," she says, voice full of confusion. Like she doesn't know who I am anymore, and maybe I don't either. "What did you do?"

Spring

Twenty-seven

Adina

A BROKEN INSTRUMENT FOR A BROKEN GIRL. MY VIOLA and I have this in common, and I like the poetry of it so much that I haven't brought it in to be repaired yet. We are both imperfect, but we still make beautiful music.

Arjun may feel differently about it, though it's been three days since I returned from my trip and he hasn't seen me or my viola. Two days ago I performed with the youth symphony and waited around to see him afterward, but he wasn't there, despite promising me earlier this month he would be. Yesterday I called him four times. Each time it went to voice mail and I hung up. Maybe he got bored of me. Maybe he went back to his old girlfriend, the one with the wild rose moisturizer who wasn't his student. I imagine him and this faceless girl in his bed. I imagine him touching her the way he touches me.

I have to make sure there is still an *us*. Adi and Arjun. Even our names sound right together. Like music.

Friday after sundown, Shabbat, Tovah is locked in her room weeping over Johns Hopkins. I am still waiting on my acceptances; they ought to arrive any day. I am not nervous, though, only eager to know which places want me.

My parents are on a walk, unlikely to notice the car and I are gone until much later. I have no patience for the unreliability of the bus, not today. Besides, if my parents are upset when I get home, I have a feeling I will get away with it.

When I get to his building, before I can get out of my car or even find a parking spot, I spy him getting into his silver Honda Civic. He's wearing a deep brown jacket I've never seen before, probably because we've never really been outside together. I'm not sure if I've ever noticed the way he walks, but he does it with purpose. Head high, back straight. Perfect posture.

I could wait around until he returns to his apartment, I suppose. Or I could head back home. He fiddles with something in his car, probably trying to find the right music. Liszt? Schubert? Mozart?

I tap my fingernails on the steering wheel. And then I follow him out of the parking lot.

♩ ♫♩

First he goes to Bartell Drugs. I park far enough away that he won't notice I'm there. He doesn't know this car, anyway, considering I always take the bus. He carries a canvas tote with the words I ♥ NPR on it, the kind everyone in Seattle uses since the city outlawed plastic bags. He must be either eco-conscious or stingy. I wonder if he keeps the bags in the backseat of his car, the way my family does.

After fifteen minutes, he emerges with his canvas bag half full, judging by how he's holding it. I wonder what's inside. Toothpaste and hand soap. Shaving cream. Shampoo. Condoms.

Then he heads to a music shop, my store's primary competitor, which makes me silently seethe. Is he avoiding my store, or does he simply prefer this one? Mine is better—I made sure of that when I applied. Arjun wanders around the store for a while, chats with a couple salespeople.

I send another text, trying to sound casual.

You around tonight?

Through the window, I watch him peek at his phone and then slip it back in his pocket.

Clearly he is so busy running errands that he cannot reply.

Next he goes to a café in Capitol Hill. I can't find a parking spot that lets me see inside, so I have to pay for street parking five blocks away. I pull my hood up as I approach the café's window. Arjun is sitting at a table toward the back. Across from a woman.

My guts twist into pretzels, tighter and tighter until I think I might collapse in the middle of the sidewalk. The woman has delicate features and a blond bob that skims her shirt collar. She's thin, entirely curveless, and I wonder if the way Arjun pinches the curves of my body and buries his lips in my hip bones is because I am the type of woman he prefers. But she is older than I am, probably in her midtwenties. Closer to his age.

She crosses her carrot-stick legs beneath the table and leans over it. Arjun is tilted slightly away from her. They each have their own cup of coffee, and while she's nibbling on a muffin, he's not eating anything. When she reaches out to stroke Arjun's forearm, he pulls back.

What the hell is going on?

I stand outside the coffee shop watching their conversation I cannot hear for ten, twenty, thirty minutes. By the time Arjun heads for the door, I have to race out of sight, but I lose my balance and slip on a square of wet pavement. I go down hard. When I get back to my car, there's a pressure behind my eyes and my knees are burning, probably beginning to bruise and bleed beneath my torn-up tights.

I tune the radio to Seattle's classical station, which is playing Dvorak, and I circle the blocks again and again until I find his car and follow him all the way back to his apartment.

I key in the access code: one-nine-four-five. No patience for the elevator, I take the stairs two, three at a time. The stairwell smells like wet dog. I don't know how Tovah runs for fun because this is torture, four flights of stairs. When I reach the third flight, I'm huffing and puffing and have to hold my hand against the wall to ground myself.

On the fourth floor, before I can make it across the hall, the door to 403 swings open. There he is, holding a basket of laundry, which he nearly drops when he sees me.

"Adina! Shit, you scared me." He sets the basket down as I draw nearer. Inside I see his collared shirts, his burgundy sweater, his underwear, black and gray and one pair that's plaid. "What are you—how did you get in?"

He didn't ask me that the last time I got in. He didn't ask how.

"I need to talk to you."

Picking up the basket, he heads to the elevator and presses the down button. "I'm busy. Can this wait?"

I wedge myself inside the elevator with him. "No. It can't. Who is she?"

"Who is *who*?"

"The blond woman!" I sputter, breath ragged. Who the fuck else would I be talking about? "The blond woman I saw you with in Capitol Hill today."

"You were there?"

"You weren't answering any of my messages or calls. I've been back for three days and I haven't seen you." My voice trembles and cracks. My stupid, young, eighteen-year-old voice. "What were you so busy with today that you couldn't take two seconds to reply to me? Going to Bartell's and the music shop and meeting *her*?"

A couple measures of silence pass between us.

"Were you following me?"

I open my mouth to either defend myself or confess, I'm not sure which.

Then, with a screech, the elevator stops.

"Fuck," he mutters, shoving his palm into the wall. "It's always doing this. It should start back up again soon."

Pushing my back against the wall, I say, "How long does it

usually take?" I wonder if we will suck up all the oxygen before it begins descending again.

"A few minutes. This building's ancient. They really need to fix it up." There's something unfamiliar in Arjun's eyes, and they won't meet mine.

That look makes something inside me snap. I want this to be a relationship. And in relationships, I think, you are supposed to talk about things that upset you.

"Who is she?" I demand again, inching closer to him. Heat radiates off his body. I soften my voice. "Please. I deserve to know."

He sighs, dropping his basket to the elevator floor in front of us, putting up a barrier. "Becca and I dated for a little while last year, but it didn't work out, and she wanted to get coffee to catch up."

"You're not getting back together or anything, are you?"

"No. We're not. We were just talking." There's a sharp edge to his words.

Our voices echo in this small space where we are stuck between floors, stuck between together and apart.

"I hate that you and I can't 'just talk' in public like that."

"You know why we can't. You said you understood. I've worked hard to build my reputation here, and even a rumor about us could ruin it." He gives the side of the elevator a light kick. "Why isn't it working yet?" he grumbles. He takes out his cell and curses under his breath. "No service."

"Why didn't you answer my messages earlier?"

Another deep sigh, and he props an arm against the elevator wall. "You're starting to worry me. You text me constantly, and I work, and I can't always respond right away like you apparently need me to. And then you follow me? I don't know what the hell's going on, but I don't like it."

"I had to see you. I—I'm really scared." I bite the inside of my cheek. "I think I'm starting to show symptoms."

"Adi," he says, an eyebrow quirking like he thinks I am making this up to mess with him. Half true, perhaps.

"I'm serious. When it first happened to my mother, she was clumsy all the time, and that's how I've been feeling. You know how she hit her head on New Year's Eve? I dropped my viola, and now it has this crack, and I've *never* been careless with it—you know that about me. And my moods are all over the place. Also—I've been hearing things, seeing things out of the corner of my eye that I'm pretty sure aren't real. Hallucinations, delusions. My mother has them." I'm bending the truth now, seeing how far it will stretch before it snaps. "I don't know what to do."

"Have you talked to your parents?" His words become gentler, though his face is still anger and hard angles.

I shake my head. "You're the first person I've said it out loud to. It's—" I force my voice up an octave so it'll crack with just the right amount of emotion to get to him. "It's really hard to say, and I'm terrified I won't be able to play viola, and that's the most important thing to me—you know that. . . . What happens when I don't have that anymore? Who am I without it?" Tears trickle down my cheeks.

269

Finally, his features soften, all his earlier rage turning into sympathy. I used to want him to want me because of *me*, but if pity is the only way to tether him to me right now, I will settle for it. At least it means he cares for me.

"Come here," he says, shoeing the laundry basket out of our way. He holds his arms out, and I collapse into them, able to breathe more deeply with his warmth around me. I grip the fabric of his shirt, hanging on tight. He feels bigger than I remember, his arms able to hold more of me. He strokes my hair, uses a finger to catch my tears. "I'm sorry, Adina."

When I lift my face from his chest, I put my lips to his neck and inhale him, rosin and soap and laundry detergent. I kiss the hollow of his throat until it rumbles with a groan. Then I move higher, bringing my mouth to his, biting down on his lower lip the way he likes.

By the time we reach the first floor, I realize I hadn't even noticed the elevator had started moving again.

♪ ♫♪

A jazz singer croons through Arjun's speakers. Two wine-glasses sit on the coffee table in front of us. Earlier we cooked dinner together, as much as boiling water for pasta and tossing arugula in oil and vinegar can be considered cooking. His refrigerator barely had anything in it—the arugula was wilted but I didn't say anything, and he didn't have pasta sauce, so we just sprinkled shredded cheddar on top of it. One day we will go grocery shopping together, and I will make sure he is well stocked.

270

He probably didn't have time to go earlier and didn't know I'd be here. Though I guess he had time to have coffee with Becca.

This cozy Friday night feels like a regular couple activity, but Arjun has been relatively quiet. It's turned me into a chatterbox. I have peppered him with as many questions as I can think of, more questions about his life in India and classical music and minute details about his family members.

"Why did you stop performing?" I ask him now. I'm wearing one of his collared shirts with the top few buttons undone. It stops at my thighs. We had sex earlier, and while it was good, if rushed—he always makes sure it is good for me—that cannot be the only language we speak anymore.

"It's nothing dramatic." He sips his wine and focuses on the ruby liquid as he answers my question. When he speaks again, his voice is weary, as though he is exhausted by my interrogations. But I don't understand it. I want to savor this adult conversation with my adult boyfriend. I want him to be so fascinated by me that he asks me questions too, but he has barely sent any my way.

"I still want to know," I urge as gently as I can. It must bring up bad memories. Maybe it's similar to how my mother doesn't talk about Israel and her life there.

He sighs. "I'd been playing since I was very young, and it started to feel monotonous. This might sound arrogant, but a lot of the challenge was gone for me. I began to dread performances because it felt like I was spitting out music I'd committed to memory long ago. There was no excitement left for me."

"Why haven't you ever told me that?"

"How can it possibly inspire my students? I gave up, but you should go for it?" He shakes his head. "My parents couldn't understand why I'd give it up, but I wanted *out* of everything. Out of that life, out of the symphony. I had a cousin in the States, so I moved here. I couldn't be entirely away from the music, so I started teaching."

"Do you ever want to go back? To performing?"

"Sometimes. I can enjoy playing simply for pleasure now. There's no pressure. And I love teaching."

I draw a quarter note on his knee with a fingertip. "You're very good at it."

He shifts his leg away from me, and my hand plummets to the couch. "Thank you." Then he rises and picks up our wineglasses. "So . . . you're okay now?"

"What do you mean?" My heart flutters into overdrive.

"You're okay to go home? It seems as though you've calmed down. You'll talk to your doctor about what's going on with the clumsiness and the—hallucinations." He trips over the word. It is always a difficult one to say.

"Yes, but . . . I was kind of hoping I could stay over tonight." *Like we're a real couple*, I don't say. He cannot be ready to banish me. I have never spent the night here, and I want to wake up next to him so badly. His face the first thing I see, his body the first thing I touch.

Another tremendous sigh, as though I am asking him to let me paint his walls neon yellow as opposed to sharing a bed for eight hours. "I really don't think that's such a good idea."

"Why not? Tomorrow's Saturday. You don't have students on Saturday. And I can tell my parents I'm spending the night at a friend's house. Easy."

I want to spend the night, but I also need him to say that he thinks about one day going public with our relationship. I want him to say that he's falling for me. I want him to say he will visit me in college. All the time.

I used to think I'd be satisfied with only the physical pieces of him, but I crave something deeper now. Love is gradual. A few more nights like this, and I know he will feel it too.

Perhaps he senses how deep that need is for me, or he realizes I have shattered all his potential excuses, because he says, "All right. You can stay. Just tonight, though, okay?"

I grin at him.

After we clean up and decide it's time for bed, I use the bathroom connected to his room. It is very small—in fact, the whole apartment is, but it has never bothered me. I don't need a lot of space. I open the drawers and cabinets and examine everything. My honeysuckle body lotion could fit right there, next to his aftershave, and I could line up my tubes of lipstick to the left of his Tylenol and cough syrup. I use his toothbrush, squeeze a pinky-nail-size amount of minty green onto it.

If I had allowed myself to continue to mope about my result, I might not be here. I might not have decided that I needed Arjun in my life not simply as a hookup or a fling, like I've had before, but as the real thing.

I've been in his bed more than a dozen times, but tonight

when I slip between the sheets, it feels different. Foreign, but in a very good way. I've only ever shared a bed with Tovah. She used to accuse me of touching her with my cold feet and hogging the bedcovers, which I insisted I never did. Arjun's sheets are too thin; at home I sleep with several extra blankets because I am always cold. But I imagine his body heat will make up for that.

He switches off the lamp, sinking the room into darkness, but he stays on the other side of the bed. I assumed he would arrange himself next to me, drape an arm across my stomach, plant a kiss between my shoulder blades.

But none of that happens. I bite down hard on the inside of my cheek in frustration. Perhaps I have one more way to keep myself in control long enough for him to realize he is falling for me. One last secret to reveal.

"I've decided something," I say, and he must be nearing sleep because he gives a slightly muffled "Mm?"

"I've been doing a lot of research about what's going to happen to me when I—when I develop Huntington's." The *when*, the tangibility of it, trips on my tongue. "I have a plan."

"That's good," he says sleepily. "I'm so glad to hear that."

I smile. It *is* good. Then I choose my words carefully. "I won't let this thing hold me back. I'll go to conservatory, and I'll do whatever I can to become a soloist as soon as possible." Even though my hands quake when I play. "I'm going to travel, too. With you, hopefully. Until the symptoms start. And then, well, that will be it. I will be done. With . . . living."

It is the first time I've uttered my plan aloud. There is a

poetry to it, a quiet sadness that lives inside all my favorite concertos and preludes.

For a while he doesn't speak, and I wonder if he's fallen asleep. But then he says, "Adina—" and I shift to face him, putting a finger to his lips. He draws in a deep breath.

"I don't want to say anything else about it. Not tonight, okay? I just want to enjoy this with you."

He nods in the darkness and finally pulls me tight against him, his chest against my back. My bones and muscles melt victoriously into his touch.

The next time I see him, I will insist our relationship cannot stay a secret any longer. I will tell him I've fallen so hard that spending these past three days without him was like living without oxygen. Without music. On vacations from school we'll go to Israel and India and anywhere else we want. We'll eat falafel and dunk bread in neon curries and paint ourselves with mud from the Dead Sea. We'll listen to symphonies in all the world capitals. And someday, even just for a short time, I'll be up on that stage, knowing that when my performance is over, he will be waiting for me.

Twenty-eight
Tovah

ADINA CREEPS INSIDE THE HOUSE WITH THE GRACE OF a cat. One of Ima's knitted scarves, a maroon that matches the flush on her cheeks, is loose around her neck. Her hair, as usual, is long and wild. Beautiful.

I sip a vanilla protein shake as she tiptoes from the hall to the kitchen, unaware I'm watching her. Waiting to catch her and interrogate her.

I quit track—which I joined only to put it on my JHU application—the day after my rejection, but I can't seem to give up running entirely. I won't allow my muscles to atrophy. My internal clock wakes me up early, even on Saturday mornings. Most exercise is prohibited on Shabbat unless it relaxes you. These days, running is one of the few things that does.

"Are you just now getting home?" I ask.

Adina jumps, startled by my voice. "Good morning to you, too."

She pours herself a glass of orange juice, and we do an awkward dance in the kitchen for a few seconds as we try to get out of each other's way. Then she sits at the table across from me. Casually. Like staying out all night is something she does all the time.

"Were you with that guy?" I ask. "Your mysterious boyfriend?"

Adina shrugs. Takes a sip of juice.

She was. She was with a guy *the whole night*. On Shabbat.

"Did you have sex with him?" The word isn't frightening anymore. After all, Zack and I are on the precipice of it.

"I have been for a while."

"Oh," I say softly.

He's not my first, she said before her audition trip. I assumed she meant first boyfriend. First kiss. Not the first everything else.

I guess I thought, even after everything we've done to each other, that she'd tell me when the first everything else happened. I can't believe I missed it. That I have no idea who it was or when it was, if it was good and if she felt different afterward.

"It isn't a big deal," she says, unwinding the scarf and fluffing her hair.

My sister looks calm. Relaxed. *Happy.* Is it because of the sex? Maybe she should be having as much sex as she wants. Why shouldn't she?

If I'd tested positive instead of my sister, there'd be no Zack. I'm sure of that. There'd be none of these Adina mind games.

Would I have been as heartbroken over Johns Hopkins? I planned so much for both outcomes, but none of this is what I expected. At all.

Adina is the person I'm going to have to take care of the rest of my life. We'll always be tied together like this. Every day of my life, I'll face this nightmare of my supreme genetic luck. Over and over and over.

I force myself to drink a third of the protein shake; if I don't, I'll feel miserable my entire run. Adina smiles at something on her phone, draws a design on her glass with a fingertip, hums something off-key under her breath. God, she really is happy. Evil eyes glint on her wrist.

"You've been wearing the bracelet every day too, right?" I say, searching for some common ground between us. Like after everything we've been through, maybe all we have in common is a piece of jewelry.

"Oh." Her eyes dart from her bracelet to mine. "The bracelets from savtah."

"Yeah." I take a closer look at hers. The bracelets are nearly identical. The beads on hers are larger, a deeper blue. I haven't noticed before.

"Well, *mine* belonged to savtah," Adina says, and when I raise my brows in confusion, she continues: "Ima only had one actual heirloom. She found yours online and told me not to tell you. I guess yours does look a little cheap."

"What are you—," I start, shaking my head, not sure if she's telling the truth or merely trying to hurt me. "You—you've been skipping school," I wind up firing back at her, fighting for leverage in this conversation. "Your teachers have been asking me where you are." To be fair, it was only one teacher we have in common, Ms. Hawkins, who teaches both regular gov and my AP US Government class. She mentioned to me yesterday that she hadn't seen Adina in more than a week and calls to my parents had gone unanswered.

"Why does it matter? I'm going to Peabody next year anyway."

A pause. I blink at her.

"You're . . ." The words dissolve on my lips. She's strapped me to an operating table and cut out my tongue. "Peabody, as in the Peabody Institute at Johns Hopkins? You're going to Baltimore?"

Her lips twist into a strange smile. She drags the scalpel from my mouth to my heart. "Yes. I am. My acceptances arrived yesterday. I got in everywhere I auditioned, but it was an easy choice. Baltimore was incredible when I was there, Tovah. I loved it. All the old architecture, and how artsy it is, and the cute little neighborhoods . . . There's so much history there, you know?"

Of course I fucking know.

"And the Peabody campus is much prettier than Johns Hopkins. JHU looks like any old college campus, but Peabody is like something out of a movie."

Any old college campus. How dare she make it sound ordinary.

She continues to babble about Baltimore. *My* Baltimore. She'll walk those cobblestone streets and absorb all the energy of a brand-new place. Maybe she deserves exactly that. Surely she does. She tested positive, so she gets everything else she wants, and I get indecision and confusion and choices, choices, choices.

"I was supposed to be there," I say hollowly, as though I had some claim to it. I wasn't good enough. Adina knows it. I know it. The entire city of Baltimore knows it.

"You didn't get in." She finishes her juice and gets up, leaving her empty glass on the table. "Hey, since you're the expert, do you think I should take any classes at Johns Hopkins my freshman year?"

I'm so numb, I can't even feel her scalpel anymore. Peabody students are allowed to take classes on the Hopkins campus, but I can't imagine what kinds of courses would interest Adina.

I shrug like I don't care, though there are few things I care about more at the moment.

She stands. "I'll figure it out later, I guess. I'm going back to sleep."

I wash out her glass and place it in the dishwasher so our parents don't have to deal with it later. Typical careless Adina. Then I roll the evil-eye bracelet off my wrist and slip it into my pocket.

Suddenly it seems like I'm the one struggling more than she is. I'm the one stuck deciding where to go to school. I'm the one suffocating beneath all this guilt. I'm the one who can't figure out how the hell to be happy with my own result.

"Why did you pick it?" I call as she climbs to stairs to her room.

Halfway up, she pauses. Doesn't even look back at me. Then she says, as though it really is that simple: "Because you wanted it so badly."

𝇍𝇍𝇍

After I get home from my run and shower—another activity only occasionally prohibited on Shabbat, but it's up to the individual and this individual needs a shower—it's time for Saturday-morning services at the synagogue.

"Is Ima coming?" I ask Aba, who's waiting for me in the hall.

He shakes his head, then readjusts his kippah. Ima knitted it for him. "Not feeling up to it. And Adi's still sleeping. I didn't want to disturb her."

I bite down on the inside of my cheek so I don't say anything. Of course, better not disturb my doomed, beautiful sister.

Our walk to the synagogue is chilly and filled with Aba's chatter about his ivrit class. He asks me about my impending college choice, but I give only vague, one-word answers.

We've been going to the same synagogue since Adina and I were children. We had our bat mitzvah here, and Rabbi Levine, a six-foot-tall man with short silver hair, still leads the congregation. Aba exchanges hellos with the Mizrahis and his other synagogue friends, both American and the few other Israeli transplants like my mother, who all pull pitiful faces when they see she's not here.

Rabbi Levine talks about this week's Torah portion, Terumah, in which God tells Moses to collect an offering from the Israelites to build a sanctuary so God can live among them. If my life were a movie, the Torah portion would parallel whatever problems I'm facing. I'd emerge from the synagogue with new energy, full of solutions.

It doesn't. And I don't.

"It's a shame Adi missed that," Aba says afterward.

Right. It would have meant so much to her, I'm sure. I pull my coat tighter around me as we trek outside. It's too cold for April. "Did you know Adina's been skipping school?" I'm a tattletale. I don't care.

"The principal has called a few times," he says. "Ima and I are still deciding how to bring it up to her."

"Seriously?" I sputter. "She gets a free pass to act however she wants now? Even with her parents?"

"She's fragile, Tov." He hunches his shoulders, shielding himself from either the cold or my accusation. "You know your sister. She can be . . . volatile. I love her, but I don't always know how to act around her. I'm still figuring it out."

"You and me both," I mutter, wondering if I'll ever figure it out.

Though there are only a few months left of senior year, I drop out of student council, too. My afternoons are now wide-open, lonelier even than my sister's. She's never been involved in school, and now it's my turn.

Since seventh period is now free, I spend it in the library mulling over my college acceptances. I got into a half-dozen public and private schools in Washington and across the country. The pain of losing Johns Hopkins has dulled to a bruise. It hurts only when I imagine Adina there next year.

Someone taps my shoulder, and I twist in my seat to find Zack.

"What are you doing here?"

"Abusing my hall pass privileges." He shows me a wooden paddle with GET OUT OF CLASS FREE written on it. Gently, he bops my arm with it. "You're cute when you're concentrating hard. What are you working on?"

I show him my pros and cons lists. "Trying to plan out my entire future."

He kneads my shoulders, and I lean into him. A librarian shakes her head at us, smiles, and looks away.

"You've been grinding your teeth a lot."

"I'm sorry. I know it's annoying."

He turns my face to him and skims my jaw with his thumb. "It's not annoying. I feel bad that you're so anxious about it all."

None of the cities or states of schools we got into overlap. That night in the tent, he was so hopeful we'd end up near each other next year, but now we don't talk about it. I like him too much to imagine losing him to distance. So when he asks me to come over later, I tell him yes, and I slide my foot up his leg until he blushes.

When the last bell rings, we walk outside with our hands linked. It's amazing how natural it feels now.

"Hey," Zack says as the school doors swing shut behind us, his voice incredulous. "It's snowing."

I blink at the flurries of white. A thin layer has begun to coat the grass. Everyone's staring up at the sky, laughing and running around. Surprise snow in Seattle turns high schoolers into children. I hold out my hand to catch a snowflake, but it disappears as soon as it touches my skin. Snow in April: another strange mystery in my strange universe.

Climate change deniers, come at me. Let my entire city prove you wrong. Maybe we'll get enough snow to bury me and put me out of my misery.

Twenty-nine

Adina

IF AN ANIMAL IS SUFFERING, WE PUT IT OUT OF ITS misery. Years ago the Mizrahis had an ancient, blind cat named Methuselah who developed a goiter on his chin. He couldn't see. He couldn't eat. He was in so much pain, I ached to look at him when we went over to their house. Tamar was devastated when they decided to put Methuselah to sleep, but it was the humane thing to do. How could they have let him go on like that?

I am not an ailing cat, and neither is my mother. But the other day when I was researching Huntington's, I learned that I am not the first person with the kind of plan I've been devising. Others have executed it successfully, and it even has a name: death with dignity.

Sufferers of terminal illnesses who are judged mentally competent can request lethal medication. It's legal in only a handful of states, and Washington is one of them. The catch is that you have to have six months or fewer left to live, and when I read that I wanted to scream. That timeline might not work for me. I searched some more and found there are some doctors who will obtain the medication for patients who have more than six months. Illegal, perhaps, but not wrong. There are even some younger people who have chosen this ending for themselves.

I wasn't going to think about the details this year, but this is perfect. I can spare myself and my family the gore of a violent death. They'd know there had been a good, peaceful ending for me, and they'd look back with fondness on the time we had together. They'd understand.

Except, perhaps, for Tovah.

My revenge has been more perfect than I could have imagined, though perhaps I felt a bitter twist of guilt when I told Tovah about Peabody and saw the stricken look on her face. I could have easily chosen any of the other conservatories, but I stole Baltimore from my sister because I knew it would hurt her the most.

It doesn't matter how she feels now, though. All that matters is the future, however near or distant it may be. Now that I have Arjun back and know for certain where I am going next year, I can truly savor the time I have left.

♩ ♫♪

Ima calls me into her bedroom after sundown. I should start counting how many more Shabbatot I have to observe before I leave for school. "Adina'le? I need some help."

She's sitting at the foot of her bed, still in her nightgown though it is eight o'clock in the evening. Her clothes are on the bed next to her.

"Do you mind?" she asks, and my heart climbs into my throat, gets stuck there.

I help shimmy off the nightgown. She isn't wearing a bra underneath. Her body is painted with freckles and wrinkles and stretch marks, physical proof Tovah and I came from her. There's the scar from her C-section, which is proof of only me. Her stomach is concave, but her breasts sag. My breasts will never sag like that. She has no shame in me seeing her like this, doesn't make any move to cover herself up.

My relief brings another feeling: sympathy.

"That one first." She nods toward the bra with the satin cups. I hook it around her back and help her get the straps up her arms. "Todah," she thanks me after we've finished with the soft pants and plain long-sleeved shirt too. It's a little easier to meet her eyes these days, knowing that I am never going to become like her.

"Bevakasha," I say.

For a moment I consider telling her about death with dignity. I am not sure it is an option she would ever consider for herself. Religion complicates it, of course, but she might agree it is the best option for me. Another look at her and I know I can't tell her. It wouldn't bring her peace, only more anguish, and she has enough of that.

Ima strokes my hair, and I lean into her touch. When I was little, she told me to brush my hair one hundred times before

I went to bed if I wanted it to always be soft and silky. I never skimped, not even once. Ima's hair, which is the rich golden mahogany of a viola, was always so smooth, and I wanted mine to be just like hers. Today, though, her hair is coarse and ribboned with gray and some white. She refuses to dye it.

Ima's hand drifts to the evil eyes on my wrist. "Where did you get that bracelet?"

♪ ♫♪

Everyone said the snow wouldn't stick, but it's snowed hard the past several nights and school is closed and my entire world is frosted. Arjun got his spring blizzard.

I lace my boots over two pairs of tights and toss an Ima-made scarf around my neck. Nothing smells nearly as fresh as the morning after a snow. I can't wait to take a big gulp of the air outside, feel ice crystals form in my lungs.

Today I will tell Arjun I love him, and he will say it back.

I've never felt quite this way before. My heart is floating away and I can't tether it back to my chest. I find the words hovering on the tip of my tongue, like they could slip out at any moment, delicate as snowflakes, for strangers to hear. "Love" is the only word for how I feel about Arjun. When he laughs, I want to make him laugh again. When our bodies come together, my skin sings. And when I told him my plan, he got it.

Before I leave, I dig around in our pantry to find a protein bar. It'll be a joke. I dodge a snowball fight as I skid and slide toward the bus stop, and the bus coughs its way slowly, slowly to Arjun's.

Absently, I wonder how many more winters I'll have, how many more unexpected snowstorms. I've always liked winter more than summer, although now it is technically spring. I am a cold-weather, cold-blooded person, from my ice hands to my heart.

Tree limbs are dusted with snow, Arjun's apartment walk-way fossilized with human and canine footprints. When he opens the door, I press myself against him, letting his hot mouth warm me to my core.

"Happy snowpocalypse," I say breathlessly. He releases me, and I wave the protein bar at him. "I brought sustenance."

He gives a small smile. "I told you it would happen."

"Yeah. In *April*." God, his apartment is freezing. Is the heat not working?

He rubs his elbow the way he does when he's nervous. After a few moments of silence, I lead us into the living room and onto the couch, unwinding my scarf.

"I made my decision," I tell Arjun, deciding to start with something easier.

"Hm? Oh, yes." He sounds distracted. "What did you decide on?"

"Peabody."

"Excellent," he says, his voice flat. "You'll be fantastic there."

I touch his wrist. He doesn't pull away exactly, but his body tenses, and it sets me on edge.

"Arjun. I have to tell you something."

He lets out a long breath, his face softening. "I have to tell you something too, but you can go first."

"I . . ." I swallow. I take both his hands in mine. There was a speech I rehearsed in my mind a good hundred times last night before I went to sleep, but now all I can get out is: "I'm in love with you."

I must whisper it because he stares blankly, blinking a few times.

"Did you hear me? I said, I love you." I laugh a little, like, *of course you heard me*. This is the part where he tells me that he loves me too, and then we'll kiss deeply. A black-and-white-movie kind of kiss, the kind where the woman's back arches so deeply you think she'd fall if it weren't for the way the man is holding her.

He withdraws his hands from mine. "I heard you." Rest, rest, rest. "Adina. You know I like you. A lot, actually. Probably more than I should."

All the adrenaline I had in me when I made my confession turns to dread. If adrenaline made me feel lighter than feathers, dread makes me feel like I'm balancing a piano on my shoulders again. Like it is crushing me. I want to snatch those words back, stow them away for longer this time.

"What do you mean?"

He makes that sigh-groan sound of frustration. "I keep thinking about what happened last week."

I shouldn't have to defend myself, but I do anyway. "I told you, I had to see you. And it worked out okay, didn't it? We talked about everything and you helped me calm down, and then we were fine."

"Adina." He makes a strange sound, kind of like a laugh, but an I-can't-believe-this laugh, a this-isn't-actually-funny laugh. "You *stalked* me."

"I didn't—," I start, but he cuts me off again.

"I like being with you, but I can't do this anymore. It's making it difficult for me to focus on my own work and music. You're . . . you're not well. I don't want to put my job in jeopardy by being with you, and I can't spend this much time with someone who's not . . . stable."

Stable. If he means it in both the physical and mental sense, I don't find it funny at all.

"I'll change. I swear," I insist. "I won't do that anymore. I won't even text you or call you. I just need to be with you."

"That's exactly what I'm talking about! This 'need' you have. It scares the shit out of me, okay? It makes me feel like if you're *not* with me, something's going to happen, and I don't want to be responsible for anything."

I cross my arms over my chest. "What do you mean? Responsible for what, exactly?"

"Your *plan.* When you said it, I was half-asleep, and it didn't sink in until you'd already left. At first I was certain you were overreacting. That you'd change your mind someday. But the more I think about it, the more I'm convinced that you need to talk to someone. Have you talked to anyone else about this? About any of it?"

"Just you."

He curses under his breath. "I think I need to tell your parents."

I cannot speak.

He wants to tell my fucking parents?

He couldn't stop thinking about it. My *plan*. Why couldn't he stop thinking about my lips, my body, my music? I swear I'd settle just for sex if it meant I could keep him.

"You can't tell my parents."

"I have to," he says. "It's my responsibility as your teacher. As the adult."

As *the* adult. Singular.

My breathing races away from me. It makes my words leap entire octaves. "So, what, I'm not an adult? You're on my side, aren't you? I thought you could keep it a secret. You're my boyfriend."

"Your boyfriend?" He shakes his head. "I'm not your boyfriend. I'm not taking you to the prom, Adina. I'm not going to buy you jewelry or take you on a weekend trip to a charming bed-and-breakfast."

And he's right. He's one hundred percent right. He is not my boyfriend. He is barely a functioning adult, living in this apartment with a stove that is *still* broken and a tiny bathroom with black mold on the ceiling and probably nothing in his fridge except expired milk.

I always liked the simple classiness of his studio, but of course, his students don't ever see the rest of his apartment. Not like I have. He told me once that he didn't usually cook for people or have anyone over. At the New Year's Eve party, his friends were so happy to see him. But he has never once mentioned other names to me.

Either there is much he's kept hidden from me, or his life is entirely unremarkable.

I suppose I'll never know.

I yank at a thread on my outer layer of tights and wrap it around my fingers until they turn white, hoping it'll balance out the pressure building behind my eyes. "Stop it. God, do you have any idea how condescending you're being?"

He springs off the couch and punches the air. "You told me you're going to commit fucking *suicide*!"

It is forte, that word. It ricochets around the inside of my skull. It pins me to the couch. Shrinks me. It's a word I have barely used even in my own head.

When I speak again, my voice is tiny. "Not tomorrow or anything. Just when I start showing more symptoms. A lot of people—"

"What do you think you're going to do? Slash your wrists? Leave the car running in the garage? Swallow a bottle of pills?"

My mind morphs those words into images, and they are red and violent and *not me*.

"No. Death with dignity. A lot of people do it."

"I'm sure they are people much older than you are."

I slam a pillow against the couch, frustrated by the pathetic *thump* it makes. "You're so fixated on age! You've never been okay with me being in high school, have you?"

"That's not what this is about," he growls.

"Is it? You're always so back and forth with me. I can never tell what you're thinking." I crush my palms into my eyes to trap the tears, but it does no good. Not even five minutes ago, I said, *I'm in love with you.* I thought this between us was more than sex. For once I wanted more than the physical and assumed I could get it, but maybe that is all I am allowed. Maybe men see me only as a pretty thing to play with.

"What was I supposed to do?" He throws up his hands. "I knew you were getting attached, and more than once I came close to breaking things off. But every time I thought about your . . . your *situation*, I couldn't bring myself to hurt you like that."

"You pitied me." My worst fear, come true. I am the one who should feel sorry for him: Where is *his* life going? What is he working toward? He already failed as a musician, regardless of what he said about not enjoying the challenge anymore. He is good, but he is not such a virtuoso that he has nothing left to learn.

"One of us has to be responsible here. One of us needs to tell your parents what the hell is going on with you, because I bet they don't have a fucking clue."

"This isn't your secret to tell. It's *mine*." The tears are falling now. I can't stop them. "What else am I supposed to do?"

"People deal with these things. It's horrible, but they do. They go to support groups. They go to therapy. They get help."

"You don't under*stand*," I say around a sob. I'm a little kid. I'm the little kid I never wanted to be. "I have to see my mother every day. Every day I look my future in the fucking face, and you know what it looks like? It's pretty fucking grim."

He waits a few beats before saying, "And suicide isn't?"

I wish he'd stop saying that word.

We're both breathing hard, sharpening our swords for the next round. Finally, I get an idea. A way to get him to back down.

"I *will* tell them," I say through clenched teeth. (I won't. I *can't*.) "But I never want to see you again. And if I find out you told them what I did, or what I'm planning, I'll—" It's the worst thing I can threaten him with, but it's also the *only* thing. Licking my lips once, I continue: "I'll tell the families of your other students. They might be interested in knowing what we've been doing, don't you think?"

"You wouldn't dare. Adina." He reaches for my wrist, but I snatch it away before he can touch me. "Please."

He looks ill. Part of me wants to shout *just kidding!* and take it all back. We could rewind to the night I spilled this secret, and instead of telling him about my plan, I'd sink into his body and keep my Siren lips locked tight, tight.

We are measures, movements, symphonies past that night now, and we both know it. I shake my head as though to show how simple it would be to destroy him. I'm not sure I could do it; it only matters that he believes me. "If I find out my parents know, that's what I'll do."

With this I am reminding him that I am the powerful one, that I can control this even when I can't.

"I don't know what else to say," he says softly.

With more confidence than I feel, I say, "Then I guess this is good-bye."

He pauses, lets out a very long sigh. Dark half-moons droop beneath his eyes, as though he hasn't been sleeping well. I haven't noticed them before. There is also a tear in the fabric of his sweater, near his collarbone, and a patch of irritated skin on his neck, probably from shaving. My final observations are all imperfections.

"Good-bye, Adina."

My fingers are shaky lacing up my boots, and finally I give up with one half untied. I abandon the three words I can never get back and the only person I've said them to, pressing *L* for lobby and glaring at the faded button between three and five, certain I will never press it again. I wipe my face on the sleeves of my coat. My nose is dripping, and the cold isn't helping.

My boots crush the snow on the walk down the hill to the bus stop. It's started up again, flurries dancing in my vision before the cold fuses my eyelids shut. I might get buried out here, become a real-life snowman.

Trudge forward. Keep moving.

On the endless bus ride home, I try to create stories for the other passengers as a way to distract myself, because if I don't, I am going to turn into a mess on public transportation, which is the last place I want to turn into a mess. The memory of making up stories with Tovah crushes me more than I thought possible.

We will never have that again. I have made certain of it.

These are the stories I create. The girl whose boyfriend's arms are wrapped around her shoulder while she's texting someone? She's cheating on him. She's going to screw some other guy later. The guy with missing teeth who's trying to hide his can of beer inside a wrinkled paper bag? He's a drunk. Probably a drug addict, too. The bus driver with the sunken eyes? She wants any job except this one and has dreams of driving this metal box into a lake . . . and one day I will meet her there.

Thirty

Tovah

ALL THE CITY'S SNOWPEOPLE HAVE AMPUTATED LIMBS and punched-in noses. Muddy slush is piled high on the sides of the road. It's the coldest spring we've had in decades: my last spring break of high school.

"Zack tells us you're very critical of his art," Zack's mom Mikaela says during dinner at his house, and I nudge Zack's foot with mine under the table. He's grinning.

"I'm not. I swear. Zack's really talented."

Mikaela laughs. She has olive skin and dark eyes. Tess, with her auburn hair and high cheekbones and lanky frame, shares DNA with Zack.

"Critics are a good thing," Mikaela says. "You don't want to be with someone who's going to praise everything you do, you know? You want to be challenged."

"That's why I tell Mikaela all her art is horrible," Tess says.

"Exactly. It's what keeps our marriage alive. Constant criticism and nitpicking."

Zack's parents make me like him even more. Make my like for him slide closer to love.

The house is decorated with Mikaela's and Zack's art. They have wildly different styles: Where Zack is abstract, Mikaela is realistic. Where he is sloppy, she is precise. When I got here, Zack tapped a hallway photo of him as a Boy Scout. "See? Proof that I was once a wild outdoorsman." In the photo and in real life he smiled his gap-toothed smile, which back then was too big for his face but now fits him perfectly.

I used to think I was lucky to have my family. My parents were present, caring, kind. They are genuinely good people. They pushed us, but not as hard as we pushed ourselves. True ambition has to come from within—I've always believed that. These days, though, at least one person is missing from the dining room table at any given meal. It makes me wonder if my family will ever be whole again. With Adina on the other side of the country in the city I was supposed to be in, maybe not.

Maybe it was wrong of me to think I was ever entitled to that place simply because I worked hard. Surely I could have done more. Taken extra classes, applied to other science programs? God, the past eighteen years have exhausted me. I can't imagine having worked any harder.

"What do you two have planned tonight?" Tess asks.

"Someone on student council is throwing a senioritis party later," I say. "We're all supposed to bring an old essay to throw into a big bonfire. Or in Zack's case, an old art project?"

Zack's decided on the Rhode Island School of Design, and I have already teased him multiple times that the RISD mascot is Scrotie, a giant walking penis.

"Senioritis party. I love it," Mikaela says.

No one talks about where I'm going because that is still a mystery. Zack's careful not to mention Johns Hopkins, and he must have asked his parents not to say anything about my college decision either.

Tess glances at her watch. "We should probably get going if we want to get good seats. We have tickets to a lecture on green homes at Town Hall. You two mind cleaning up here?"

"Sure," Zack says as he starts stacking plates. "I'd hate for you to have bad seats for a lecture." Meanwhile, I try to act casual about the fact that Zack and I are about to be left alone in his house and nearly drop a glass of water.

After his parents leave, it takes us only ten minutes to clear the table and load the dishwasher. I don't know how long a lecture about green homes can last, but probably not an insignificant amount of time.

"Your parents left us alone," I say, stating the obvious, anticipation forming goose bumps on my skin.

"They did."

"Your parents trust you to be alone in the house with . . . me?"

"Are you not trustworthy?" he asks with a sideways grin, leaning back against the counter next to me, bumping me with his hip. "I've racked up a lot of good-son points over the years.

I may not get the best grades, but my moms and I talk about everything. So, yes. They trust me."

I position my body in front of him and run my hands up his chest. "Does that mean we shouldn't go upstairs to your room?"

"It means we absolutely should," he says, but once we're up there, something pulls my attention from him.

"Quite a collection you've got," I say, pointing to a shelf of Holocaust books.

"Yeah. I went through a phase when I was younger."

"Didn't we all?" I say.

He sits down on his bed next to the bookshelf. "You too?"

"My shelf is practically your shelf's twin."

"My grandparents gave me Jewish books every holiday, every birthday. I got worried I might get desensitized to it all, but nope. I'm not." He pats the bed next to him, and I sink down and lean my head on his shoulder.

"Did you feel different from everyone else? Like, because you didn't celebrate the same holidays?"

"My family's pretty secular—not nearly as Jewish as yours, as you know—but yes. Every December my teacher made me get up in front of the class and talk about Chanukah, so I told the story about the light burning for eight nights and that's why we my parents gave me eight presents, one on each night. I probably embellished a lot. I don't think Batman or Spider-Man were in the original version." He gives a sheepish grin. "I didn't know why I celebrated Chanukah or why I didn't celebrate Christmas. I just knew that it made me different." Zack wraps an arm around my shoulders. "For a while I didn't get it," he says, "why we didn't have a Christmas tree or lights, or egg hunts for Easter. But you understand."

"I do. Have you heard the phrase 'klal Yisrael'?"

He shakes his head. "Something . . . about Israel?"

"Ha-ha. Yes. It means all of Israel—that all Jews are connected."

He smiles. Warm. "I feel that way all the time."

No matter what else changes, religion is constant. Every time I read a portion of the Torah at synagogue or say a prayer in Hebrew or observe a holiday, I'm awed that people have been doing this exact same thing for hundreds of years.

I don't know if I can verbalize exactly how important Judaism is to me, how it makes me feel that I'm not alone. With Zack, I feel less alone too, even when everything else is falling apart.

"Tov? What's wrong? You're quiet."

I attempt to count the things that are wrong. My mother is dying. My sister is dying. Then the selfish things, the things that occupy too much skull space: I don't know what I want to do next year, where I should go or what I want to be. I could study medicine somewhere else, of course, but the idea of becoming a surgeon was linked to Johns Hopkins—that was where I fell in love with it. And becoming a surgeon means facing death nearly every day of my life. Am I sure I want that?

Adina was wrong. Choices aren't easy, and I have an entire lifetime to continue making stupid ones. Lucky me.

All I want is to know exactly *what I want* in this moment. To become a surgeon, to go to school nearby or leave this place behind, to do nothing at all. I want to fucking pick one thing and be happy with it.

I glance up at Zack. There's this way he looks at me: like he's awed by me, even when I've disappointed myself. Suddenly I know exactly what that one thing is.

"Tov?"

Adina stole Baltimore. I'll steal her confidence.

In one quick motion, I press my lips to his and push him back onto the bed, kissing him harder than I ever have before, until I'm dizzy with the scent and feel of him. I never thought when I got a boyfriend that I'd want to touch him all the time. I never thought I'd want so much of someone else.

"Whoa, whoa," he says, his hands roaming down the sides of my body. "Where is this coming from?"

"I really want you." And I really, really need to feel good again.

He clutches me tighter. "God, you're beautiful." His mouth travels from my jaw to my neck to my collarbone. "And hot. You're hot, too." No one has ever, *ever* said that about me. That's something they say about Adina. I'm smart, and she's beautiful.

It's working: I can be both. I am both.

Our shirts land on the floor, and my fingertips memorize the curve of his spine, the feel of each individual vertebra. I've always tried to hide my double-D-cup breasts beneath layers of loose clothing, and now I'm hyperaware of the way they react to

Zack's hands and lips. With him, I'm not shy about it.

I reach between us and splay my hand over the front of his jeans, fumbling with the button.

"Hey," he says. "Hey. Wait a second."

He doesn't get it. I have to go fast, fast, before I lose this fragile confidence I've only just claimed for myself. Finally I undo the button and mash down his zipper. My hand finds what it wants, and Zack groans. I hold my mouth to his ear. "Do you have a condom?"

He wraps his hand around mine. Gently removes it from inside his boxers. "Tov. Slow down."

Breathing hard, I blink up at him, unsure what he's saying. "You don't want me?"

"It's not that. I do want you." He makes a strangled-sounding laugh and glances down. "That part should be pretty obvious. But I just—this would be my first time too. I don't want us to rush into it or regret anything."

"So you'd regret having sex with me." I get off his lap and cross my arms over my chest, feeling a hundred times less hot than I did a minute ago.

He scrapes a hand over his face. "I'm not saying any of the right things."

"No. You're not." I snatch my bra and shirt and dress faster than I ever have before. Then I press my back against the wall and pull my knees up close to my chest.

Zack zips his jeans. Puts his shirt on inside out. Neither of us can look the other in the eye. "I'm sorry," he says quietly, fingers searching for mine on the bed, but I keep them out of reach. "I guess I thought we'd talk about it before we, you know, did anything."

"What was it you said when we went camping? About corrupting each other? We've done just about everything else. And we barely talked about that."

"I—I know. But this feels like a bigger deal, I guess. We could . . . talk about it now. If you want."

I choke out an odd laugh—odd because I don't find this funny at all. "I really don't." What's there to talk about? He doesn't want me: that's all I can focus on.

A silence hangs between us, heavy as a meteor.

"You don't have to stay," he says.

"You want me to leave?" My voice cracks. I don't know if I can take getting kicked out, doubly rejected.

His eyes widen, and again he tries to grab my hand, but I won't give it to him. "No! I meant, maybe you wanted to leave? If you're . . . mad at me? I want you to stay. If you want to."

Great. We're stuck in this loop. "I guess I'll stay, then."

All the amazing things I usually feel with him—beautiful, admired, even sexy—are gone. The confidence I stole from Adina is gone too. I flick my gaze between his striped sheets, the jacket with elbow patches draped across his desk chair, the canvas boards mounted on the walls. I finger-comb my hair, trying to erase the evidence of what we didn't do.

"Do you still feel like going to the party?" he asks.

"I don't know that I could handle a party right now."

"Yeah. Same here." Zack stands up. "Maybe we could go downstairs and watch a movie or something?"

"Sure."

We sit a cushion apart on the couch watching an old Wes Anderson movie. All I can think about is how this would never have happened to my sister. She's the girl who always gets what she wants, and I'm the girl who tries and tries and tries but can never quite get there.

Two of the walls in my room are still bare, a result of my Johns Hopkins meltdown. It's nine thirty and I'm home from Zack's and ready to fall asleep for about a week. But something stops me from collapsing onto my bed.

Several dozen scraps of red paper are spread across the sheets like confetti. At first I assume they're from when I tore this place apart, but I was meticulous in my cleanup. I can't have missed something as obvious as this.

I pick them up with my fingernails. It takes me only a few seconds to puzzle them together, and when I do, my stomach plummets so quickly I nearly drop to my knees along with it.

It's the Nirvana ticket that used to hang above my desk. The only thing on my bedroom walls I loved enough to keep. A connection to Aba my sister can't begin to understand.

"Adina," I hiss under my breath, and it sounds like a vow of vengeance.

I have no idea what I'd have done had our results been

flipped, but I wouldn't have destroyed something that meant the world to her. I wouldn't have smashed her viola or sabotaged her future.

I've been kind to her—as kind as I could. So understanding. I've held myself back when I wanted to explode so many fucking times. I'm done with that. We're both the evil twin.

I want to scream at her. I want her grab her by the shoulders. I want to force her to piece together the ripped-art concert ticket until her fingers are covered in paper cuts. But I'm not allowed to do any of that, am I? Because she tested positive, and I tested negative.

"Where is she?" I ask my parents as I race downstairs. "Where's Adina?"

"She went out," Aba says. They're eating a late dinner. He's cutting a piece of chicken into more easily chewable chunks for Ima. She struggles with a fork and knife, and she continues to have trouble swallowing. "Some kind of senioritis party? What does that mean?"

Ima's face scrunches with concern. "What's going on?"

I ignore her. How could I possibly explain what her darling daughter has done? I grab my keys and then I'm out the door, touching my fingertips to my lips and then to the mezuzah and praying I finally have the strength to tell my sister exactly how I feel about her.

Thirty-one

Adina

I DON'T WANT TO BE ALONE TONIGHT, SO I AM GOING to drink until I can't remember how monumental a mistake Arjun was, and maybe I'll keep going after that. The scene from earlier today in his apartment repeats over and over and over in my head with no coda. Perhaps the coda is the successful execution of my plan.

Most of the faces in the living room are familiar, but no one says hi to me. I don't say hi back. This is nothing like the New Year's Eve party. The windows are fogged up and it's hot and it's loud and I don't recognize the music and no one is dressed up. You should have to get dressed up to go to a party. When I used to imagine my future, I conjured more parties like the one on New Year's Eve. Then I replay what Arjun and I did in the coatroom at that party. I was trying to control him with my body, hoping that would make him love me. Stupid,

stupid, stupid, thinking he might actually love me back.

Tovah's friend Lindsay waves at me, but she doesn't say anything. She's glued to her boyfriend, Troy. Thank God she doesn't ask me if I want to hang out with them again. I am done being pitied.

Maybe I should have joined student council, or tried track, or taken "at least one AP," like Aba always said, and then Tovah and I would still be close as we were when we were kids. Or at least I would have had someone to talk to at this party, someone who cared that my heart broke this week, someone who could help me put it back together, if such a thing is possible. Someone who will hold back my hair later if I drink too much.

After I get another drink, I stagger into the next room, where a few people are playing pool and others are watching a superhero movie on a giant TV. I watch a girl from my English class make out with a guy from my physics class.

Did I really think Arjun and I would become a real couple? That I could introduce him to my parents, not as my teacher but as my boyfriend? He is twenty-five—what kind of future could we have had? He was right—at some point he would have had nothing left to teach me. I will become a better musician. I know it. He is stagnant, stuck in that shitty apartment with no aspirations. He wanted me for only one reason—the same reason the other guys wanted me.

But I fucked up too. I threatened the one man I've ever loved. The tornado of emotions in my mind flashes with a guilty bolt of lightning. Childish. That is how I acted.

"Hey, Adina."

I pull my gaze up from the carpet. Connor Mattingly. Double bass guy. Nice enough guy, completely age-appropriate guy.

"Hello." I toss back my head and laugh. At absolutely nothing at all.

"I don't think I've ever seen you at a party."

"I haven't seen you either." I laugh again. Sweet, inoffensive Connor is the kind of guy I should have dated. The kind of guy who could have loved me. "Come here," I whisper, crooking a finger at him, even though he's standing right next to me. "I want to talk to you."

He gives me a quizzical look, like why would I want to talk to him when I've gone out of my way to avoid him in the past. Still, I take his shoulder and steer him into the hallway. Down, down, down the hall we go, until I find an unoccupied room.

I close the door, set my drink down on a table, and push my hair out of my face. "You got your braces off."

"Yeah." Alcohol's reddened his cheeks. "Months ago."

Then I lean in and smash my lips to his. He returns the kiss at first, his hands coming around my neck, and I'm thinking, *I was wrong; he's not a good guy.* His fingers fumble around in my hair, and his mouth is sloppy, as though he is trying to retrieve something he lost inside mine. His body is soft—well, most parts of it—probably because he's so young. He hasn't grown into it yet.

We stumble backward, and I push him onto whoever's bed this is.

"Adina—"

I reach for the belt of his jeans. I hope he has a condom. Because I don't. I crave the feeling of hands gripping my hips, fingers pulling my hair, weight on top of me.

But then he groans and breaks away.

"Whoa." He holds his hands in front of him, a barrier between us. "Um. This is . . ."

"What? You don't like it? You seemed to be enjoying it just fine."

"I'm sort of . . . seeing someone. We went out once last week and I really like her, and I don't want to screw it up, okay?"

"Who?" I drag the back of my hand over my mouth, smearing my lipstick, erasing him.

"Gina. You know Gina? She plays violin."

"Right. Gina." I do not know Gina.

"Plus, I'm a little drunk, and I think you're a lot drunk, and—"

"I get it, okay? You don't need to give me a whole dictionary of excuses."

The room tilts and flips over. I'm on the ceiling now. I fold my hand over the bedpost, trying to keep from crashing to the floor.

"I'm sorry," Connor says. There's red all over his mouth. He doesn't seem to notice, and I decide not to tell him.

"It's whatever. I thought you liked me. My sister said . . ."

He flushes deeper. "I—I do. Or I did, but . . . we barely know each other. And you've always seemed sort of . . . distant. Gina's, well, I think she likes me too." He fixes his hair back into place, redoes his belt buckle. "Look, do you want to talk instead? You seem like you could use a friend right now."

No. I can't use a fucking friend. That wasn't what I wanted. I leave.

Guys used to want me just for sex, and now they don't even want that.

A pretty girl like you should have a boyfriend. Fuck that. For years I have been stared at and told over and over that I am *such a pretty girl*. Like nothing else about me matters. I used to love it, even the looks from guys who were too old to have been looking at me. Now I am nauseated. That is not all I am.

A body. A face. A pair of legs. Hips. Breasts. Lips. Someone to stare at. Fantasize about. No one cares about the music, only that the girl with the viola under her chin is beautiful. That is all I was to Eitan; I know that now. Even Boris Bialik, who is probably triple my age, said it after my showcase performance.

The reality, I fear, is that it *is* all I am.

♪ ♫

"What the fuck did you do?"

I hear her before I see her. Tovah comes at me from out of nowhere, eyes blazing. I'm in the backyard, leaning against the porch railing. She grabs my shoulders and shoves me so hard the railing digs into my back and the liquid in my cup sloshes over the side and spills down my coat. A few people are smoking pot, and everyone's old assignments are burning in a fire pit a few yards away.

For a split second I'm convinced she's talking about the

failed hookup with Connor Mattingly, but then she throws red confetti in my face.

She found my grand finale. For now at least. Surely I'll find other ways of destroying her. I'm deep in it now, no way to crawl out. It happened earlier today, after Arjun but before this party, when she was out with her precious Zack. Stealing Baltimore wasn't enough. I thought Johns Hopkins was most dear to her, but then I realized there was something else.

"I figured you weren't coming," is all I say as the paper scraps flutter to the ground. It doesn't answer her question. I rub my back. If there is a bruise tomorrow, I'll only be able to see it in a mirror.

"What does that have to do with anything?" Her teeth are clenched and her fists are clenched and she looks like she might hit me. She is feral. The people by the fire pit are so loud that she has to practically scream for me to hear her. "You know how much that ticket meant to me."

The watery beer I've bring drinking all night loosens my lips, slurs my words. "I don't have as much time as everyone else does. I figured . . . why not do exactly what I want to do now? When I don't have any consequences? Nothing's stopping me."

"Nothing except basic human decency," she spits. "That's what all this has been about? All the shitty things you've been doing to me? Living life to the fullest?"

I say nothing.

She pinches the space between her brows. "Okay, so let me make sure I get this right. I want to examine all the ways you're living your life to the *absolute fullest*, since that seems to be really important to you right now. You're making my life hell, that's one. You're on the verge of not graduating. You're sleeping with some guy you won't tell me about. Oh, and I can't remember the last time you went to synagogue because I guess you're always 'too tired.' Really, well done. That's a life well lived. I'm sure you'll be in history books someday."

Someone throws an entire textbook into the fire, and the flames lick the words from the pages. A couple people have taken notice of us. They have started pointing. *Look at the Siegel twins. Aren't they sad?*

Yes, yes, we are. I stay silent, unsure how to respond when there is no way she could possibly understand.

"God, at least fucking *talk* to me!" Tovah says.

It's an electric shock to my spine, to my vocal cords. I straighten to my full height, an inch taller than Tovah, and step closer so we are eye-to-eyebrow.

"You want me to talk? Or do you just want to know who I'm sleeping with? Since you're clearly not going to shut up until you know, I'm sleeping with Arjun. Arjun Bhakta. Or at least I was."

"Your viola teacher?"

I take another sip of my drink. "Well. Not anymore. We broke up."

"You broke up with . . . ? You were dating him?" People are watching, and a couple guys catcall, "Oooooh." Tovah turns to them. "This is private," she growls, and there's enough venom in her voice to shut them up.

The people by the fire pit are singing an old song about

314

school being out for the summer, though it's not summer and there is still snow on the ground.

Tovah must feel the same because she yells at them, "School isn't even out yet!" But they either don't hear her or don't care, and they keep on sing-shouting.

God, it's so cold. Our breath makes clouds in the cold night air, white against midnight black. I inch off the deck, closer to the fire. I crave its warmth.

"How old is he?" Tovah asks. "Your teacher. Are you at least on birth control?" Practical, smart Tovah. She'll be such a good doctor one day.

"It doesn't matter how old he is. I'm eighteen. And yes, I've been on it since I was fourteen, so I don't think we need to have a safe-sex talk. Ima took me to get it because my period cramps were so bad."

Tovah sets her jaw. "Mine were bad too. I never said anything about it." She grips the deck railing, starts saying "oh my God" over and over and over. Finally, she drags her eyes back up to mine. "You said he wasn't the first."

The alcohol makes the words tumble out easier, destroys my filter. *Eitan*, I mouth.

"*Mizrahi*? He's engaged!"

"Not recently. Like, four years ago." Lifetimes ago. Who was I then?

The oh-my-God symphony starts again. "You were fourteen?" Her face is solemn. Scared, even.

I nod.

"And you didn't tell me?"

"I didn't tell anyone."

She runs one hand through her hair and pulls at some of the short strands. "I've never understood it. The attention has never been enough for you. Not when it comes to your music, or to guys. Is that why you sabotaged me, because you couldn't stand to see me get any of the attention? You realize, don't you, that that could be why I didn't get into Johns Hopkins?"

"Maybe you didn't get in because they didn't fucking want you."

One of the fire pit kids is filming a video of us. Cool. Glad to know we are entertaining someone.

Relishing the control I have over the conversation, I get louder. "You were ready to leave us behind, go off on some grand adventure. Hooray for you! You were the only person who could understand what I was going through, and you wanted to leave. I had to do what I did."

"Why did you even need me when you and Ima are so close?" Envy drips from her voice. "You guys have your little club with your old movies and helping out in her classroom."

"It's not the same," I say, though it has been a long time since Ima and I have watched a movie together, and she no longer has a classroom. "There's always been someone better for you. Your friends and your homework and now Zack. You have so much that I've never had, and you don't even realize it."

"Is that really what you think?"

"It's not what I think. It's our history."

Tovah clenches her jaw. Scrape, scrape, scrape is the sound her teeth make. I don't care if she can't help it. I fucking hate that sound.

"Here's the deal with my supposedly amazing friends, because I really only have three of them," she says. "There's Lindsay, who's been ignoring me most of the year. There's her boyfriend, Troy, who really doesn't care about me one way or the other. And then there's Zack, and"—she gestures wildly at the empty space surrounding her—"do you see him here with me tonight?"

I tilt my cup to my lips, but Tovah snatches it away and turns it upside down over the lawn.

"What the hell?" This action of her pisses me off so much that I push a hand into her shoulder. Hard.

She stumbles back, shoe skidding on the icy deck, but she grips the railing before she falls. "Haven't you had enough?"

I hate you, I think, though I'm not sure it's true.

"Part of the reason I wanted to leave," she starts back up when I don't say anything, "is that I wanted to be on my own for once. I didn't want to be half of the Siegel twins. I wanted to see who I could be without your shadow constantly threatening to overtake me."

"So you were jealous."

She grunts like she cannot actually admit it.

"You don't have to act like you're above it," I continue. "I'm jealous too. Okay? I don't have the perfect relationship like you and Zack."

"My boyfriend doesn't even want to have sex with me."

Tovah lifts her shoulders in a dramatic shrug. "So there you go, another thing you're better at."

"Getting guys to sleep with me?"

"Sure. If that's what you want to call it."

I shake my head. She doesn't get it. "You think you're so much better than me. You're going to save the world. All I'm going to do is play silly music, right?"

"Maybe you don't have friends because you only think about yourself and your music," she says. "You think you're so grown-up, but you're immature. Reckless. You can't keep acting this way forever."

Inside the house, something shatters. Someone yells. But we remain near the fire, the flames casting shadows onto Tovah's face.

This is me, Adina, a girl on her way to becoming a ghost.

I stare at her. It's still the plan, still the only choice I can make for myself. "I won't. I'm not planning to be here long enough to find out how Ima's disease is going to destroy my life too."

Thirty-Two

Tovah

"WHAT DO YOU MEAN?" I BLINK AT MY SISTER A FEW times, certain I've misunderstood her.

Adina pulls her lower lip into her mouth with her teeth, as though regretting her words. She must realize she can't take them back. Can only go forward. When she speaks again, her words are measured. Tentative. "Have you heard of death with dignity?"

My whole frozen world stops spinning. Silvery puffs of breath hang suspended in the air. And my sister, this person I'll always be inexorably linked to, turns herself inside out.

I expected several things when I stormed into this party. I expected I'd yell at Adina. Tell her she's been acting fucking terrible. Push her, shove her—not enough to hurt her, but enough to get my anger out. We haven't physically fought since we were little kids. She bit my arm once. Stamped a teeth-fossil onto it that lasted for weeks. I can't remember why; surely it was over something insignificant. Until Ima's diagnosis, we only fought about insignificant things. Maybe it makes sense that when we touched each other again after our test results, it wasn't to hug, but to hit.

I was not expecting a confession like this.

"I've heard of it." I bury my head in my frozen hands. "Tell me you're not serious. Tell me you're being melodramatic as usual." But I can tell, already, that she is and she isn't.

"It's the best choice I have," she says quietly. "The only choice I have."

I claw at her shoulder. This time she can't push me away. She may be taller and prettier, but I'm stronger. "You think Ima and Aba would let you do this?"

"I don't need their permission."

"We all have bad shit, Adina. All of us. This isn't—you can't—"

"Yeah?" She stares at me hard. I smell alcohol, the citrus shampoo we share, the ashes the smokers left behind. "What's your bad shit? Not getting into your dream school? Boyfriend problems? Friend drama? Is it really as bad as this? I'm doing this so that I can have *more* time to do the things I like. I have to condense my life into a smaller timeframe, so why can't I spend the rest of my good years doing exactly what I want?" She tries to shrug my hand off her shoulder. Fails. "Don't I deserve that?"

"No," I say simply. "You can tough it out like the rest of us. You can have good things and bad things like the rest of us. You can talk to someone. You can go to therapy. What you're doing is selfish. You've always been so fucking selfish, Adina."

"This is the least selfish thing I could possibly do!" she yells. "I won't be a burden to you, or to Aba, and I won't break Ima's heart." She's crying now, sloppy tears she tries to mop up with her sleeve. "I want to die before this fucking disease can take away every good thing in my life."

"You've already done a pretty great job of that yourself."

Her eyes turn predatory, and she glares at me with tears streaming down her face. "I hate you. You've been an awful sister to me these past couple years, and I hate you. Ani sonet otach."

Her words take the air from my lungs. She's stung me in both languages as poisonously as she can.

There's a pause between us. Ima's reprimand from long ago comes back to me: *You don't hate Adina. Do you know what that word means?*

She's waiting for a response. Expecting me to copy her. Instead I release my grip on her shoulder and say: "I don't."

Thirty-Three

Adina

I DON'T KNOW WHERE I AM AT FIRST. THE PILLOW IS lumpy and unfamiliar beneath my face, and something heavy is crushing my stomach: a guy's bare arm.

Rubbing my eyes, I throw the arm off me. The boy attached to it is Dennis Kim, second-chair violin. He stirs but doesn't wake. After the fight with Tovah, I was distraught. He was sitting alone, and I was sitting alone, and we decided to be not alone together.

I stare at his sleeping face. The night clarifies itself in my mind. Dennis lives down the block from the party and we sneaked into his bedroom. He was too drunk to stay excited, so nothing happened besides some sloppy making out. He begged me not to tell anyone at school about the not-getting-it-up part and then promptly fell asleep.

I grab my tights from the floor, and before I put them on, I glance at my legs. The scar on my right thigh still hasn't healed—maybe it never will—and a new one slices down my left. I added it last week. To match.

I am a mess.

Supposedly, I came to terms with everything months ago, didn't I, when I first devised with this plan? The entire point of it was to make my result easier to bear, pursue my passions with manic vigor, knowing I would end my life before I became my mother. But my supposed choice has only sunk me deeper, back into my old habits. I am the same Adina I've always been. Doomed and pretty and utterly lost. The center of attention for all the wrong reasons.

I am more than this. I am not just a pair of legs or breasts or hips. I am a mind and a soul and I know with certainty that Dennis Kim didn't care about any of that.

"No more," I whisper to myself as I finish getting dressed and slip out the window, my traitorous feet once again failing to keep me from stumbling.

With eight percent phone battery, I google the early symptoms of Huntington's disease.

Difficulty concentrating

Clumsiness

Mood changes, including aggression and/or antisocial behavior

Short-term memory lapses

Closing my eyes, I conjure my Debussy prelude, trying hard to remember the notes.

Thirty-four

Tovah

I USED TO THINK BEING A TWIN MEANT I'D NEVER BE the center of attention. For a long time, I didn't mind sharing the spotlight with my sister—but secretly, I wanted to be her.

Back when our bodies started changing, she was so confident with her new shape. I hid my curves in sweatshirts and baggy jeans. Adina knew how to handle it. Knew how to own not being a straight line. Knew what to wear and how to style her hair and how to walk without staring at the ground.

She has always known exactly what she wants.

The day after the party, I lie in bed until morning turns into afternoon, until afternoon becomes evening. Adina crawls into her room sometime in the midafternoon, and I sag with relief that she made it home okay.

There isn't enough room in my head for all the new knowledge that's been crammed inside. Death with dignity. I'd heard of it, but I assumed it was only for the elderly, exhausted by the agony of a terminal disease. Not people like my sister.

I can't stop the visions in my head: harshly lit rooms and metal tables and cold blue skin. A dark-haired cadaver sliced open from sternum to her last rib, ready to be examined and analyzed. A girl taking a razor blade to her wrists. A car smashing into a tree. Red. Too much of it.

On my nightstand next to me, my phone lights up with a message from Zack.

Heard you and Adina fought at the party. You okay? Here if you need to talk.

I turn the phone over. My relationship is the least of my worries right now.

Adina wasn't wrong that I wanted to leave her behind. I had school and I had goals and if I didn't try my hardest to get where I wanted to be, I was going to collapse with the weight of Ima's diagnosis. I had to be selfish.

Death with dignity. It's something many Jewish scholars agree should be condemned, but I guess that's another item on the list of things that no longer matter to her.

If Adina . . . *committed suicide* . . . would I still be a twin?

Would I still be a sister?

I used to think I could separate myself enough from death that the darkest parts of a career as a surgeon wouldn't faze me. I'm years and years away from that still, but death has taken on new meaning. Now I'm terrified of it too.

༒

For days Adina and I don't talk. I should tell my parents—I know I should—but I need to talk to her first. I'm still letting it all sink in, doing my own research. Death with dignity is reserved for people with six months to live, but Adina has a long time before she hits that stage. Doesn't she?

On Passover, Adina and I are forced to interact.

"I guess this is our last seder all together for a while," Aba says once we start eating.

"Unless I have a break that coincides with Passover," Adina says.

Will you be alive then? My stomach twists until I'm no longer hungry.

"Why would this be our last seder together?" Ima says. "What's happening? Where are the girls going?"

"Adi is going to conservatory in Baltimore," Aba says. "Remember?"

Ima's head bobs up and down quickly. "Oh. Yes," she says, but she doesn't sound convinced. "And Tov is going to Johns Hopkins! My talented girls. I can't believe it. Wait until I tell my mother. She'll be so proud of her granddaughters." She looks to my father. "Do you have her phone number?"

"Simcha," he says in a quiet voice. "Your mother—"

"—is on vacation!" I say quickly. I don't want to break Ima's heart. I can't fathom forgetting your own mother has died. "She, uh, doesn't have reception where she is."

"Right," Aba says.

"Oh," Ima says, her smile drooping for a moment. "Well,

we'll just have to phone her when she gets back!"

My eyes meet Adina's, whose shoulders slump in relief. Part of me opens up and understands: she never wants to become this version of our mother. And I have no idea how to feel about that.

Ima's memory lapses are beginning to scare me. She must know I'm avoiding her, because one night when I'm coming back from a late run, she calls me into the living room. A blanket is draped across her legs. She finally finished knitting it a couple weeks ago. It's chocolate and caramel with some patches of bright blue, and it took her months because she's been moving so slowly lately.

"I can't sleep," she says, sliding a biography of an old Hollywood movie star onto the coffee table.

I head into the kitchen. "Do you want some tea?" When Adina and I used to get sick, Ima made tea with a scoop of honey and a pinch of cayenne pepper. Sweet-and-spicy tea, she called it.

"Tea sounds nice." When I return with two mugs, she says, "Todah." We blow on the tea. Sip in silence for a while. "How was your run?"

"Fine." I pull my knees up tight against my chest.

"We don't do this very much. Talk, the two of us."

"I know." My fault. "I'm sorry."

"You and Adi have so much going on. I understand that. But if you're not too tired, and I can't sleep . . . tell me what's going on with you, Tovah'le," she says, and it sounds like begging. "Something about school, or about your friends, or your boyfriend . . . You're going to have to help me with his name."

"Zack," I say quietly. "Zack."

"Right, Zack."

There's no Adina around. This is just my mother and me.

"Actually," I start. "I'm not fine." Suddenly I want to confide in a mother who's been a mystery to me for so many years, but I'm not sure where to start. It's not just losing Johns Hopkins that's thrown me completely off course. But I don't want to—*can't*—admit what's been on the edge of my mind for weeks. That I don't know who I am without a definitive path toward med school and residency and operating rooms.

That I don't know if that's the right path for me anymore.

What comes out is this: "I don't want to make the wrong choice."

"About college?"

My jaw is tight and I don't know how many more words about this I can spare, so I nod. Pressure builds behind my eyes. *No*, I don't want to do this here. Not in front of her when she has so many other troubles to deal with.

"I don't know what to do once I get to college, wherever I end up going, and if I'm supposed to take bio classes for premed, and I'm . . . freaking out." Finally saying this out loud feels *good*. "Everything's different now, and I'm really freaking out."

"Come here." She wraps me in the blanket like a burrito. I've forgotten how comforting it is to be taken care of. If I'm too old for this, I don't care.

My lungs fill, and I suck in big breaths. They come fast, like I'm starving for air. She kneads my back, whispering "hakol yihyeh beseder" over and over until I start to believe her and my breathing returns to normal.

"You think about the future so much," she says softly.

"Is that a bad thing?"

"Not necessarily, but . . . I think sometimes you live more in the future than in the now. You're so young. You should be thinking about the now."

Right. My own mother's now is so grim I can't imagine how she could think about the future. As always, I'm acting so selfish.

"How are you feeling?" I ask gently.

"I'm all right. Some days are worse than others. I am struggling to remember more things than I used to, and this new medication is supposed to be helping with the hallucinations. It's an adjustment, though. Not teaching. I have . . . a lot of time on my hands."

She has good days and bad, and so far it seems this is a good one. She's not the stammering, confused Ima she was a few nights ago, the one who forgot I wasn't actually going to Johns Hopkins.

Tonight I can almost remember who she used to be.

"I like all your knitting projects, though," I say, and she smiles sadly. "Can you tell me about savtah?" It feels weird to call her "savtah" when I never had a chance to use the word.

It makes me think of the evil-eye bracelet, currently buried in a dresser drawer.

"My ima." She waits a while before continuing, like she's digging around in her memory. "She used to let me stay home from school every year on my birthday. She didn't think you should have to spend your birthday in school. We'd go to the market, and we'd get something to eat, or we'd go to a park, or we'd buy a new outfit." A sigh. "But I don't remember much of anything else. I wish I did. I barely remember her going through this. She progressed so quickly, and the doctors weren't able to determine what it was. They wouldn't have known if it was genetic or not, if it was something I would inherit too. That you girls were at risk for it."

"Is that why you left? Because she got sick?"

She shakes her head. "That was a long time before I left. I was eight years old when she died. My father . . . he changed after she passed. He had always had some trouble with alcohol, and her death made that even worse. He wasn't abusive, not physically. Emotionally, perhaps. He yelled and swore constantly, came home late or sometimes not at all. I couldn't stand to be in my own house."

"Ima." My heart twists. "I'm so sorry."

"You can understand why I wanted to do my service and then get out of there."

"What about your grandparents?" Optimism grabs hold of me. They could still be alive, just really, really old, living in a tiny house somewhere in Tel Aviv.

"They passed when I was a teenager."

"Is your dad—"

"I stopped talking to him after I left the country, but I heard from some friends that he died a few years ago."

"And you never told us."

"No. I wouldn't have wanted you to meet him. After I left . . . There were no good memories there, Tovah'le." A smile crosses her lips. "Do you remember when you were little, you asked why I took Aba's last name? Why I didn't keep my own last name?"

I nod. I thought her maiden name, Shapira, was better than Aba's because before I could spell I associated Siegel with the bird. And her names sounded so good together: Simcha Shapira. I wouldn't have changed my name if I had one like that. In fact, I'm certain I'll never change my name even if I get married.

"That was the one thing that tied me to my family," she says. "To my father. I needed a new family."

Growing up, Adina and I only knew Aba's family, sprinkled all over the Pacific Northwest: an aunt in Portland, an uncle in the Tri-Cities, grandparents in Bellingham. We used to think it was odd that we didn't have photos of our mom's parents. We always wanted to know more about them. Our mysterious Israeli side.

Now I know why.

"The bracelets you gave us." I say it quietly. "You told me they were from savtah. But . . . was it only Adina's?"

She's silent for a moment. "Ani miztaeret, Tovah'le. I should not have done that."

"So you found mine online. You lied to me about it." I'm more resigned than upset. Ima and Adina have a bond I'll never understand, but my relationship with Ima doesn't have to be identical to hers.

"Ani miztaeret," she apologizes again. "I only had the one, but I wanted you each to have something special. And after the test . . . it seemed like she needed it a bit more. That connection to our family. It's difficult, sometimes, trying to keep everything equal between the two of you."

"I'm not sure that's possible."

"Perhaps not."

"Does Adina know the reason you left Israel?"

"No," Ima says, and that makes me feel like maybe things are more equal than she thinks. Adina has the bracelet, but I have the story. "I've been waiting for the right time to tell both of you. But it's okay. I'm not upset about any of it anymore. I have my family here. I have you and I have Adina, and I have your father, and my friends . . . and it's okay." She takes a deep breath. "How did we get off topic? I thought we were talking about you."

"I don't know what else to say about me. I'm completely stuck."

She sips her tea. "You know how many times I changed majors in school. And careers, too. You understand that you don't have to know now, right this very instant, what you want to do for the rest of your life?"

The rest of my life. That suddenly sounds like a long, long time.

"I mean, yes, but . . ." I've always thought I had this one path, but maybe I'm more like my mother than I thought. "I like biology.

I like the idea of being of a surgeon. And I had the right test scores and took all the right classes and the right extracurriculars. . . ."

"The *right* ones," Ima repeats. "Were they the ones you wanted to take?"

"Some of them." Not all of them, though. Not student council, not really. And I always thought it would be fun to try an elective like photography or newspaper, but I filled my schedule with APs instead.

"When you get to college, you can take anything you want. It doesn't have to be biology, or premed, and you can join clubs just because you want to." She touches my hair, her fingers gently combing the short strands. "I know it seems overwhelming now, but you are going to love college."

I picture all the torn-up pages of *Gray's Anatomy* in a dump somewhere. Adi found her niche so early on; is that why I was so desperate to claim one for myself? I found something I liked, something people told me I was good at, and suddenly it became my *thing*. I wasn't the invisible twin anymore.

Surgery and medicine don't have to be my entire life, though. I have time—time my sister may not have—to test out another path. I can try something new and fail at it a dozen times until I find a passion that fits me as well as viola fits Adina. If I stay at home this year, maybe I could learn more about my stranger-mother, too.

"Have you ever seen *Singin' in the Rain*?" Ima asks.

I shake my head, and her face lights up. So I turn it on and we drink our tea and watch a movie together just the two of us, no Adina, for the very first time.

Thirty-five
Adina

THE LAST TIME I WORE THESE JEANS, I MUST HAVE BEEN twelve or thirteen. They're too tight on my hips and they flare out at the ankles, a style I'm certain hasn't been popular for years. I keep reaching down to pick at loose threads, but there aren't any, so instead I scrub away fuzz that's accumulated over years of living inside a drawer. I didn't want to wear any of my dresses today. I don't care about looking good.

When I explained my symptoms, Dr. Simon told me she could do a whole neurological and psychiatric exam. So we did the tests and now I'm back. Waiting.

If she tells me I'm sick, I have to begin preparations. I will have to figure out what to do with my viola, obviously, because I do not want it to wind up at a thrift shop or in a Dumpster. I will have to come to terms with the fact that I will never hear music again, never watch another black-and-white movie, never eat another cheeseburger, never see Israel. I will never see Ima or Aba or Tovah or Oscar at Muse and Music or Connor Mattingly or Laurel the pianist or Boris Bialik or the woman who drives the 44 bus.

I will have to find a doctor who can give me lethal medication. Will it be a pill or an injection? Would I feel each organ shutting down, feel my blood stop flowing, my heart slowing? Do I have to write some kind of good-bye-cruel-world letter, or is that just something they do in movies? What should I wear before I do it? My nicest dress? Pajamas? Many Conservative Jews are against cremation, so would my parents bury me? Where? Would my eyes and kidneys go to someone else? There is a little heart on my driver's license that means I am an organ donor. . . . Is this what that is for?

I'd have to figure all this out, and oh my God, I'm not ready. The night of the party, I was so sure I'd still go through with my plan. I assumed it would mean ultimate peace for me. An escape from what I've seen Ima endure.

Now I am really fucking scared of everything I'm going to miss out on. I have been so glib about suicide—possibly because death terrifies me more than I can admit.

Please, I think to myself. *Please. Not yet.*

♩ ♫♩

"Adina," Dr. Simon says when she finally calls me back. "There's nothing on our tests that indicates you have Huntington's right now."

"What?" This was the answer I wanted, but I don't quite

believe her. "But, but the clumsiness, and the delusions . . ."

Dr. Simon leans forward, propping her elbows on her knees. "Here's what I think is happening. Sometimes anxiety can bring on delusions and occasionally hallucinations. You're dealing with a tremendous amount of anxiety. You likely experienced an auditory hallucination on the train."

"So this is all in my head. That's what you're saying."

"It does happen. I've seen many patients go through it."

I don't want her to tell me how many other people go through it. I want her to tell me how to fix it.

"How do I make it stop?"

"Counseling is a good option, and we can discuss medication for anxiety."

But I have more questions. "Honestly, how much time do you think I have? I'm not trying to be morbid, but . . . a ballpark. Like, how much time before it starts getting bad?"

"I wish I could give you a real answer, but that's the tricky part of this disease," she says. "There's a chance you won't experience symptoms for another twenty years."

"But there's also a chance they could start in my twenties. Or before."

"A chance, yes," she says. "A very small one. There hasn't been enough research about those cases to have really solid statistics, but some numbers indicate about five percent of all HD cases start that early. But you know we can't predict that."

With my fingernails, I scrape harder at the fuzz on my jeans. In this room, talking to Dr. Simon about this disease I am surely

336

going to start suffering from at some point, with Tovah know-ing my secrets and limited time, I'm certain, before she tells our parents, I feel trapped. I am utterly trapped in this body, my skin stretched too tight across my bones, my ribs about to snap. With-out the plan, there is no escape, and the unknown terrifies me.

"But *why* don't we know? We have cures for all sorts of dis-eases, and we can't predict when this one in particular is going to start ruining my life?"

"Adina—"

"No, you know what?" I prop my boots up on the coffee table between us, kicking aside a few magazines and a box of tissues. My relief's gone. I'm not sick, not yet, but I'm going to be. I'm going to have to keep waiting. Worrying. I haven't actually escaped anything. "I'm so fucking sick of waiting. For the rest of my life, I'm going to wake up wondering if today is going to be the day. The day I can't play viola anymore. The day I can't feed myself. *Why* don't you know when this will start happening to me?"

"I can guarantee you, Adina, people are researching that very thing right now."

"I thought I was here for you to help me. Isn't this your job? Aren't you an expert? I just"—I draw in a deep breath, hiccup—"I just—"

I'm breathing hard, my skin getting tighter and tighter. Can't look at Dr. Simon, a doctor with no answers and no cure, only platitudes about living my life normally and blah-blah-blah.

If I'm going to be stuck like this with no way out, I need

something from her that apparently she cannot give me.

When my breathing returns to normal, after my panic attack or whatever it is subsides, Dr. Simon says, "I know it's not fair. I hate it too. I hate this disease. But this is why I do this job. To show people that it's horrible, yes, but it doesn't have to be life-ending. Or life-ruining. Not at all. It changes things, and I think you'll find that human beings are surprisingly good at adapting to change."

I say nothing.

"We have a support group that meets the first Tuesday of every month," she continues gently. "Would you like to try it next month?"

I've always dealt with things on my own, or with Tovah, or when I didn't have Tovah, with Ima. Or maybe that's the problem: that I have no one to talk to about this anymore, no sister, no friends. And I'm not sure how much longer I will be able to confide in my mother.

"Fine," I say, though I'm not entirely sure I'll show up.

"And like I said earlier, Adina, it seems as though you're going through a lot of anxiety. And probably some depression, as well, based on everything you've told me."

Depression. The word feels a bit like a missing puzzle piece. I think about the scars on my legs, my occasional inability to enjoy viola. The darkness in my mind.

"Oh," I say, but I am not angry with her anymore.

"We could start you on a low dose of an antidepressant," she continues. "It can help with the anxiety and the depression. I

338

can also recommend a therapist who specializes in working with teens dealing with both."

"That would be good," I tell her. "I . . . I think I want to do that."

She gives me a prescription, and then I'm done and it's Ima's turn with Dr. Simon. I'll have a lifetime of doctor's appointments, but Ima doesn't seem to hate them. In fact, she's never shown anything but graceful acceptance toward the thing that's killing her.

On the drive home, when we are waiting to turn left at a red light, I say, "Ima, can I ask you something about Huntington's?"

"You can ask me anything, Adina'le."

"Didn't you ever get angry that you have it? I don't remember it."

The blinker goes *tick, tick, tick*. It shouldn't sound like a countdown, but it does.

"Of course I was angry. I tried my best to hide it from you and Tovah. I couldn't put on anything except bravery in front of you two. You were old enough to understand what might happen to you, too. But I've accepted this machala arura, this damn disease . . . and that's made it easier."

"When?" I press as I swing left. All the snow is gone, and in its place are spring blooms, tulips and rhododendrons and cherry blossoms. "When did it happen? That acceptance."

"It took a while. It didn't happen overnight or in a month or even a year. I don't know if I can give you an exact moment. My mind is a little muddled today." She pauses. "Actually . . . do you remember the day you got into the youth symphony? That was the same day, if I recall correctly, that Tovah got her PSAT scores."

"I got mine too," I say. "They weren't that good."

"But I was so proud of you," Ima says. "I knew how much effort you put into practicing. You wouldn't have been happy if you scored well on a test. The symphony was what mattered to you, and it mattered to me that it made you happy. And in a similar way, Tovah was thrilled with her test scores. I realized I wanted to be able to enjoy those things with the two of you. And that meant realizing life was going on around me, outside of this disease."

We've reached the garage, but neither of us moves to unbuckle our seat belts.

"What did it feel like? When it first started?"

"At the beginning, I started to forget things. You know that part," she says. "And I felt . . . 'off' is maybe the best word for it. Left and right didn't match. I was clumsy, and I'd never been clumsy before that."

"Ze lo fair," I say quietly.

"I know it's not fair."

"And I'm still angry. Sometimes . . . I think I'm angry at *you*." I allow myself to look at her after I say this. Her deep dark eyes are stormy with guilt.

"It's okay to be angry. I am too," she says. Soft. Gentle. "I feel responsible. If only I had gotten tested. If only I had known earlier . . . But I didn't. Adina'le, I'm so sorry this is happening . . . but we're all here for you. You know that."

My head is heavy as I nod. I wish I had an ounce of my mother's strength, wish she had passed that along to me too. The two should go together, this disease and that strength.

"Aba and I have been trying to figure out how to talk to you about this, but we know you've been skipping classes."

"Oh."

"The school has called several times, and we've told them we would talk to you about it." She sighs. "You can't keep skipping classes. You have to graduate. You have to go to conservatory."

"Am I not going to graduate?" I ask, suddenly worried.

"Your principal said that if you maintain perfect attendance through the rest of the year and make up the work you've missed, they will allow you to graduate. We explained . . . your situation."

I squeeze my eyes shut. I wonder how many times this will be used as an excuse. I vow not to let it happen again. "Okay. I'll make everything up, and I'll stop skipping. I promise."

"And then you won't have to deal with Hemingway ever again." She smiles. "If you're not busy right now, will you play for me? I haven't heard you in so long."

"I play all the time," I say, though in the past couple weeks, I have not played very much. When I left Arjun's, it was clear I was no longer his student in addition to whatever else I'd been to him, and I have no desire to begin with a new teacher I'd work with for only a few months. I told my parents I quit private lessons because I want spending money once I'm at Peabody.

"But it's in your room. With the door closed. Like the music is private." She touches my arm. "I love hearing you play. I always have."

"Okay." So I set up my music stand in the living room and pick a piece she loves.

I hold my breath as I unpack my viola, patting its scar. I'm still unsure if I'll fix it. There is no way to fix me, so perhaps I should let my dearest possession remain unfixed too.

I let myself collide with the music, unable to stop thinking about my mother, my future. Aba gets home from work and sits beside my mother on the couch, sliding an arm around her shoulders as they listen together. This tragedy has done so many things, but it hasn't affected their love for each other.

I play, and play, and play.

This is still who I am.

This is who I will always be, even when I lose it.

Thirty-six

Tovah

ONCE AGAIN, BEING A GOOD KID PAYS OFF. I PERSUADE the art teacher to let me into the classroom early Monday morning, so I'm there waiting to startle Zack when he flips on the lights.

"Shit, you scared me," he says when he spots me at his table.

"Sorry. We should probably talk."

He drops his bag on the table and leans against it. "We should." When I don't immediately initiate the aforementioned talking, he says, "Feels almost ridiculous to ask this, but how are you doing?"

Lately we've seen each other only at school. I've invented excuses for not seeing him on weekends, but I've missed his floppy hair and paint-stained jackets and the space between his teeth. I've missed the way he looks at me like he can't be disappointed with me.

"I've been better, to be honest." I think of Adina and say the only thing I can manage. "Things are difficult at home right now."

"I won't pretend to understand what that's like, but I wish I could have been there for you."

"Me too," I say, surprising myself. Although I haven't been able to repeat Adina's plan to anyone, maybe I could have told Zack, and even if he didn't have any magical solutions, he could have at least shared the weight of it.

He lowers his voice then and flicks his eyes around the room to ensure we're the only two people here. "I'm sorry about what happened at my house."

I sigh. "Yeah. That."

"Your mind was a hundred different places that day," he says. Not an accusation. A fact.

"I—I know," I admit. "It was. I'm sorry too."

"Is it cliché to say that I want our first time to be perfect?" He brushes my knuckles with his thumb. "I don't want us to have to rush in between parents getting home. I want us to not be thinking about anything else except each other. I want to have plenty of time because"—he blushes—"well, whenever I've imagined it in my head, it lasts a *long* time."

My heart flutters at those last words. "That . . . sounds extremely good to me."

"Yeah?" He brightens.

I force myself to say what I've been thinking since I said yes to the University of Washington a couple days ago. "But we only have a few more months before college, and you're going east for school, and I'm staying here."

"You'll be great anywhere. I have no doubts."

I swallow this down, trying to believe it. Wanting to believe it. "Even though I have no idea what I want to do? Or who I am?" It feels like I'm turning my brain inside out for him to examine. Waiting for him to diagnose me.

"Maybe you're not supposed to know what you wanna be in high school," he says, like he and my mother discussed this together beforehand.

"But you with art? And my sister with viola? And everyone else who seems to have the rest of their lives mapped out?"

He shrugs. "I could change my mind, and that's okay. Or I could never make any money and have to figure out something else. Who really knows for sure?"

I did. But everything I used to think has changed.

"I don't want to force you to do long-distance," I say, switching the conversation back to what I'm sure we're both thinking about.

"Is that it? Or do *you* not want to do long-distance?"

I chew on this for a while. "I'm not sure. And I hate not being sure. It's not that I don't like you. You know how much I like you."

"Yeah. I think I do." He grins. "Hear me out a sec, because I have an idea."

I lean forward, my heart twinging with hope. "I'm listening."

"What if we agree to see where things go? If we're still together by the end of the summer, well, we'll figure it out. And if we're not . . . then there's not much to stress out about now, is there?"

I nearly open my mouth to protest. To say that we should have a concrete plan. Instead, what comes out is: "I like that idea. We'll see where we are at the end of the summer."

Beneath the table, his sneaker bumps mine.

"I've missed that," I say softly. Across the table, we connect our fingers. "There's one more thing I want to ask," I add after a while.

"Fine, I'll show you my mutant toes."

I raise my eyebrows.

"Sorry," he says.

I take a deep breath. "I love you. A lot. And I'm wondering if you'll go to prom with me."

The way he looks at me melts me from the inside. He isn't smiling—this is a different emotion from happiness. It's gentler. Softer. "I love you a lot too," he says, inching even closer and putting his hands on my knees. "And yes. Of course we're going to prom together." He opens his backpack and pulls out a canvas board. "Before everyone starts coming in and ruins our privacy, I have something for you. Something I've been working on."

The canvas is covered with a variety of found objects: the receipt he found the night of our first date (ginger ale, cold care tea, cough drops, beer), tickets from a science museum we went to, the stub from the movie at Rain City Cinema.

My heart is full. Throat dry. I can't speak.

"This one does mean something," he says, "but I'll let you figure it out."

DNA

Someone raps lightly on my bedroom door.

"Come in," I call without glancing up from where I'm lying in bed with my laptop.

"Hi," Adi says, and I sit up straight. Her hair is in a whatever ponytail and her face is makeup free, her mouth not its usual red. "What are you doing?"

"Browsing the University of Washington's course catalog. What do you think, should I take History of the Circus or the Anthropology of Chocolate?"

"Both." She perches on the edge of my bed, but barely, like my sheets are made of lava.

"When do you sign up for classes?"

"They're all basically decided for me, but, you know, that's what I want. All viola, all the time." She doesn't say anything about taking classes at Johns Hopkins.

"It'll be the perfect place for you," I say, because it probably will be. Adina can have Baltimore. She deserves it.

Adi gives me a slight smile. "Thanks for saying that."

She stares up at my walls, all of which are bare now. My room is no longer a museum of all my accomplishments, all my dreams. It's one big blank slate.

"I don't hate you," she says to the walls. Quietly. The opposite of how she said that statement's opposite.

For about a minute I don't say anything.

"Tovah?"

"I heard you," I say. "I—I think I knew that. But . . . thanks for telling me."

Adina crosses her legs, the bed squeaking beneath her. "I shouldn't have said it. I shouldn't have said a lot of things to you that night. What I said about death with dignity—that's not happening. I don't want that. I hadn't thought anything through, and I was acting reckless, like you said, and . . ." She trails off, as though waiting for me to say something.

I shut my laptop. I wanted more time to prepare for this conversation, if it's something I could ever be fully prepared for. I want to do what I wasn't able to do after our mom was diagnosed. I want to hold her in my arms and keep her there and make sure nothing bad ever happens to her. I want to *be there*, because maybe if I am, it'll stop her from thinking such horrendous thoughts.

I should have planned some grand speech. Convince her that life is still worth living. Fill it with quotes and statistics and facts about how people with this disease aren't doomed the way she thinks they are. But with Ima getting worse, that's tougher for me to wrap my brain around. Tougher for me to believe.

"I want to believe you," I say. "I really, really want to believe you, Adina."

She stares at me, unblinking, and there's a rawness and sincerity in her gaze that makes me realize: she wouldn't lie to me about this. It's too massive. "I swear to you. When I went to the doctor last week, I was terrified, really fucking terrified, that they were going to diagnose me with Huntington's and what that would mean. That I'd have to start going through with this 'plan.' And I didn't want that. I couldn't envision it. I thought that was the one way I had to control this, but I can control so many other things. I'm still scared of what's going to happen to me someday, but . . . I have some time. To do the things I want. And"—she chews her lip—"those things don't have to involve destroying objects that are important to you."

"You have *so much time*." I want to hug her, or touch her shoulder, but I don't have the courage to do either yet. "If you ever feel that way again, tell me, okay? Or tell Ima, or tell your doctor, or . . ."

"I'm starting some antidepressants. And the doctor mentioned a support group. I'm going to go. See what it's like."

"That's good. Really good. I could go with you, if you want."

She twirls the end of her ponytail around a fist, checking for split ends she doesn't have. "I think I have to go on my own. But thanks."

In the silence that follows, I mimic her, running my hands through my own short hair. It may never look like hers, but I don't think I want it to.

"I need to confess to something. I was jealous of you. You were right. I spent most of elementary school and middle school being jealous of you. You had—still have—this confidence I wish

I had most of the time. And you've always known what you were meant to do."

Adina's eyebrows crease together. "But you couldn't stand my music."

"I couldn't stand that because you could play an instrument, you were the music expert, even though I love music too. But viola became who you were, and that was what I wanted. Something for myself."

"You accomplished that," she says. She lies down on my bed, increasingly more comfortable in my space. "Pretty well, in fact. And you have to know now that I'm not confident all the time."

"That's the thing. I don't know if what I picked out for myself is the right path, and I'm okay with that. I don't think I need to have everything figured out yet. I don't know why I was in such a hurry." I tap my laptop. "Hence the course catalog."

She sighs. "Since we're being honest, you have to know, Tovah, that when you wanted to leave for those programs—that killed me. I couldn't have handled Ima all alone. And I understand that what I did was wrong and I could have done something else, but . . . that was the only thing I could think of to get you to stay."

I push my pillows out of the way so I can lie down next to her, prop my head on one arm, and turn to face her. "We're past that now."

"I know. I just wanted to make sure you knew. That I'm sorry. Ani miztaeret."

"Me too." She sighs. "Hard to believe high school's almost over." It's such not a very Adina thing to say. She's barely shown interest in high school. "I just think . . . no, never mind."

"What?"

"I don't know. I wonder if I missed out on anything. I haven't been the most . . . social person in high school."

"I don't know, you have a pretty good shot at prom queen."

Adi holds a hand to her heart. "Like, oh my God, thanks for voting for me!" she says, and I wish this ease with which we joke felt more familiar. It feels good, though, like picking up a book you read years and years ago, remembering certain passages you loved while some twists feel brand-new.

"I think," she continues in a small voice, "that I might want to go to prom. Is that weird?"

"Very weird," I say, and then grin. "Do you want to go with me? Zack and I are going with Lindsay and Troy, and I could find you a date. Or you could go without one. Whichever you want."

"As much as I like the idea of making a statement by going solo, I want the full experience. Find me a date."

We talk plans for a while longer, until it's after eleven and she starts yawning. I almost ask if she wants to have a sleepover in my room like we used to do, but it's too soon. Things still feel—not fragile, but newly rebuilt.

As she's about to go across the hall, she turns to me. She holds my gaze, dark eyes hard, a hurricane inside them. "There's one more thing I need to ask you. If it had been you, Tovah . . . what would you have done?"

And at this point, even after everything we've done to each other, I truly don't have an answer.

351

Thirty-seven

Adina

EVERY COUPLE MINUTES THE DATE TOVAH FOUND ME sends an awkward smile in my direction. Henry Zukowski has slicked-back blond hair and light stubble on his chin, and his spicy cologne stings my nostrils.

"I'm sorry about your girlfriend," I say to Henry, straining to be heard over the music in the hotel ballroom. She broke up with him two weeks ago. I am his backup.

"Nah, it's fine. Thanks for agreeing to go with me. I hope I'm not completely pitiful."

"Only partly," I say, and he grins.

We've been around Tovah and Zack and Lindsay and Troy all night. They're on the dance floor, leaving us alone for the first time. This whole thing feels so high school. For four years, I avoided all this, and it strikes me as funny that it's all happening tonight. When the three of us got ready earlier, Lindsay watched me braid my hair in a crown around my head and asked if I'd do hers. Then, at the restaurant, I ordered fettuccine with sausage in a ricotta cream sauce, and Tovah stared at me. "Oh—I don't keep kosher anymore," I told her. Tovah wouldn't quit looking at me like I was a stranger, but then Zack nudged her arm and told her a joke and no one said anything else about it.

The music changes, and Henry's face lights up. "This is my favorite song." His eyes plead with mine. The song is quick with a pulsing bass line. Its patterns are obvious, but tonight I find the simplicity refreshing.

I give him my hand. "Let's go."

I don't realize how fast the song is until we start moving along with it. I'm too aware of my arms and legs for a while, so I copy his movements. Gradually, I start to relax—and then the song ends and the crowd erupts into applause. As I turn back to our table, Henry's fingers graze my arm. "One more?" he asks.

This song has some strings in it, which I like, so I say yes. We dance a little closer this time, though we're still not really touching. We dance the next one too, and by the one after that, my feet are throbbing and I'm out of breath, so we take a break.

A slow song comes on, and the DJ invites all the couples onto the dance floor. Tovah and Zack are at the edge of the crowd, moving in time with each other. Together they look effortless. Her head is against his chest, and he pushes hair away from her ear, whispers something into it that makes her smile. His hands drift down, settling around her waist, and her fingers curl into the hair that grazes the back of his neck. No one has ever held me the way Zack is holding my sister.

I want that.

And it is stronger than any want I've experienced before. It's a longing, an ache deep in my belly. It is not the same as the way I've wanted sex from guys, when that was the only thing I focused on.

I make another vow. One day I will be loved for my music and my mind by someone who puts me above everyone else. Maybe someone who is discovering love for the first time too. I will not be a secret. I will be a declaration.

I cannot believe I spent so much time making Tovah miserable. We could have been growing closer with the time we have left. I don't wish our fates were reversed—how could I wish this on anyone?—but knowing what will happen to Ima and me and being unable to stop it must be its own kind of torture. She deserves this happiness.

Henry catches where I'm looking. "They're cute together, huh?"

"Yeah," I say around the knot in my throat. "They really are."

I tear my gaze away. I've always been good at getting what I want . . . and one day, I will have that.

A bridge and a chorus later, the music switches to something fast again, and Henry says, "I've clearly gotten you out of your comfort zone enough for one night, but would you believe this is my *second* favorite song?"

I shake my head, laughing as we head back to the dance floor.

♪ ♪♪♪

After the dance winds down, the six of us hang out in a hotel room upstairs. Troy pulls out bottles of rum and Coke and pours them into the Styrofoam cups next to the coffeemaker.

"Classy." Lindsay accepts a cup and raises it to him.

Troy loosens his tie. "Anyone have a deck of cards? We could play strip poker or something similarly debaucherous."

"I'm not playing strip poker," Tovah says.

"Fine, what about Ten Fingers?"

"How do you play?" I ask.

"Everyone holds up ten fingers, and we go around saying something we've never done. If you've done it, you have to put down a finger. First person to put down all ten fingers wins."

"Or loses, depending on how you look at it," Lindsay puts in.

We go several rounds of this game. *I've never had sex in a public place. I've never cheated on a test. I've never read Harry Potter.* It lasts an entire hour. Maybe these are the experiences I should have been collecting, hanging out with people my age, playing stupid games, laughing until my stomach hurts.

"I can call an Uber whenever you're ready to go home," Henry says

"I have a little bit left in me." Our cups are empty, so I get to my feet and say, "I'm going to get more ice."

I grab the bucket and head into the hall. After I fill it, I check my phone out of habit. There's nothing new on it, but I put my thumb on Arjun's name anyway. He sent me one text last week, which simply said, **I hope you're okay**, and I replied, **Fine. I** must have frightened him because he hasn't said anything to my parents, and I'm certain he won't. Whenever I think about it—and I try my best not to think about it—I realize Arjun was not this great love of my life. It was doomed from the beginning.

I thought I could force him to love me. Relationships are not about control, though, and perhaps that is why I have never had a real one. I want to always feel strong when I am with guys. That isn't going to change. I am always going to wear my dresses and red lipstick because *I* like them. I am always going to have people watch me when I am onstage, but my looks are not the only things that make me Adina.

Arjun knew I was vulnerable and perhaps took advantage of that, but I shouldn't have threatened him. My last words to him were cruel. That is not who I am anymore.

I send him one last text: **I won't say anything.** Then I delete the entire conversation and erase his name and number too. I won't check to see if he replies, and I doubt he will. Gone from my phone, from my mind, from my life.

I'm not settling for another relationship that revolves around my body.

A *click*, and the door to our room opens. Tovah makes a strange face when she sees me sitting across the hall.

"Hey," she says. "I was wondering where you were. Had to make sure you didn't have a tragic ice machine accident."

"Nope," I say. "Needed a little break, I guess. I'm not used to . . ." I wave my hand in the direction of the room. All those people.

She nods, getting it. I realize she's wearing her evil-eye brace-let again. We both are. "Can I sit with you?" she asks.

"Go ahead."

"It looked like you were having a good time with Henry." She slides down onto the carpet next to me.

I feel my face flush. I was having a good time. I've spent so much time trying to convince myself I'm not young, that I'm old enough for all those guys, but the truth is . . . I *am* young. And I've spent so much time isolating myself that I've missed out on countless things. There's still so much to experience. I want love like Tovah has, like my parents have, but I want *more* than that. There's more than that out there. More than viola, even. I feel greedier than I have ever felt, for friends I can confide in, and dancing with strangers, and sitting in a room playing a stupid, fun game. The miniature orchestra swells in my chest again, but this time it is playing something new, something I have never heard before.

"He's nice, but I'm taking a break from boys, I think." I pluck a stray thread from the carpet. I'm not wearing tights tonight. "I can tell. With Lindsay. That it's not . . . that things aren't how they used to be with you." At dinner, the two of them didn't speak to each other, only to the rest of the group.

Tovah sighs. "It's been like that all year. She cares more about Troy, and that's her choice. We might never talk after high school. Apparently you meet the best friends of your life in col-lege, though, so maybe I'm not losing all that much."

But she still looks sad.

"I'm sorry," I tell her. Maybe this whole year, she was as alone as I was.

A silence falls over us. We exist in silences these days, but I suppose it is better than yelling, than slamming doors, than destroying prized possessions.

I unzip my bag and pull out an envelope. "Tovah. I know I can't begin to apologize for what I did, and I know it's not as special because it's not Aba's, but . . . I wanted to give you this."

She turns the new Nirvana ticket over. "How did you get this?"

"I found it online, and it arrived in the mail earlier today. I swear I'll get it framed for you, but I wanted you to have it tonight. That was such a shitty thing for me to do. I'll continue making it up to you however I can—"

Tovah holds up her hand. "No. I don't want there to be any more debts between us. I don't want one of us to owe the other."

"Okay."

"Thank you." She regards the ticket with a sad smile, and then her head jerks up as though she's just remembered something. "What time is it? I left my phone in the room."

"Quarter to ten. Why?"

"Get up. We're going somewhere."

I raise my eyebrows. "Where? And what about Zack and everyone?"

She holds her hand out to me, pulling me to my feet, and grins. "It's a secret. And they'll be fine. This is just for us."

Thirty-eight

Tovah

THE CROWN OF THE SPACE NEEDLE VANISHES AND then reappears as I steer us up a steep hill and into a neighborhood I've been to only once before. I've lived in Seattle all my life and it's still full of mystery. Cities are a little like people that way. I didn't know Adi no longer kept kosher, but that's her choice, and I can't force her devotion to our religion. Maybe one day she'll find her own way back to it.

"Are you going to tell me where we are?" Adi asks as I wiggle into a parallel parking spot. She pulls down the mirror to check her makeup. Dabs at an imaginary lipstick stain on the side of her mouth.

"You'll see." I unbuckle my seat belt. "And your makeup looks fine."

"Only fine?"

"You look beyond stunning, as always. Is that what you wanted to hear?"

She smirks. "When you say it sarcastically like that, it doesn't sound genuine."

Our heels clack along the sidewalk, the fabric of our dresses rustling. I lead us down a stairway and across an old bricked street and into an alleyway, and when I knock on a door at the end of it, a honeyed voice asks me for a password.

"Blotto," I say.

"Are you serious?" Adi says, laughing. "What is this, a speakeasy?"

That's exactly what it is. Bernadette's is sepia-toned, tea lights strung across the ceiling, old movie posters on the walls. A cluster of round tables faces a stage, where a pianist plays a tune I vaguely recognize. Maybe it was in one of the films Ima loves so much.

Zack got the password from someone in his art class. We did some reconnaissance here last week and learned they're very lenient about the under-twenty-one policy as long as you don't order alcohol and you tip generously.

"I love this." The awe in Adi's voice is clear. "I didn't know this was your scene."

"It's not. But this is about you. Not me. They do an open mic night once a month, and tonight is that once a month."

"I'm . . . playing?" she asks, finally connecting all the pieces. "I can't do it without my viola."

"I planned ahead." I dig a scrap of paper from my purse and

360

hand it to the coat check, who returns with Adi's viola case. She stares at it, her mouth ajar.

"Why are you doing this?" she asks. "How did you know I'd go along with it?"

"I know how much you like being the center of attention."

"Ha-ha." Her lips wobble like she's struggling not to smile. At last one corner bends upward. Soon I'm copying her.

"I wanted you to have your chance to be a soloist," I say. "To be the only person onstage. To have everyone watching only you, listening to your music."

While I'm not sure what my future holds, I know I have so many opportunities for a spotlight of my own.

Adi bites down on her red-lipsticked lip, as though trying to keep whatever emotion she's feeling from spilling out. "I don't even know what to say," she says. "I guess I don't owe you, but it feels like I do. Todah. Todah rabah."

A host approaches us. "Your table is ready, Miss Siegel," he says, and Adina raises her eyebrows at me, trying not to laugh at the forced formality.

He shows us to a table to the left of the stage, and we order virgin mojitos.

"Now your lipstick is smudged," I tell her as we sip our drinks.

She shrugs. "Eh, whatever."

When the pianist finishes with a flourish, the emcee calls Adina to the stage for her viola solo.

"Make me proud, Adi," I say, and she rolls her eyes, but

361

her hand grazes my shoulder as she heads for the stage.

Our relationship probably won't ever be what it was before we started growing into our own skin. Before we hurt each other. Before the world hurt us. Maybe we'll never fully understand each other or know all of each other's secrets, and surely we'll never recapture our childhood innocence. But we can have something new. Something messy and real and imperfect, because that's what both of us are.

Adi raises her bow, and I let myself sink into her music. It's been a while since I really listened to her. When she was little, she hauled out her music stand and performed for our family all the time. But over the past few years, she's kept the music locked in her room. I think it's because I used to complain about how annoying it was. Sure, the music's not my favorite. It's not catchy, and it's definitely not Nirvana, but I can't remember why I claimed to hate it so much.

A single buttery light illuminates her and only her.

She glows.

Summer

Thirty-nine

Tovah

FOR THE FIRST TIME IN MY LIFE, I TUMBLE HEADFIRST into uncertainty. The last summer before college stretches before me, and I'm not scrambling to add anything to my résumé. I have zero obligations. Nothing to do.

I kind of love it.

This year I'll live at home and begin college as an undeclared freshman. I don't need to be one hundred percent certain what I want to do with the rest of my life now, and it's okay if it's biology and it's okay if it isn't. There are so many things I want to try that I can't believe I almost narrowed myself to just biology. I did place into a lab class, one of the prerequisites, but I'm also planning to take Introduction to Jewish Studies, History of the Olympics, and Anthropology of the Middle East.

Unlike Adi, Lindsay doesn't seem to think whatever happened between us this year is worth talking about. Maybe it's because I have my sister back, but I'm not as heartbroken about it as I thought I would be. Lindsay and I were not the best friends I assumed we were, and while I may never understand why, I do know I tried too hard to force her into an Adina-shaped space.

I see her one last time after graduation, at a beach party I go to with Zack and Adi. Adi is dipping her toes into the water, and Zack and Troy are playing volleyball with a big group, and somehow I find myself alone next to Lindsay by the likely illegal bonfire.

"Hey," Lindsay says, lifting her hand to wave. Her sweatshirt sleeves are pulled over her hands.

"You were a shitty friend to me this year," I say.

She winces. "Did you really need to say that?"

I stand up. "Yeah. I did. And even though you were a shitty friend, I still really hope you like college. I hope you figure out what you want to do. I hope you find what it is that you love." I say it genuinely, and she mumbles something back that sounds like *you too*, but I'm already walking away.

In the middle of July, Zack and I take another camping trip. Alone. I tell him what I want and what feels good and I'm not shy about it, so there's one thing Lindsay wound up being right about.

This time we have all night to figure it out. And after some stumbling and laughing and rearranging of sleeping bags, we finally get it.

"You're going to miss me," I say afterward, and while I meant it as a question, it comes out as a statement.

He holds me closer against his bare chest, fingers moving through my hair. My cheek rests on his heartbeat. "So much. But we'll talk all the time."

He might be my high school boyfriend or he might be the one true love of my life. We might be back in this same place next year, commemorating the anniversary of our first time, or we might be smitten with other people. I might be a surgeon and he might be an artist, or we might be completely different things.

Right now, though, we're just Tovah and Zack, reckless in love with each other, and I like that most of all.

Something on Aba's laptop screen, open on the kitchen table, freezes me in place.

"Aba?" I was about to go on a run, but my feet have turned to lead. I set my protein shake down on the table. "What's this?"

"Not now." He shuts the laptop and the website listing long-term care homes. "But you know we're going to have to talk about it sometime."

"I know." I bite the inside of my cheek, hard. It'll happen for Ima, and then for Adi. And I'll visit both of them all the time. Regardless of what my own future holds, I'll spend much of my life in a hospital.

He slides into a chair. "Do you have time to help me practice my ivrit, or are you on your way out?"

"On my way out," I say in Hebrew. "Could we do it later?"

He nods. "Betach," he says.

"How does dinner and a Hebrew lesson sound?" It's something we've gotten in the habit of, cooking dinner and speaking Hebrew. "I can stop by the grocery store. And the pharmacy, for Ima's meds."

"Todah," he says before switching back to English. "You've always been my girl, right?" He squeezes my shoulder.

"You can be so sappy." I roll my eyes so he can't tell how much this touches me. "It's not like I'm going anywhere."

"Not now, maybe," he says. "But you will."

Fall, again

Forty

Adina

I MISS THE COLD. I LONG FOR RAIN. I DREAM OF OVERCAST skies. In Baltimore the summer bleeds into fall, and September is punishingly hot. What I want is an East Coast winter, snow and closed streets and that fresh chilly scent. A few more months. A few more months and I will have my cold.

I unpack in my dorm, a small bricked cube with a window the size of a piece of sheet music. I take a photo and send it to Tovah.

My clothes fill the closet and my viola finds a spot in the corner of the room. Then I sit on the creaky bed and . . . wait. This is the first time I've been truly alone. Tovah and I went to Jewish day camps when we were little, and one weeklong overnight camp in Eastern Washington. But that has been it, and it barely compares.

At first I relish my alone time before it can turn lonely. I go for long walks around campus, or I play viola in the rehearsal spaces before classes start. Then I meet my roommate, Corinne, a flute major from North Carolina who has an accent and says "y'all."

Corinne tacks up photos of her friends on her side of the room. "My boyfriend's at school in Asheville," she says with a sigh, smoothing out a picture of the two of them. "Do you have a boyfriend?"

"No."

Her eyes flash with mischief. "I saw some cuties on the fourth floor. Piano players, so you know they're good with their fingers. . . ."

I laugh hard at this. I have never had a friend like Corinne, who talks too much and has no filter.

We eat dinner together in the dining hall the first night, and while there is a kosher meal option, it dawns on me that there's no one here to say anything about my not keeping kosher. There's no one to disappoint if I don't spend Shabbat resting.

This is an intensely freeing thought.

It felt good to go to support group over the summer, learn how others like me are coping. It took a couple weeks for my body to adjust to the antidepressants, but now that I have been on them for several months, I sense a definite lift in my moods. My doctor recommended a therapist in Baltimore, and I'm going to see her next week. What I am trying to do is focus on what's in front of me: how much I loved the dining-hall lasagna I had for dinner, classes starting tomorrow, the party I am going to with Corinne tonight.

Evil eyes jangle on my wrist. I put on a short-sleeved dress, leave my hair long and wild, outline my lips with Siren, then fill them in. Dab. Reapply. Perfect. In this moment, I feel genuinely content, though there is something in me that could alter the trajectory of my life at any second, something not even Tovah will ever understand.

All beautiful things in life lose their sheen. Gardens wither. Skin wrinkles. I might be waiting for a while—hopefully for a very long while—but some parts of my future are inevitable.

As Corinne and I wander through campus at night, my heel catches on a crack in the sidewalk, and I stumble.

"Careful," she says with a smile, reaching out to catch my elbow. "Clumsy, clumsy."

I steady myself. "Thanks. I'm okay."

The fear is never far away. My broken heel reminds me the disease could sneak up on me at any moment. One day I will twitch when I want to be still, rage when I want to be happy, forget when I want to remember. It has happened to my mother, and it will happen to me. We are a doomed family—but we are not done fighting yet.

I jam my shoe back onto my foot. "This party better have good music," I tell Corinne.

One thing is certain: before I go, I am going to make a hell of a lot of noise.

Acknowledgments

THIS BOOK'S JOURNEY HAS SPANNED FOUR YEARS AND a half dozen drafts, and this final version owes its existence to so many brilliant, generous people. I must begin with a tremendous thank-you to my agent, Laura Bradford, the first person to believe in this book. I'll never forget what you said about Adina during our first call: "She's not nice, but she's interesting. You root for her." Here's to many more characters who are more interesting than they are nice. I feel so lucky to have you in my corner.

Massive thanks to my editor, Jennifer Ung, for loving Adina and Tovah as much as I do, for inspiring me to dig deeper, and for just generally being amazing to work with. I'm so proud of what we made together!

Thank you, Sarah Creech, for designing such a stunning cover that conveys the tone of the book so perfectly. I wrote this book partially because the only Jewish stories I read growing up were Holocaust narratives. We cannot stop telling those stories, but they are not the only stories we as Jewish people have to tell. Thank you to Mara Anastas and the rest of the Simon Pulse team for believing a book with practicing Jewish characters could appeal to a wide audience.

Thank you to Rachel Simon, one of my very first critique partners, my online BFF turned real-life friend. Your generosity and enthusiasm are unparalleled in the book world, and you have the kindest heart. I know I can always count on you for an honest opinion.

I am grateful to have had such insightful feedback from this book's early readers: J. C. Davis, Nikki Roberti, Natalie Williamson, Natalie Blitt, Richelle Morgan, Maya Prasad, Jamee Kuehler, and Paula Garner, who first encouraged me to venture into a darker place. A special thank-you to Jennifer Hawkins. Without you, I may have put this book away forever.

Thanks too to my more recent readers: Heather Ezell, Tracy C. Gold, Rachel Griffin, Carlyn Greenwald, Kelsey Rodkey, Allison Augustyn, Brianna Shrum, Gloria Chao, Jeanmarie Anaya, Jenny Howe, Sarah White, and Al Rosenberg.

I feel so fortunate to have found the Pitch Wars community, and through it, some very meaningful relationships. Thank you, especially, to Joy McCullough, Helene Dunbar, Kit Frick, and Brenda Drake, for making it all possible.

To my fellow Electric Eighteens, I cannot imagine a more

supportive, talented group of writers. I can't wait to fill my shelves with your words and see where your careers take you.

I doubt I'd have written this book, much less shown it to anyone, if I hadn't summoned the courage to share my first finished manuscript in the Seattle critique group formerly known as Ladies of the Write. Thank you for being so nice when I showed up with three info-dumpy chapters of character backstory in a thinly veiled autobiography that will never see the light of day again. Thank you in particular to Janine Southard and Lara Doss, my first post-college, "real-world" friends.

Thank you to the helpful folks at the University of Washington Genetic Medicine Clinic, especially Robin Bennett, who took me seriously during this book's early stages, when I wasn't yet sure what it would be. Thank you to the Huntington's Disease Youth Organization, a group providing young people with so many valuable resources. Thank you to the Stroum Center for Jewish Studies, also at the University of Washington, and especially Hadar Khazzam-Horovitz, for the Hebrew transliteration help and for letting me borrow the "die, die" story.

My life would not be as rich without the community of dancers and teachers at eXit SPACE. Rachael Enderle, thank you for listening to me talk about publishing in between tap classes.

To Ivan Vukovic, thank you for listening to my author neuroses and assuming weekend mornings are for writing. Thank you, too, for agreeing to go to El Chupacabra many more times than you would like. You bring out the good parts of me.

Thank you to my sister, Michelle, for the enthusiasm and inside jokes. Please don't read too much into the sister relationship in this book. I swear, it's nothing like ours.

Last, thank you to my parents, Jenny and Brad. I don't know if I was an exceptionally good kid or you are exceptionally good parents, so let's just go with both. Thank you for always assuming *when*, not *if*. I love you.